PUSHED DOWN, THEN OUT

PHILIP WYZIK

Pushed Down, Then Out

©2021 **Philip Wyzik**

Print ISBN 978-1-09839-480-6

eBook ISBN 978-1-09839-481-3

To my daughter Elizabeth and son Daniel,
you add so much to my life and bring so much to the world.

CONTENTS

PART 1

PART 2

PART 1

TEN YEARS BEYOND THE PRESENT DAY

"Be kind; everyone you meet is fighting a hard battle."

– IAN MACLAREN (1850–1907)

CHAPTER 1:
HOW ABOUT BRISTOL?

THE TEENAGER WASN'T SURE WHETHER IT WAS THE POWER-
ful clap of thunder or the slamming of the heavy metal door echoing
through the dark and empty warehouse like a tidal wave of sound that
made her nerves tighten and Bristol's ever-vigilant eyes fly open wider
to scan for danger. Huddled in the safety of a long-forgotten corner of
the massive room, she froze and hoped that whoever opened the door
wouldn't see her there, crouching and silent. The rain outside fell on the
aging roof of the cavernous building, steady and determined. It easily
found the many holes made wider by time and neglect so that showers
of water puddled on the dirty concrete below.

The rugged, middle-aged Black man navigated these wet columns
as if he'd done it many times before, zig-zagging towards the corner at
a steady pace while shaking the water from his soaked pale green army
coat. With the muscular build of an ex-football player, the man was
nearly six feet tall and carried himself with a commanding presence.
He wasn't trying to be silent, and as he walked, his thoughts went to the
quarry he hoped to find, wondering if she would run, engage, speak, or
fight. His tattered hiking boots made a clomping sound with each step,
despite the drumming of the rain.

By the time he reached her, Bristol had curled up as low as she
could, thinking that the navy blue of her dirty pea coat and her jeans

might hide her sufficiently in the dimming twilight brought on sooner than usual with the heavy gray clouds moving ominously outside. She knew that her slender body would make a camouflaged target, but she regretted not using the adjacent corner where she slept last night, hidden by the two stacks of broken pallets. For a few hours, at least, she felt safe. It wasn't apparent to her whether the twitching in her legs was from the chilly temperature or her fear.

"Hey Bris," he said calmly from ten feet away, "it's me, Frank. You there?"

His voice was familiar, its nonchalant tone doing what it had always done these last few weeks. She felt her taught muscles relax just enough to be noticed but not enough to give her any respite from her fear. Of course, he didn't know he had that sort of effect on her for sharing something that personal, or anything at all for that matter. By his words and actions, she knew he didn't care that she didn't speak at all and it was fine, in her mind, that he didn't even know her name. Even if the others there teased and taunted her about her muteness, she took the leap of faith to trust the big man standing before her—but just a little.

She vividly remembered the night, several weeks ago, he decided to call her Bristol. There must have been a dozen or more that night, people much like her, running from demons both real and imagined, homeless and looking for any oasis that would shield them from the elements, even a dirty old factory filled with pigeon droppings and dust.

They sat with Frank and the teen trying to warm themselves around a tiny fire in the middle of one of the smaller rooms in the maze of structures that still bore the name Mohawk Mills in rusty red letters near the main gate. The factory, like many scattered throughout New England, shut down decades ago when both the economic vibrancy and the manufacturing bedrock of the community both slowly vanished like a steady and inevitable sunset. Hugging the bank of the Pennebec River that supplied the flowing energy that turned the pulleys and belts that powered the factory's mighty machines of yesteryear, the acres of masonry block buildings, some of which were erected in the early 1800s, now showed the unmistakable signs of age, neglect, and blight. The structures were forlorn and grim, their cracked and dirty walls, smashed windows, and weathered wooden doors fitting enough to rival what Charles Dickens called Ebenezer Scrooge's house—"a dismal heap of brick." Many wings were linked together by elevated wooden walkways, conveyer shafts, and a rickety assortment of passageways on second or third floors throughout, so employees and material could move from place to place. Over the years, the Mills were put to many purposes, depending upon the financial prospects of the long line of owners who made their money in diverse products like leather goods, radiators, truck parts, or metal toys. In its heyday, manufacturing jobs at the Mills, no matter what product was loaded on to the daily boxcars for shipment all along the Eastern Seaboard and beyond, were the best career that any resident of Hallet Springs, New Hampshire, could ask for. They afforded a comfortable middle-class existence and the promise of a pension.

But those days were long gone. They were a distant memory for most who remained in the region, and foreign history to the cast-aside collection of souls circled around the small fire. Some were there because they had nowhere else to sleep; others were fortunate to have a rented room somewhere in the town and came there during the day for the fragment of bonding that happened between strangers facing the same battle—surviving the current moment. Either way, the scene was fitting: abandoned buildings and abandoned people.

The room was their gathering place, picked because of its placement at the outermost edge of the complex, as far away as possible from the entrance on Market St, where the old railroad line separated the parcel from an expanse of woodlands, thick with pines, hemlocks, and a smattering of maples. They sat on plastic milk crates, up-ended wooden boxes, and a few heavy metal bins they had scrounged from the many massive rooms in the derelict factory. A few molded plastic chairs that must have been white at one point were the sought-after seats.

The hesitant, guarded, and soon-to-be "Bristol" was part of this rag-tag, informal community and was sitting on the dirty floor with her legs folded almost in a yoga position next to the large African-American man who had invited her in. It was about a week since their first encounter, but the look of hunger and desperation on her face reminded him of the war-ravaged people he had seen throughout his tours of duty in Afghanistan. Her eyes spoke volumes of vulnerability, fear, and some deeply hidden pain, the same wary eyes through which so many innocent children used to look at American soldiers throughout the Kandahar Province. No question he asked her was answered, but the unmistakable sadness she bore spoke to Frank loudly. Clearly, she needed more than food and shelter, but that would have to be the place to start for now. Be it the distrust or injury she held inside, he would not let her muteness be an obstacle to his attempt to help her.

"So, since you won't talk to us," he said, looking at her casually, "what'll we call you?" At this, her stare at the flames remained unchanged. "I know you can hear me," he said playfully. "Either you tell me your name, or I'll pick one for you."

Though her silence continued, her mind considered the possibility of an honest answer. She wondered if it would be dangerous just tell him the truth, or to vocalize a lie as a way of fitting in and making some casual connection with these fellow outcasts? *No,* she concluded as the familiar feeling of fear flooded her insides, *best to keep dead silent and, therefore, safe.*

Another member spoke up next. "Let's call her Beatrice," Tommy Hodges suggested. "That was my mother's name; she was a freakin' jerk; can't remember the last time I saw her. Maybe it was Japan, but that's another thing. Those people were wonderful. Most of what you hear

about Washington is just plain wrong. I do like the Patriots, though."
The forty-year-old was wearing a grimy Red Sox hoodie and his speech
petered out as if his memories took him to a private place somewhere
in his mind.

"Shut the fuck up," added Margie Karpinski. "You always talk non-
sense, Tom, and I'm getting sick of it. Everyone is." The heavy-set Margie
stood up, straightened, and stepped towards the small fire. Grabbing a
stick of firewood piled nearby, she tossed it onto the orange embers.

"Careful," a voice came from the group, "we don't want it too big."
It was Derek Hale, a 50-year-old rail-thin and lanky man who pointed
up to the ceiling two stories above where the gray clouds of smoke were
collecting because the hole in the roof, the size of a washing machine,
wasn't sufficient to free it all. "We don't want them to see the smoke."

"I'll do what I please, thank you very much," she replied, looking
at Derek sternly and pulling both her sleeves up past her elbows as if
to signal to everyone she was a woman not open to advice and physically strong enough to make any point she needed to. In doing so, he
saw arms that revealed scars from years of razor cuts every half-inch
or so, some longer and thicker than others, from her wrists right up to
the elbows.

"How many times have you tried to kill yourself?" Derek asked.

"I don't know," Margie said, her voice suddenly calmer. "I've
lost count."

"Now take my cousin," Tommy blurted out. "He was a piece of
work too. He'd just as well break your neck as look at ya. It was because
of the drugs; those damn spiders—they're everywhere. But they were
never in my Toyota. I had one years ago. Yellow."

"I told you to shut the fuck up, didn't I?" Margie lashed out, her
anger returning as she edged herself towards a fight.

Tommy looked at her sheepishly as if he was ready to apologize
for a transgression.

At the same instant, Margie, catching herself mid-explosion of emotion, looked over to the Black man sitting next to the teen, sensing he disapproved of the brewing conflict she was provoking. "Sorry, Boss," she said meekly, then retreated slowly back to her milk crate.

"How many times have I told you," Frank Stringfellow replied briskly to Margie and then scanned the group, "I'm not your boss. My name is Frank and that's it. But you know what we all agreed—respect." It wasn't clear to the people there how or why they started to call Frank Boss. He did what he could to reject that title. But they sensed that it was just a natural thing to do, seeing in him not someone who barked orders or made rules, but someone who had their backs. He was their constellation amidst chaos, a wise coach who would try to help even though he might not have much by way of material things to offer. Had the cognitive compromises of the mental illnesses they possessed not been so great, they might have said that the man just had an innate leadership aura and quiet warmth that couldn't be ignored as it gathered people closer with a subtle magnetism.

"Yes, Boss," Tommy said. "We got it. I'm sorry, I messed up again."

Frank looked over to the pile of unburnt wood and saw that some were strewn on a handful of collected sheets of cardboard, paper forms, and old newspapers someone must have found on one of the office floors that they would use to start the only source of heat the group would have. He reached for some of the sheets and examined them, finding an old shipping order for items probably delivered 20 or more years ago.

"OK then," Frank said, turning back toward the young girl. "One more chance. Got a name?"

"Let's call her Chatty," said Tommy, who looked at the girl with a teasing brotherly smile on his face.

"That won't fit," Margie suggested. "She ain't talked one bit since she got here."

The teen stayed silent and unmoved, except for her eyes that nervously hopped from one person to another, scanning the group for threats.

"Then your name is Bristol," Frank announced, "cause that's where this order went—Bristol, Connecticut. Looks like it was 1998. Way before you were born, probably." The teen gave no sign of acknowledgment, as if lost in thought while transfixed on the flames.

In the weeks that passed since that naming, Frank demonstrated to Bristol that he was looking out for her in a cautious way, just distant enough to make her feel safe, but not close enough to make her feel threatened. He didn't talk to her a lot, nor did he expect anything from her, but in some instinctive and perhaps magical way, his look and manner made Bristol think he might just be OK, though she was never certain what his intentions were.

Making eye contact with the man, or anyone else for that matter, was a fearful thing for the girl because even such a fleeting moment made her feel nothing but shame. Still, when he wasn't looking at her, she would watch Frank closely. It struck her that his quiet but assertive manner was much like those of her father, at least from what she could remember.

Even though she said not one word to him, nor anyone else for that matter, Frank didn't ignore her, and he didn't turn away.

So, amid the thunder in the damp warehouse, as his extended dark hand to invite her to get up from her dingy little corner, Bristol felt a tiny bit less afraid. "There's got to be a better place than this around here. Let's see if we can find you something to eat," the Boss said.

The teen started to extend her hand towards Frank but then quickly pulled it back. *A better place?* she thought to herself. *You must mean a better world. Tell me where I can find that.*

Frank stayed motionless, neither stepping forward nor stepping back, merely waiting. "OK then; suit yourself—it's all the same to me." Sometimes, the adage is true: it does take one to know one.

After a second more, Frank turned and headed to the hallway door that led to the interior spaces of the mill, and Bristol got up to follow. Between her spot and the hallway was a cascade of rainwater, spilling down from one of the holes in the failing roof. While Frank circumvented the shower like anyone would do, Bristol purposely walked right into it, and, closing her eyes, tilted her head straight up and into the stream. The next thunderclap came with lightening such that the flash made the droplets around the girl sparkle. There she paused as the steady drops of rain bounced off her young face and brown hair and soaked into the wool of her coat.

"Come on, Bris," the Boss encouraged, watching her get wet, "this hotel don't come with any towels, ya know."

CHAPTER 2:
A GROUP OF CONCERN

FRANK LED BRISTOL DOWN A LONG HALLWAY FROM WHICH a variety of large, dark rooms with wide plank floors flanked the passage. In their day, they must have housed huge machines and material, but now only the immense glass windows remained, most either cracked or punctured by rocks. If the sun was shining, the glass would have allowed bright light inside, as would the many skylights spaced carefully in a row in the middle of the ceiling. They might have made the dust hanging in the air seem like glitter. The two made right turns and left turns as the corridor snaked through the quiet complex, the structure seeming to swallow them up with the solemnity of a forgotten necropolis for discarded dreams. They reached the far end of the factory and what once was a workshop. Some of the regulars were assembled there.

Dinner for the loose association of people was their only communal meal, if scraping together some meager stew or pasta dish without sauce could be called that. Over the open fire on the concrete floor of the far back work room, someone had fashioned a portable metal grill like the kind that might be found in one of the many nearby tourist campsites which fill up in the warm months with people and their RVs or pop-up tents, trying to escape the heat and congestion of bigger cities like Boston, Hartford, or New York. While such vacationers find an open fire a romantic or enchanting novelty, the outcasts that night in the

Mohawk Mill saw one as a vital necessity, especially when the weather turns cold.

Some Hallet Springs residents wanted more tourism, but so far, the city had not found the "secret sauce" that would bring them to the area in any big number. It was, by all accounts, a fairly nice place to be if you already lived there, but it was situated just far enough from the major mountains with their hiking and winter attractions, just far enough from the interstates and remaining rail lines, and just far enough from exciting cities that might make it a destination of significance. Only one yearly event, the Craft and Gem Festival, brought in large crowds to the town—tourists, antique collectors, mineral hunters, craftspeople, and food vendors—and their week or more of spending was a temporary blip in the economic fortunes of many a Hallet Springs business.

For others, the region was fine without the event and the problems that outside money brings in. To them, the small local college planted conveniently on one end of Main Street, brought enough culture and outsiders to satisfy the local economy while not taxing the public services too much, which, truth be told, were getting harder and harder to maintain at sufficient levels.

Recently, Mayor Peter Haddad thought he found a way to satisfy both constituencies and more besides. Writing in the *Observer* about the upcoming budget decisions that the City Council would face in the coming months, Haddad tried to make the case that no matter what future unfolded in this "gorgeous gem in the Granite State," municipal services, particularly "population monitoring and management" would have to improve. He described how the city's small fleet of monitor drones were getting to the end of their life, and that if the citizens still wanted what they had come to expect from their public safety services, an investment needed to be made in the latest versions of the flying surveillance technology.

"We're a small community," he wrote, "but thanks to potential funding by the U.S. Office of Homeland Security and matching financial support from the New Hampshire Department of Population Management, Hallet Springs can purchase six new state-of-the-art drones and the necessary computers that will equip our valiant Police Department pilots with the tools they need to watch and control the groups of needy who blight our streets and neighborhoods." If he made any mistake in his last article, it was that he failed to use the more politically tolerable term "groups of concern" instead of the word "needy"; the later word was considered risky because it carried the potential for sympathy. "And, if we can move ahead with the demolition of the Mills to make way for new development," he remarked, "we'll finally put Hallet Springs on the map."

If the reaction from the voters who wrote letters to the newspaper after the Mayor's columns was any indicator, the citizenry supported the acquisition, especially if it increased the control, hiding, or removal of the poor and mostly those with mental problems who lived outside government-sanctioned containment protocols. Most people thought the Mayor and City Councilors would get their drones, remove the blighted complex from the heart of town, and become inevitably, if not magically, attractive to investors.

Frank made it a point to read the newspaper too, and his reaction contrasted markedly from what he judged to be the popular response. Each small story of this ilk in this tiny unknown city in this small and unimportant state was for him the raw material in some evil structure, rising tall and confident for all to see like the pyramids at Giza, not as a tomb for a beloved king but more as a burial spot for a long-dead ideal. Though he had only been in the area for less than a year, he had seen this unfold many times in his travels up the Eastern coast of the country, a land he once admired. His patriotism propelled him to military service where he learned much and saw many tragedies. But that seemed like a lifetime ago.

They're coming for us, he thought to himself as he read, anger rising in his body. *Is this where I make a stand?*

In the Mills' dingy workroom, the group of friends was assembling themselves for their Tuesday night dinner. When the Boss entered with Bristol, the bustle momentarily stopped as all eyes fell on the pair. Frank went to each person in greeting, and each one smiled as they shook hands.

"Remember," Frank told Brian and Mary, the two whose turn it was to cook, "not a big fire; watch the smoke. They can see the smoke."

He took a two-day old copy of *The Boston Globe* from the inside of his wet coat and placed it on the makeshift table, as was his custom. Bristol went over to a milk crate she'd come to think of as her spot in the circle and sat quietly. Mary left her station at the fire and went over to her, putting her hand on her shoulder. "Hey Bristol," she said, "good to see you. How are you?" The teen smiled but neither answered nor looked up. "Let me see if I can find something to dry your face."

Mary stirred what looked like a stew in a big pot perched on the grate above the small cluster of orange embers. "Yes, Boss," she said, as her husband Brian carefully placed a foot-long stick of birch sapling on the hot coals. "Looks good, Mary," the Boss said after peering into the pot, but he knew his comment was a stretch.

While the couple were new to the group and still getting to know the routine they fashioned together by necessity, the old timers welcomed them eventually because whatever illness Mary or Brian had, or whatever demons they were running from, they didn't steal from their peers. Mary would talk if someone else started a conversation, and Brian was glad to take his turn with the ancient handsaw they used to cut up a pallet from the warehouse, when the need arose, for the fire. That chore was essential when any rain fell outside, making wood from

14

the forest that still made up one edge of the Mill's property impossible to light. Used sparingly, the lumber from the pallets was also needed for winter, when footprints in the snow from the forest to the factory might be spotted.

They didn't talk about it much, but Mary and Brian could point to something that made the couple distinct. When they were married at the Town Hall three years ago, a photographer from the *Observer* was present covering the event because the nuptials were considered newsworthy. They were the last couple of their kind able to be married in Fontange County because, the very next day, state law number RSA 5511.4 was taking effect, which prohibited marriage between two people known to have "cognitive processing or emotion dysregulation disorders detrimental to individual health and/or social order." No one knew whether the couple's ceremony was the last in the state, but most people thought it was about time New Hampshire followed the numerous examples of such laws in almost every state in the nation.

The cadre of people there were busy, too. A few were removing what plastic plates, bowls, and such they had from an old footlocker someone had found in one of the factory rooms in the Mills, and utensils that came from the dumpsters of a smattering of thrift stores around Hallet Springs because the tableware was too far gone to sell. Others were arranging the crates and makeshift chairs in a circle.

From another doorway, Tommy arrived with another person the group did not recognize. This man looked to be in his 40s or 50s, and his backpack, jeans, and torn jacket looked to be half that age and owned by someone living on the road.

"This is Zak," Tommy announced to the group as he made a few steps into the room. "I met him today near the bus station. He needs something to eat and a place to stay tonight. Sorry, everyone, I didn't tell you yesterday, but I just met him today."

Derek went over to the men and stood between the members and the newcomer. "Hi," Zak said, offering his hand to Derek. "Pleased to meet you."

"Tommy," Derek said, still looking at Zak seriously, but reluctant to take the stranger up on a handshake. "What's his story? Did you bring anything?"

"No, I forgot," Tommy replied, his eyes cast downward. "Sorry."

"Got anything to contribute?" Derek asked Zak. Zak looked confused and scanned the room to judge, if he could, the type of place his new acquaintance had led him to. "No," he said apologetically, "Tommy didn't say anything about that."

"You got to pay for your meal," Derek said. "We all do, every day. That's the rule." Tommy reached for Zak's elbow as if to signal him that the two should reverse their steps and leave. Zak shook him off.

"Look, man," Zak said, "I just got out of Rikers a few weeks ago. I'm trying to get to Canada, but I don't have any cash. I'd give you some if I had it."

"What's Rikers?" Derek asked.

"A prison. What are you, some sort of retard?"

From a distance but within earshot, Frank was monitoring the exchange among the three men. At the last statement, he walked towards the group, which made Tommy smile.

"Hi Boss," Tommy said. "Sorry, sorry, sorry," his sheepish voice growing meeker with each word.

"What's up, Tommy?" he replied. "Who's this?"

"This is Zak. I met him today in town. He needs a place to stay for a while and some food, but we forgot to get anything. We don't have any money either."

"No problem," Frank said. "You know what to do. Zak, here's the deal: First, we don't put anyone down. If you can't do that," he said firmly, "you need to leave. Second, if you want to join us tonight, you are welcome to, but everybody brings something. It's either something to eat, something to burn on the fire, or a rock—something the size of a baseball that someone can throw. If you don't have anything to share for the meal, you and Tommy can head back to the woods and find something else."

"Got it, Boss," Tommy said, "sorry I messed up. We'll find something, either a stick or a stone."

Frank nodded and turned to Zak. "We're happy to share what we got," he explained to Zak. "You can have this food or stay here if you like, but we want you to have dignity, too. If you don't have some food, go find a piece of wood or a rock. A stick or a stone. If it's a stick, it's big enough to burn; if it's a stone, it's no bigger than a baseball."

Looking at the sizable pile of rocks next to the fire, Frank thought that maybe tomorrow's task was to get everyone to help him bring them to the top floor of the building, next to every window that wasn't already broken.

Their meager meal concluded, each in attendance seemed to follow their own sense of when they needed to leave. Tommy and Zak left quietly but not before both expressed thanks to Mary and Brian for working to prepare the food everyone shared. Frank announced his departure, saying he had an early day of work in the morning. The last person he glanced at was Bristol, who looked up at him in acknowledgment as he said "good-bye" to her. She offered back a half-smile and a momentary gaze that he took to mean they were friends.

When the room emptied out, she got up and started to walk to the spot she'd found in the drafty maze of buildings she claimed as her own. She walked down two long dark hallways away from the workroom, strewn with broken furniture, file cabinets, large wooden crates, and other forgotten remnants of the place's heyday. Like every other room in the forlorn Mills, this detritus was covered with layers of dust and pigeon droppings, the stale air rife with the smell of mold. Had she thought about her destination, she may have deduced that the warehouse area of the factory would have held either the raw material that would be transformed by the manufacturing process the Mills housed in one chapter of their history, or the finished products of that transformation as those goods waited for their journey to the customer who would pay for them. Bristol's mind didn't have the luxury of such speculations; it was fixed on survival and finding whatever respite she could from the tornado of emotions—fear especially—that colored her most of her awareness.

To her, the corner she selected was perfect; to any person with a house or apartment, the place was a barren, dirty, and dismal old cavern of cinder block and brick whose roof was made from tired timbers and whose floor smelled of grime and oil. Rainwater pooled in places from the leaky roof, but she knew from her time there the last few weeks that the puddles would dissipate soon enough.

While the massive room contained many stacks of wooden pallets, the girl found a pair nestled in one corner and ideal for her purposes. Whoever arranged them there years ago, instead of piling them snug against the block corner wall, left a four-foot gap on either side of a row of three stacks. In this space, Bristol had rolled out her sleeping bag, her backpack, water bottle and whatever useful items she'd managed to scrounge in her travels. Of particular significance was the cardboard she snagged from the dumpsters behind grocery stores, for they made the only weak insulation she could manage between her bag and the cold floor. She liked the protection that the six-foot high collection of pallets afforded. With her head down to sleep, she could easily glance through the slats of the pallets, scan the area in front, and spot if some interloper or noise roused her from her slumber. After a few days of using this nest, Bristol felt happy that it turned out to be useful, yet not comfortable enough to drop her guard.

Thankfully, most of the night sounds the girl heard from his safe spot were not threats of harm. With the pallets before her and the chilly thick wall behind her, she had the liberty to relax, if just a bit. Since most of the windows in the room were already weakened with age or smashed, the natural noises of the wilderness beyond the buildings were her consistent lullaby. After a strong rain, the revitalized Pennebec flowed over a series of rocks and waterfalls on the other side of the building such that the sound was audible, steady, and peaceful. Sometimes, the branches of the one oak tree just outside her corner would rustle and tap against one of the windows. Like clockwork, one bird's music from that tree rang louder than the others, a haunting riff that she thought must have come from an owl. Each night, it was there in the air no matter when she felt safe enough to sleep, the phrase of six notes somehow comforting and familiar, as if in some mysterious way, nature was wishing her "good night, sweet dreams" since no human being would. The vocalizer of that melody could not have any notion that it had been years since Bristol had either.

CHAPTER 3:

MAX GETS THE MINIMUM

THE NOVEMBER AFTERNOON WAS GRAY AND CHILLY WHEN Max Cherryfield walked past the front door of a simple two-story brick building on Main Street with the only friend he had in the world, a ten-year-old Cavalier King Charles Spaniel, aptly named King Charles. It was far more than the ratty black leash that linked the two together and Max knew, from the moment he saw the dog at the humane society in Hallet Springs, that he'd found his soulmate, a companion of infinite patience, understanding, and love that only dog-lovers know. Befitting his name, Max found the dog a gold-colored collar at a local thrift shop.

If thrift-store clothing were ever to make a fashion runway in Milan or New York, Max would be a trendsetter who would send the clothing industry into the stratosphere. The tired and sickly middle-aged man was squarely entrenched in a poverty-shaped existence, alive only because his financial support, medical insurance, and social benefits were just sufficient, if he was careful and smart, to keep death from starvation, isolation, and homelessness at bay. It hadn't always been that way.

After a promising start in an academic career at Dartmouth, the genetic timebomb of mental illness exploded with a vengeance in his first year as an adjunct in the history department. Undergraduate work at Notre Dame and doctoral years at Harvard prepared him well, he thought, for the plumb Ivy job in Hanover, where he and his wife happily settled—which, to the client now trapped in the state's mental health monitoring system of the day, seemed like a lifetime ago. But, like a thief in the night, schizophrenia had other plans, robbing him of his marriage, career, friendships, self-esteem, and the capacity to hold down a job. In fleeting moments of mental clarity, Max often thought of John Nash, the Princeton University mathematician made famous by the old movie "A Beautiful Mind," wondering why no one would be interested in making a film about him—a promising career of a brilliant scholar brought low by some mysterious monster in his DNA. But, unlike Nash, Cherryfield hadn't had the triumph of a Nobel Prize and now, thanks to fate, his clean and trendy Dockers and North Face jackets were replaced by two-dollar jeans and faded gray sweatshirts from the bargain bin at the Salvation Army.

Inseparable from his friend, his lifeline, the fifteen-pound canine pranced happily alongside as Max strolled past the entrance of the office of the Mental Illness Management Service, its MIMS understated black sign screwed into the red brick walls, to the end of the block. After taking a turn at the corner, the two entered a small alleyway that led towards the rear of the building. It was a route they had to take every second day of the month. Coming to a thick glass window in the wall of the building, he waved to the uniformed security guard who acknowledged him with a nod and pressed a button, which made the steel gate in front of Max and the dog pop open.

King Charles followed his master through the gate, which allowed entrance to the rear parking lot that was surrounded by a chain-link fence that protected the expensive cars of employees from unauthorized interlopers. There, Max could see that the queue of people lined up in front of another window was not terribly longer than usual. He recognized some of the people in the line ahead of him but made no attempt at conversation. As Max waited, the dog sat calmly by the man's muddy sneakers.

In time, Max found himself to be the second person in line. In front of him, an elderly woman in a tattered sweater too thin for the cold temperature addressed a female worker behind a two-inch thick glass where she sat at a small metal desk that looked like it might have come from a bank teller window some years ago.

"I can't really hear you," the woman said to the worker, getting her mouth closer to the small microphone in the glass.

A garbled reply came back to her from a speaker embedded in the window: "That's all the money you have left in your account this month, dearie. Next, please." The woman turned away dejectedly, leaving Max free to approach the window.

As he came forward, a small door no bigger than a mailbox in the window just beneath the speaker hummed opened automatically. Max rolled up his right sleeve halfway to the elbow and put his bared hand and arm in the slot, onto a computer screen scratched by years of use. A blue laser light moved up and down the screen and when it faded, Max removed his hand.

"Cherryfield," the worker said stoically, her eyes studying the computer screen at her desk far more seriously than she did in her fleeting glance a Max.

"Let's see," she said, more to herself than to Max. "Says here that your next injection is in two weeks. Be sure to report to the clinic about fifteen minutes ahead of time. Your appointment will be sent to your minder, but it's not until the twentieth. Your microchip will need to be replaced in two months. It's a day surgery thing, but you've done that before."

Max nodded, recalling the time five years ago when, under local anesthesia, a nurse cut his arm to remove a bloody implant just above his right wrist, a wafer thin disk no bigger than an aspirin that contained his full medical history, financial and academic records, a DNA sequence chart, and a GPS tracker. Thanks to the artificial intel algorithms in the programming, the computer also gave the reader any important answers they might need were they to be asked questions by the person whose record this was.

"It also says that your rent has gone up this month," the worker continued, "and that the rental charge for your minder is now due." The woman turned and opened a cash drawer, counted out a few bills and some coins, and put them in a white envelope. She turned back to the screen to read the next instructions:

Diagnosis: Schizophrenia, mixed type.

Remind the individual that his long-acting injected medication is not the only drug he agreed to take. Inform him that one tablet of Praxisidryl is to be taken with food every morning to control hallucinations, delusions, and other symptoms like anxiety. Remind him that should he experience any other symptoms, he should contact us via his mobile minder text message service. Remind Maxwell that he agreed to two hours of community service with the Hallet Springs Parks Department every week, Fridays at 10 a.m. Tell the man that the City of Hallet Springs needs him to comply with everything he's been instructed as part of his plan.

The worker turned to Max and casually said, "This says you agreed to take other pills, so do that."

Max nodded, knowing from experience that it was safer to say nothing than to offer anything verbal for the audio recordings being made of this interchange. He had been in the monitoring system of services that the state euphemistically called "treatment" from time to time. That tenure also taught him that if you were to survive that system with any modicum of freedom or self-respect, the best way was to have the authorities think you were a docile participant, adhering to the plan of steps, measures, and medications you were shaped into accepting, and not causing them to expend resources to solve any problems you might present. Some training material for new employees in this system reduced the overarching goal of this "vital public function" as designed to achieve "compliance, with a smile" from participants. He also knew of the tragic consequences that fell to those who hadn't figured this out.

The woman returned to the envelope of money on her desk and sent it through a slot in the window so Max could retrieve it. "There you go," she said without expression. "There's $22.56 for the rest of the month."

The shock in the man's face was a significant change in his presentation just seconds before as her message came like a blow. "Wait," he demanded, "there's got to be more left than that. Is there a mistake?"

The worker looked back to the computer screen and paused to study a square of information that contained Max's budget until his next U.S. Social Security check arrived into the system. "No," she said, "no, there's no mistake. Like I said, the landlord is charging more rent with your new lease, the utilities where you live have gone up for everyone, your minder rental fee hits this month, you got your $2 per day meal allowance here, and, well, that's about it. Look at your minder and find the budget app. It will show you all this and show you how much you can spend per day."

Max was already doing that before the worker was finishing her accounting. He removed the government-issued smart phone from his pocket and his thumbprint was sufficient to have the money application software the woman was referencing light up on the tiny device. "I see it," he told her, the look of anxious surprise still on his face. "But I need to take Charlie to the vet this month. His license is due, shots; what about food?"

"As I said," the worker replied, "you have a $2 per day meal allowance; you should be able to find something with that."

"No," Max said, "you don't understand. I don't care about food for me, but food for Charlie. As long as he can eat, that's the important thing." His tone carried more panic than there was a minute ago as his thoughts and emotions started to boil within him at the news.

The woman returned to the computer screen and she reached for mouse that moved the information upward, her eyes darting around the display as she clicked here, searching for the proper predetermined response to the increasingly agitated man in front of her.

Then the familiar cavalcade of sinister voices erupted in Max's mind, hijacking his awareness with a vengeance. The first was that of an old nameless lady he thought to be a witch that haunted his dreams: *She can smell your stink clear through that glass, you worthless boy. Why are you so dirty?* The second sound was from a group of men, speaking some unfamiliar language Max did not recognize, but their laughter and jeering he did. The next came from the familiar Clara, a ten-year-old child prone to singing: *Row, row, row your boat, skipping down the street....* She never had the lyrics right. Then came Professor Tice, an advisor from college: *You can make something of yourself, man; be confident because you will bring great things to the world.* The angry old witch then returned: *Just get the hell out of here before I kill you, but not before I slit your mangy mutt open so you can see his guts spill all over the street!*

After a minute of silence, the worker turned back to the window to address Max. "It says here that there are six states in the country that could provide you with a different budget for monthly expenses that might be easier than New Hampshire: Arkansas, Wyoming, Ohio, South Carolina, and Alabama. We can arrange a transfer of your Social Security to any of these places. There are bus vouchers available at City

Hall if you need help getting there. You can't take your dog on the bus, however." Her monotone delivery of this message was slow, clear, and devoid of feeling.

Max took a deep breath, mustering his efforts to tune out the malevolent mayhem only he could hear, hoping that the technique he had been taught by Frank would help him calm down, think, and collect his thoughts in the face of this useless information cloaked in the guise of a helpful instruction. Even with the shock of this message and his mounting anger, he remembered that everything he told the worker behind the window was being recorded and could be used to build a case that he was hostile or some sort of threat to the service system at the MIMS office.

There was no prompt on her instruction screen to tell her that for Max, going anywhere, let alone to some other state, without Charlie was like asking him to cut off his right arm, for losing an appendage would have been preferable to losing his dog. The worker had no way of knowing this because Max, like other participants in the "treatment" program at MIMS, never told anyone the important things about themselves— not the doctors, the psychologists, or service coordinators whose job it was to keep society problem-free.

"No," he told her eventually, "that won't be necessary. I'll figure something out." Max lowered his head and reached to pat King Charles, who responded by getting up from his sitting to wag his thick fan-like tail, energized that they would be walking together again. "Good boy," Max said, hoping his companion wouldn't detect the sadness that had overcome him. The two turned to leave.

"But," the woman said, looking at him squarely in the eye this time, "there are plenty of squirrels in the woods. Maybe he'd eat that."

Max looked back at her, thinking in a micro-second that the idea of killing anything, even for his best friend, would be impossible for him to do. Dejected, all he could manage to say was "Thank you." As he left the window, all he heard the worker say was, "Next."

CHAPTER 4:
CLIMATE CHANGE

JUST ABOUT THE SAME TIME MAX LEFT THE PARKING LOT AT the office of the State's Mental Illness Management Service, Fontange County Sheriff Bertrand LaBounty was sitting down with *Observer* reporter Paula Damascus in his courthouse offices in downtown Hallet Springs, the county seat. LaBounty, a forty-year veteran in New Hampshire's public safety community, was a large officer who always reported to work in a dress uniform, tactical gear, and Ruger sidearm. Radio and shoulder-harnessed microphone always at the ready, the stocky, gray-haired Sherriff prided himself on staying vigilant on the events of the day, particularly those he felt needed his personal command involvement.

But in a few days, LaBounty would put all that stress aside, climb into his RV with his wife, head off to see America, and then arrive at a retirement community in Florida. Damascus was assigned to write a farewell biography of the officer, whose departure, for some in the department, marked the end of an era.

"Sheriff," she began, "your years with the county have been nothing short of remarkable. You've witnessed many changes in your time; what stands out?" The young lady moved a small tape recorder closer to the high-back leather chair just large enough to accommodate the imposing lawman sitting behind his mahogany desk.

The man pondered the question carefully, just as he did the 22-year-old interviewer, taking his time to answer her. "That's an interesting question," he said. "It's hard to pick one or two things."

Damascus looked at him patiently. "Take your time," she encouraged.

"When I graduated from the Academy, let's see, that would have been just before the turn of the century, life seemed simpler, I guess. Then came 9/11, then the recession, then Trump, the first pandemic, then the weekly shootings and terror attack in DC, then the hack wars, the bioterrorists in California, then the second pandemic—where should I start? People won't like me saying this, but I miss the state, the country in fact, we had when I was young."

As LaBounty's time in service to the county was waning, his candor with people about his perspectives on things he chose to share was waxing. The advent of retirement brought him a mounting freedom, he felt, but embracing the opportunity would require a calculated risk.

"What was it like?" the reporter asked.

With an Associate's Degree from a state community college, LaBounty developed himself into a studious man in his leisure time. Other than to his wife Margaret, he didn't talk much about the book he'd been reading, nor anything about his political views or social leanings regarding current events in the New Hampshire, the nation, or the world. He stuck to his work with dedication and professionalism and to his family with a love that stood the test of time. Besides keeping current with law enforcement trends, he was fond of deepening his command of world history, economics, whatever the Sunday *New York Times* dished up, and some spy novel mixed in between.

"To me," he began, "the last few decades have been about climate change. It's been insidious."

"For sure!" she agreed, "I can't remember a winter when we had any great blizzards."

"That's not what I mean," he said, correcting her. "It's a metaphor. It's the social climate. We've lost the connections, the idea of what it means to be a community, any notion of the common good. We've become so focused on public safety and the wealthy, nothing else matters. I think we spend so much on safety only because it serves the private good."

Damascus looked surprised but didn't interrupt. "Don't get me wrong," he continued. "Most would say that the county has gained by all this infusion of federal dollars for technology; it's meant to protect the community from more terrorism, lone-wolf shooters, and groups that radicalize the disenfranchised. That was what it was supposed to do, I mean."

"What has it done, then?"

"Let's take a walk and I'll show you." With that, the lawman got up from his desk and loosened the straps on his Kevlar vest, which then he removed with ease. He opened his office door to the hallway, and the reporter, grabbing her recorder, exited first.

LaBounty took her down a hallway and used a key code to unlock a security door and enter the rest of the command center. Taking the first left, he opened another door to show her a darkened room full of large flat screen monitors, about twelve in all, arrayed on the far wall in a gradual curve. In the center of the room was a console where two officers were seated, scanning the images in front of them, astutely and quickly studying every screen. Each had their right hand on a joystick and their left on a modified computer keyboard.

"Closed-circuit TV?" the reporter asked.

"Nope," the Sheriff replied. "That's in another room; these are the aerial images from our drones. We've got four in the air for every patrol vehicle deployed at this moment in the city. These technicians fly each drone, and the video is monitored here. We can send any footage to the cars on the streets and give them a live feed of things they can't see.

That way, the monitoring of the area is more effective. The military term for this is 'force multiplier.' You'd be surprised at how this gives us the upper hand."

Damascus was transfixed. She glanced from screen to screen and saw many familiar locations: the Main Street shopping district, the parking lot outside the emergency room of the hospital, a residential neighborhood with each home complete with high wall and gated driveway, the area's only feeding station for the homeless, and the green lawn of the common in the center of Hallet Springs. She could even make out the image of the white Congregational Church at the far end.

"And these aren't even the latest models. We'll be getting the next generation from U.S. Dynamics very shortly, assuming they pass the budget down at City Hall, but the mayor tells me he knows they will. The new ones can stay aloft about two hours longer, have greater AI that should intuit the operator's wishes more effectively, and automatically return to their base before the batteries drain just like the robot vacuum sweeper does in your home."

"This would have been science fiction when I left the Academy as a rookie patrol officer. But, because of all the terrorism and violence in the teens and twenties, added alongside so many tech leaps we've seen everywhere, then you put the two trends together, you get a massive public investment in new tools that make law enforcement far more advanced."

"Looks great," the reporter said. "But where's the climate change? I still don't understand.

CHAPTER 5:
WE'VE LOST IT

"MY THEORY," THE SHERIFF CONTINUED, "IS THAT THIS SAFEty-oriented technology has morphed into a type of social control cloaked in the red, white, and blue of cost savings in tax dollars. The U.S. has spent so much on security that we've slowly made nonexistent our capacity to assist some social groups who need the government's help. Nowadays, we call them 'populations of concern,' and before they might have been called people beneath the poverty level, the disabled, the unemployed, or what have you. People don't appreciate how much our role has changed over the years."

"Let me show you what I mean," he said, turning to one of the officers at the control desk. "Officer Bianco," LaBounty directed, "bring the closest drone to any residential section in West Hallet Springs if you would please. Put the image on screen one."

The officer nodded and moved the joystick from left to right while typing in some keystrokes with his other hand. The image on screen one quickly sped up as if someone had engaged the unit's accelerator.

"Keep an altitude of fifteen feet above street-level," he instructed Bianco. Turning to Damascus, he asked, "What do you see?"

"I see a typical neighborhood," she answered, "same as always."

"Tell me."

"A two-lane street, leaves in the gutters; sidewalks on both sides, someone walking a dog, cars back and forth." She paused to look more intently at the screen.

"I see every house on either side; driveways have iron gates closed to the cozy two- bedroom ranches beyond. Front yards have different high fences."

"Right," LaBounty said, "and each with razor wire or decorative spikes on top; see that?"

"Yes, right," the reporter answered, "like I said, nothing unusual."

"It is unusual, however; property owners get funds from the government to protect their homes because the risk of crime and terrorism is too high for law enforcement to address. It was not like that when I started my career. Then we lived in vastly safer times; but no more."

"Let me show you something else," he continued. "Officer, what drone do you have near to St. Theresa's? Isn't it about the time they open?"

"That would be unit seventeen, sir," came the reply. "It's screen six."

LaBounty gently touched the reporter's upper left arm to prompt her to move a few steps to her right, getting closer to screen six.

As the two looked carefully, the image showed the back of a large stone church coming closer and closer into prominence. The drone was at a treetop perspective as it glided to an elevation at a spot that looked to be the edge of a parking lot behind the building. There seemed to be a long line of people queuing up in front of a steel brown door.

"Pan the crowd, please, but not too close," the sheriff instructed his officer. Soon the image was of the line of people who, if they looked in the right direction, might be recognized by the people controlling the drones. At the end of the line stood a man, looking downcast and pensive, with a little dog with a shiny gold collar sitting at his feet.

"Looks like the usual customers," Bianco reported, "waiting for the doors to open for their dinner." In the bottom third of the screen, a row of facial recognition applications, working at lightning speed, showed photos and biodata on every individual standing in the queue, which it could find in their vast library of digital files.

"What do you see?" LaBounty asked Damascus.

"Poor, tired people? They look dirty," she answered.

"Exactly," he said. "Let's go back to my office. Thank you, officer; continue your routine patrol." At that, Bianco nodded.

Back behind his large desk, the sheriff resumed making his point to the young reporter. "In short, you saw something of two groups of people in the country these days: when I was a kid, my dad told me that the people like us were called 'middle class' because they worked, paid taxes, sent their kids to school, coached soccer, made it through paycheck-to-paycheck, made their car payments, you know? Then we have the wealthy class, neighborhoods where most of the drones were deployed if you noticed, bigger houses, higher fences and gates, private security for their kids until they go off to private colleges while the parents travel."

"Nobody else matters now," he said. "Those people in line at the soup kitchen? They aren't really part of society anymore. I bet you haven't paid much attention to them, Ms. Damascus, because you've grown up in a time where there's been a subtle marginalization of them here, just like in all the other states. You might want to write a story about that—but then you'd be looking for another job probably."

"How have we done that?" the reported asked.

The sheriff looked at his wristwatch, then to a laptop on his desk to glance at the latest subject lines in his inbox, particularly for any alerts from the state police HQ in Concord. Damascus sat patiently, understanding that he couldn't give her his undivided attention.

Looking back to her, he said, "In my opinion, it's been done over the last 20 years or so with a subtle manipulation of public policy that was, for the architects behind it, part cunning and part luck. I've been a student of this move because of some family reasons."

"For example, the people you saw waiting in line for St. Theresa's Community Kitchen are some of the victims of these policies. They probably have drug addiction, though God knows where they get the drugs; or they have mental illness, or some disability, or a learning problem that prevents them from working. That means that something prevents them from contributing to the wealthy class like the rest of us. As consequence, we've slowly taken away most of their civil rights."

"Sheriff," the reporter said, "the article I'm supposed to be writing is about your retirement and your career as a civil servant for the State of New Hampshire. Seems like we're getting off topic, but then again, maybe readers will want to hear your opinions too. Should we stick to your resume, or continue?"

The man looked at her and smiled. "Let's keep going," he said, "I bet the owners of your paper won't publish it anyway, but you might learn something."

"What about 'civil rights?'" she asked.

"Besides not having the right to vote anymore, they've slowly lost freedoms that those in the other classes take for granted. For example, the only housing options open to them are in certain community-designated set-asides, and in most places like Hallet Springs, that means the area of the city or town that other people don't want to be in, like flood plains, orphaned properties with potentially hazardous waste buried someplace, or buildings that don't meet current safety codes but 'grandfathered' to house people of concern."

"You might not know this, but we've also taken away their right to purchase things of their choosing. They get financial assistance from the government, right? It's called SSDI, or Social Subsistence Discretionary Income. Out of that entitlement, their rent is automatically deducted, as is the cost of their monitoring. What's left gets to them in the mail in the form of a debit card. When they go to the SafeMart, or any other store, Uncle Sam dictates what items they can buy. In other words, they can buy from a select list of food, canned soup, mac and cheese mix, canned tuna, and peanut butter, but not much else. If they need, say, toilet paper, while there may be ten brands on the shelf, the government only allows them to purchase one brand. Even if it's not the cheapest."

The reporter looked surprised. "Sounds like you know a lot about this. I never heard of that before. Sounds like it's all regulated. Why is that?"

"Sadly, I know about this for personal reasons, but again, that's another story. If you ask me," the man replied, "it's due to the deficit."

"Economics?" she asked, trying to clarify the sheriff's point.

"No," he said, "not the budget deficit. The empathy deficit."

The reporter knew that her time with LaBounty was getting short and that his busy schedule would not accommodate this diversion much longer. She concluded her interview with a few final questions about his retirement plans and family background. She expressed her thanks for his time and indicated that her story would appear in a day or two, after her editor reviewed it later that afternoon.

The sheriff rose from his desk and started to walk her out of the office towards the main entrance. In the hallway, he felt the courage to add one more piece of information for her article.

"You know why they can only buy one brand of toilet paper?" he asked seriously. "It's because the paper company wants it that way. They made it so."

"Huh?" the reporter asked, "what's that?"

"Have you ever heard of Benjamin Franklin?" LaBounty asked her, seemingly to change the subject.

"Yes; wasn't he someone who fought in the Civil War?"

"No, he was one of the founding fathers—you know, Revolutionary War. Anyhow, he helped write the U.S. Constitution. Once, the story goes, when the Constitutional Convention was finished for the day, a lady on the sidewalk in Philadelphia yelled to him, 'what sort of

Government have you made for us, Mr. Franklin?' He yelled back 'a Republic, madam, if you can keep it.'"

He stopped his pace in the hallway and the reported did the same. He looked her in the eye. "We haven't kept it," he said. "Print that. Now we just have an oligarchy."

CHAPTER 6:
I'M DONE WITH BEING BRAVE

THE NEXT WEEK, WHEN FRANK STRINGFELLOW GOT OUT OF the Uber in the parking lot of the Veteran's Affairs Hospital in White River Junction that morning, he looked up at the stately old façade of the original facility with its large white columns against the red brick walls of the main entrance, and the sinking feeling in his stomach that started the night before intensified. The mind is a funny factory. It can take the raw material of strong emotions, blend them with stress, add the glue that memories afford, and press them until a visceral sensation that lasts, never far from consciousness. Frank was all too familiar with this phenomenon and the blow it brings to the mind and body.

He wondered how many soldiers walked through those old and now unused front doors; how many wounds, surgeries, experiments, or amputations could be counted among the records within. It would be impossible to say, but judging from the age of the old building, now flanked on either side by newer buildings grafted on to the original hospital like an old New England farmhouse, it was undoubtedly in the millions. The "elephant in the room" question for Frank these days, was whether all the battles, bombs, and bullets over all these years had been worth it if you consider that, in the end, all those warriors were risking their lives for some ideal of America and its village values that seemed to no longer exist.

For his biannual visit to the VA, Frank spent an hour waiting for a ten-minute test and the frustrating realization that this pattern needed to repeat itself three times before he would finally have the thirty-minute interview that was the finale of the visit. He was no stranger to this draining ordeal since, given his service injuries, he had been through it for years, which was, he knew, a requirement for his ongoing disability benefits. Perhaps the most uncomfortable part of each trip was the way the staff there looked at him, which try as he might, just made him feel guilty.

Like the other times, the social worker who introduced himself to him to start the last element of his experience that day was an unfamiliar actor in his care.

"My name is Captain Frank Lawton," the portly man began. "I'm glad to meet you, Lieutenant." His brown shirt and pants bore all the symbols of his rank, clean and pressed to Army standards, as was his short haircut.

"Hello, sir," Frank replied.

Though Lawton brought with him a paper file that Frank assumed might be his medical records, the captain also looked at the laptop on the table beside him. "Do you know why you have to come here for these tests, Mr. Stringfellow?"

"I haven't forgotten."

"In keeping with the study protocol, I have to repeat the message anyway, and it's good to know that you remember. Lieutenant," he intoned, "you have a service-related disability commonly known around the VA as a 'double tap.' Your service to your country caused you to experience both injuries to your body, which have been treated and remediated, and to your brain, which may or may not have healed. The first assault you experienced in a missile attack on your base that killed or injured ten others there at the time, and the second from the many assaults that came upon you in combat. You have both post concussive syndrome from the first and post-traumatic stress disorder from the second. Upon discharge, now almost ten years ago, you have been required to participate in the biannual tests like you had today."

Frank looked out the small window in the office. "I remember all this," he said. "The last time I was here, the doctors thought my memory was still intact but that they would have to keep an eye on me in case of decline. One can only hope."

Lawton looked surprised. "How's that?" he asked. "Do you want your memory to go?"

"Every damn day," Frank replied, looking at the captain directly. "Sir."

Lawton's tone of voice changed, going from interviewer to admirer seamlessly. "Lieutenant Stringfellow, I'm not sure you understand, this but you might not realize how famous you are. As the commander of Alpha Company, your accomplishments on the battlefield that are examples of bravery, innovation, leadership, and determination are now written about in textbooks at the Norman Swartzcoff War College. Do you know that? Hell, look at your record of medals! I haven't seen a list this long in some time. You should be proud, Lieutenant. You're a freak'n hero."

"If you say so," Frank replied, dismissing the accolade like some predictable cliché.

"If you made one mistake," the captain added, "it was that you didn't tell'm how bad you felt after the missile strike. By rights, your brain should be mush right now, but it isn't. We now understand that the shock wave and sound blast of their weapon harm the limbic, occipital, and prefrontal cortex regions of the brain. You must have had crippling migraines for months, and yet you still went into fight."

"My men, sir. I had to."

There was a pause in the conversation and Frank looked at the floor, sensing what was coming next from the Captain's lips.

"As you know, the VA follows soldiers like you after their discharge because they know that double tap veterans have more risk of harm to themselves or others. We ask you these same questions at every visit; you know the drill. Have you purchased a firearm since your last check-in? Have you felt like hurting yourself or anyone else?"

Frank looked at the interviewer with the same poker face he used to end this sort of questioning many times before. "No, sir," he answered, but it was only half the truth to both.

In the back seat of the Uber that Frank found to take him back to Hallet Springs, his body relaxed from the ordeal; but his mind did not. His awareness was flooded with images and sensations parading through his consciousness like some disjointed movie with no perceptible plotline: Faces of his fallen friends and former soldiers, his parents on the stoop of their Virginia farmhouse, girlfriends he had loved and lost, glimpses of medal ceremonies he endured that were to him often more painful than firefights. This collage of memories would be bearable were it not for the emotions triggered by each one in turn, the wave after wave of guilt, sadness, and grief that seemed to rest in the depth of his stomach showing itself as physical pain there, which he knew from experience, arrived before the stinging in his eyes and the migraine.

If I'm a hero, he asked himself, *why don't I feel like one?*

In times like these, Frank had to direct his memories to the helpful treatment he experienced at the VA hospital in Pennsylvania many years ago. They taught him a technique called "tracking." He had to think about and feel the bodily sensations he was experiencing as the painful flashbacks of trauma steadily took over his thoughts and emotions. Creating gentle awareness of how his body kept score enabled the veteran to shift from painful thinking to something positive.

To practice that now, Frank reflected upon the next task he would accomplish back at his apartment, namely, to continue with the restoration of an old Smith and Wesson revolver he stumbled upon in a desk drawer in some random office at the Mills. The thought of getting the rusty gun to work was both attractive and somewhat soothing.

CHAPTER 7:
SOME CLEAN CLOTHES

SINCE IT WAS WEDNESDAY AND JUST LIKE THE OTHER CAST-asides, a dinner meal at St. Theresa's was Bristol's destination, too. The cool late afternoon temperature caused her to zip up her blue-gray denim jacket as she walked along Park Street, which ran parallel to Main, a block or so away. Crisp brown leaves on the sidewalk crackled as she shuffled through them, and the stirring unleashed the signature fragrance of oak and maple so telling of October in New England. Just days ago, she knew, these leaves had been part of the big trees that lined both sides of the street, just like their counterparts all over the region, small elements of the yellow, red, and orange quilt of foliage that wraps every hill and valley like creation's masterpiece this time of year. She looked down carefully as she walked, hoping to find a brilliant one to retrieve and study.

The teen passed by the chain-linked fences that protected the parking lots of various stores struggling to stay viable in the declining city of Hallet Springs, sprinkled in between many that were boarded shut or vacant, victims of the digital transformation of the U.S. retail system that altered the traditional shopping models at the heart of a consumer economy. Those establishments still open—hardware, liquor, consignment furniture and clothing, rare book and antique or specialty food shops—tended to share a common parking lot so that the gated security costs could be shared. They also shared a common armed guard service that scanned the identifier code embedded in every windshield for the driver's criminal history, residence status, and credit history.

Bristol wished she had even something as small as ten dollars to buy a luxury from any one of the stores she passed. Finding herself straining to recall the last time she had a candy bar, a new scarf just for show, earrings, or sunglasses, she couldn't pin down the specific memory and pushed this reverie aside. Looking to her left, she saw the SafeMart grocery store with a poster in the large plate glass window advertising a sale called "Taste the World" in big black letters.

How do I taste the world? she thought to herself. *What would that be like? Sour or sweet, stale or fresh, earthy like a carrot or light like cotton candy?*

Two boys about age 10 were walking towards her, bouncing a basketball between them, laughing, and smiling like any other kids at school dismissal. Carefree and happy, they came within a few steps of Bristol and, making quick eye contact, cheerily said, "Hi" as they passed her.

"Hi," she replied, the smallest hint of smile appearing in a flash.

Taste the world, she thought again, as if it was not a slogan but an instruction or a friendly piece of advice. Then some phrases assembled in her mind.

Today, let unconquerable gladness dwell.

Let me delight in every sight,

savor every taste and scent and be gracious even before gratitude arrives.

Let me come to life with joy.

Even if it's blasé, I'll say hurray!

The poem made her recall a creative writing teacher she had in her high school in Omaha, Nebraska. Ms. Li was perhaps the only member of the faculty who could see that the girl had an insightful mind just waiting to blossom. After school, the lady would tutor her in poetry and fiction writing. Teacher and student would have long conversations about the latest books on the best-seller list. A voracious reader and clever writer, Li saw her student as a shy but bright kid who would go far, do well, and eventually shine, no matter where her fortunes took her. By the end of her freshman year, Li was sure that girl would do advanced placement English in no time.

Lost in these memories, Bristol continued onward to the section of Park Street dotted with three-story brick buildings with small storefronts on the ground floor and apartments above, the front doors of which abutted the sidewalk. The once deep red brick, so familiar to old New England communities like Hallet Springs, was faded and weathered into a dirty rust color mixed with patches of brown and black from years of grime and pollution. Some storefronts had been converted into coffee shops and restaurants and, at irregular intervals, groups of two or three such places were separated by dark alleyways that lead to parking lots or small side streets in the back.

He must have been hiding in one of these alleys. A man grabbed her from behind before she even knew what had happened.

The rush of adrenalin started even before her placid and poetic thoughts exploded into panic. By the time her instinct to run came into her consciousness, his two large hands had a tight grip on her arms just beneath her shoulders. In that position, he could manipulate the thin girl with ease, despite her wiggling and the protest of her muscles.

"I know you won't scream," he said, speaking close to her left ear. "Just like before. You don't speak, you don't yell." She recognized the voice in an instant and the man's smell, a blend of alcohol and cigarettes.

Muscling the lithe teen into the alley with speedy force and efficiency, her struggles to get free had no influence. In the motions, she looked down into the poorly lit passage and realized there was no one there, just the presence of trash bins and liter mixed with leaves. Even if she did call out, the thought of a rescuer would be only a fantasy.

Dreams, fantasies, hopes...Bristol knew these well from her journey away from her ordinary life in Nebraska running up through the Ohio River Valley, eventually up to New York state and across Vermont to New Hampshire. Where she was going after Hallet Springs was anyone's guess as she herself didn't really know or care, just that she had to keep going, keep running, keep living as best she could.

It wasn't always this way for the intelligent and curious girl. But after the overdose death of her mom two years ago; three foster families and four schools after that; more than one attempt by the state's Children's Welfare department to track down her biological father; and one rape by a gym teacher at her last school, the teen fled, hoping that miles and miles of roads, the rainy nights in the woods, or the crowded conditions in whatever homeless shelter she came upon might insulate her from years of pain so that the memories and thoughts would stop.

But if there was one thing Bristol knew from the last year or so of her still-unfolding life, it was that hope was a bipolar friend, something you weren't exactly sure you could trust. One day, it would be an encourager and motivator, a personal life coach prompting you on with optimism and giving you some needed strength. The next, it would be a sneaky trickster laying out something wonderful ahead like an oasis and then showing you it was only a mirage, blown away as easily as dust on a table.

The man threw her to the ground and straddled himself onto her waist even before she could wrangle free. Grabbling her jacket just underneath her chin, he yanked it open, making the five buttons pop free, revealing an old gray T shirt that said 'Harvard' across the front.

"I like educated women," he said as he smiled. As his left hand moved to her throat, his right started to unbutton the girl's blue jeans and then he fumbled with her zipper.

Bristol's rush of panic intensified. She tried to raise a knee into the man's back but his weight on her thighs made such range of motion impossible. *Not again, you bastard,* she thought to herself, *not again!* Next, she heard the distinctive sound of her zipper's metal teeth separating from their mates and the tight grip of the Levis around her waist loosening.

Unlike her pinned legs, her arms were free since, in the violence of her tackle to the sidewalk and the man's fall on top of her, he hadn't worried about the teen's skinny arms. She moved them back and forth searching for something to grab. At first, her right hand perched on something that felt like a tin can buried in the leaves. In another frantic repositioning, it found something that felt like it might be a beer bottle. She suddenly felt for the neck.

With whatever reserve of energy she could muster, fueled by both adrenalin and fear, Bristol sensed from the weight that her weapon still contained some liquid and, in a lightening quick motion, struck the man in his right temple with the bottle. The glass shattered when it hit her assailant's face, spilling the beer it contained onto his face and then onto her chest and face. The man leaned over and fell beside her, using both hands to clutch his face, blood dripping through his fingers. "Shit!" he screamed.

The aroma of cheap brew never smelled so good. With her attacker down, she leaped to her feet and started to flee back to the street, grabbing her still open jeans with one hand as she ran. In a quick pause, she zipped and buttoned them and continued her escape. A car or two passed her but she thought against flagging them down to get whatever help their drivers could offer, assuming, of course, they stopped to help a clearly frightened teenager. Instead, she kept running towards her original destination of the soup kitchen, hoping that with each passing block came the lesser likelihood that her creepy attacker was too injured to follow.

Rounding the corner onto Dover St, Bristol could see St. Theresa's in the distance. She could tell that the normal crowd of needy—called 'guests' by the parish community—were already filing into the back entrance of the church, to the attached hall that served as a dining area three evenings per week for the area poor, homeless, forgotten, or destitute. Though her legs ached from the run, she kept pushing herself, thinking that even if the man were following her, the open area of the parking lot would afford her some safety.

As the line of people approached the door, each guest stopped in front of Sr. Isabel Gakunde, who stood there like a drill sergeant, the demeanor of authority conveyed by her business-like approach to her task at hand, but tempered by a sincere concern for the people she greeted. Her black skin shown distinctively against the collar of her white blouse that peeked out underneath the navy-blue overcoat she wore. As each one came closer to the woman, they rolled up their right sleeve and, palm up, allowed them to be scanned by the small device the nun held in her hand. A small beep signaled that each scan was tallied.

Bristol joined the end of the queue and her heavy breathing slowed. She clutched her jacket closed so that no one would see the torn buttons. When it was her turn for the scan, the nun stopped short, the look of surprise on her face noticeably different from what was there seconds before. She took a deep breath as well.

"Hello dear," Sr. Isabel said, her distinctive African accent unmistakable. "I'm so glad you are joining us again." Her tender smile made Bristol smile too, if only for a second. "But, I'm afraid you cannot go in," the nun continued loudly. "There's a state inspector here tonight, you see. I can smell that you have been drinking and that is against their rules. If they think we give food to alcoholics or drug addicts, they will take away our license, and that is too large a risk for us. I am sorry that I cannot give you food tonight." Her tone was straightforward as she enunciated every syllable, but what was delivered was not callous, just business-like.

Bristol offered nothing in return, but her large, frightened eyes must have not escaped Gakunde's attention. Shoulders drooping, the teen started to turn around and the nun, taking a step forward, whispered in the girl's ear. "Go to the side of the church and wait for me by the steps near the garage door. I'll bring you a meal in about five minutes. What they don't know, won't hurt us." The nun then looked around to assure herself that no one might have overheard the instructions.

The teenager found the stoop covered by a small roof that had no outside light to ward off the increasing darkness and decreasing temperature and she sat on the steps. True to her word, the nun appeared a few minutes later with a china plate that held a hamburger, a few French fries, and some soggy green beans.

"Damn," she said, "I forgot a slice of cheese; did you want cheese?" Bristol didn't answer but her face showed gratitude for the food. Gakunde sat next to her, almost rubbing shoulders but not quite. "Oh," she said, relaxing next to her young guest, "it feels good to sit down for a while. I've been on my feet for hours." The teen took a bite of the burger.

"Last time you were here, I told you my name; do you remember? Isabel Gakunde. I told you I was from Rwanda, you know, in Africa? You didn't tell me your name, and I wish you would, but only if you want to."

Bristol was silent as she chewed, but her eye contact with the nun never faltered. "Do you know what my name means?" she asked. "Tonight, I will tell you. It means, 'cuddly, gentle lioness.' My father gave that name to me the day I was born. I am supposed to be a lovable lioness—kind and warm but fierce. I protect my cubs."

The girl looked at her intently, a gaze that contained both pain and exhaustion leavened with a wordless plea. She put her plate aside and dropped her head in the woman's lap, a flood of tears and shaking unable to be restrained. Gakunde's large arms embraced the girl and she started to rock the girl slowly back and forth.

The nun began to stroke the girl's tangled brown hair as she sobbed, finding bits of leaves and some twigs tangled in the snarls. After a minute or two of silence, Gakunde said, "Child, you smell like a brewery. Let's go to my apartment above the garage, get you a shower, and I'll find you some clean clothes."

CHAPTER 8:
POR FAMILIA

ABOUT THE SAME TIME BRISTOL LEFT OMAHA YEARS AGO, her father, Miguel Mindaz, exited his makeshift home in the dirt-poor village of Talnique, El Salvador. Tanned by the hot Central American sun, the 45-year-old picked up the green backpack near his door that contained a few items of his clothing, a water bottle, and what was left of a simple first-aid kit left by a non-governmental group last month after their week-long visit to the community to bring health and dental service to the region after their hour-long, bumpy ride from the capitol.

Miguel looked at the clear sky above, judging it would be another hot day, the humidity already rising in the strengthening morning light. It would be a good day to start his journey, he thought to himself, knowing what might lie ahead. The man hauled the backpack over his right shoulder and went to find his mother. The rutted road to her house was sticky with mud from the rain shower that had fallen during the night. Though he had seen them many times before, he took a careful look at the small cinder-block homes with their corrugated metal roofs, uniform in their style and aqua green color, each nestled close to one another on the hillside like a convivial family. He wondered to himself how long it might be before he came back to this homeland.

He found Ruffina walking up the steep dirt road in the middle of their cluster of cement-block homes that were about the size of a small two-car garage in a developed country. She was tired from the climb from the small store where she bought rice and some vegetables. Seeing him come towards her, the aging and wrinkled lady was confident that she already knew the purpose of his arrival.

"Otra vez?" the old woman asked her son, knowing he was there to say goodbye. It was a message of fatigue and resignation, in between those two simple words, because they had been through this parting before; this would be the man's third attempt to get back into the United States. The two-thousand-mile trek to the border would take him about three months; but even had he known then that he would need to cover twice that distance to achieve a goal he didn't even have in his mind at this moment, the determined Salvadoran would not be dissuaded.

"Si, mama," he replied, "I have to."

"Por que, hijo? Why?"

"They might be alive, mama; I must find her."

"Tienes dinero?" she asked, looking at her son.

"Un poco," he said, "I have enough."

It was a lie. Miguel had no idea what the smuggler, the coyote, would charge for the tunnel beneath the wall. Still, he felt that his best chance was to meet up with the migrant caravan that walked northward to the U.S./Mexico border each year about this same time for the last decade or so, since the first year that the Trump administration shut down the government over building a "protective" border wall. Since those days, the trek of disorganized and tousled hopefuls had become a yearly event, a collection of poor and desperate families again imploring the people of the once greatest country on earth to remember the immigrant foundations of their centennial's old rise from middle-ranked nation to world superpower, and grant them asylum from the chaos and violence of their own failed states.

Perhaps it was his experience in previous caravans that gave Miguel enough confidence to fib to his mother, a woman like any other mother, prone to worry about her children. In previous attempts, he and the hordes of others with him were helped along the arduous walk by aid groups and locals throughout Guatemala and Mexico who, with little help from their governments, were able to establish food, first aid, referral services, and even legal assistance services when the parade of travelers came into their region. Oftentimes, these pop-up humanitarian centers offered hot water, showers, and sanitary facilities. Miguel knew that he would not be alone, but, nonetheless, walking about twenty miles every day for the next ninety or more days was far from a leisurely stroll.

"Miguelito," Ruffina said. "Recuerde. Solamente con Dios."

"Yes, mama," he replied. "I know, only with God."

He kissed her and turned to go, walking down the dirt road that led to the macadam going northward out of the small village.

"I will write, or call, if I can," he shouted back after taking the few first steps of his journey, looking again at his mother who was now standing to watch her son walk out of sight.

Ruffina wondered whether she would ever see her son again, and the worry made her thoughts focus on the vast number of people she had lost in her life. As a young girl, she was one of three survivors of what came to be known as the massacre of Mozote, the village of her childhood. The vivid memory of the days in which the army rolled into her poor community on a mission to root out the identities of guerilla fighters they suspected were being hidden by the villagers. In the civil war ripping El Salvador to shreds at the time, Mozote was a haven for refugees because of its majority of evangelical residents who took a neutral stance in the conflict. That wasn't convincing to the soldiers, who, when it became apparent that they were not obtaining the information they hoped for, decided to murder every man, woman, and child in Mozote just to be safe.

In the chaos of violence, the young girl managed to hide in some bushes on the perimeter of her home, which was a sufficient vantage point to witness the soldiers kill her father, rape her mother and older sister, and set their home ablaze.

For his part, Miguel's thoughts were also a jumble of emotions and worries as he walked, and in the first hour they tempted him to retreat from his goal. The thought of familiar things, even in the impoverished mess of his birthplace, carried the allure of comfort, perhaps enough for him to forsake his wife and young daughter in Nebraska. After all, he had only been married to Louisa for a year or two before they moved from El Paso to Omaha and, when he was finally found and deported from the U.S. by Immigration and Customs Enforcement, his young daughter was only nine years old. Maybe in the intervening years since then they had given him up for lost or forgotten about him? After all, even though she knew her Salvadoran husband adored her and would do anything for her, his wife found the comfort of narcotics too seductive to keep her faithful and ardent to their lower-middle-class existence. Maybe she divorced him for abandonment, so that a new and more stable life could surround their daughter? After all, maybe his little child had learned to forget her father, an absent and illegal immigrant who receded back into the poverty from which he transiently emerged. Maybe she was better off without him. After all, Louisa probably realized that Miguel could not risk prison if he were caught in the U.S., his third illegal entry making him subject to a higher price than mere deportation. Maybe, they were better off forgetting about him.

But, as the miles and hours passed, a stronger conviction emerged in the man's consciousness, a familiar one that had motivated him for years and launched him on this same journey more than once before. This time, when he made it to the U.S. border in Texas, he would ask for asylum instead of doing what he had done in previous attempts, namely, to forge the Rio Grande and take his chances on foot or with a smuggler.

In truth, he could tell the Border Patrol that he feared for his life in his home country of El Salvador. He could tell that the gangs overrunning the lawless capital of San Salvador were forcibly conscripting members from the outlying villages like Talnique, needed, they said, to add what amounted to cannon fodder in the various wars between one drug cartel or another. Miguel could only evade them for so long, he would tell the U.S. immigration people, knowing that sooner or later that they would injure his mother to blackmail him to join them.

Still, his reasoning wasn't without risk. While he could honestly make his case for sanctuary, there was no telling that he wouldn't be thrown into a 'hielera'—Spanish for 'ice box'—a term that migrants used to name the Immigration and Customs Enforcement detention centers in the States to house people waiting for their interviews by agency officials, where they might languish for months. From there, he could be sent back to El Salvador or he could obtain a legal entry status until his court date arrived so he could plead his case before a judge.

Each step forward was like a grain of sand falling on one side of an imaginary scale in his mind. The weight of each insignificant speck piled up and the accumulation slowly tipped the pan downward. Miguel would cling to this resolve, day in, day out, no matter what the grueling miles before him presented. *Por familia*, he said to himself.

CHAPTER 9:
SOMETHING TO BE PROUD OF

WHEN THE FIRST SNOWFALL CAME DOWN UPON HALLET Springs that first week in December, the white blanket made every tree and structure in the sleepy city sparkle as the morning sun illuminated nature's nighttime surprise. By six a.m., the road crews were busy clearing away the arteries and streets that today would be less crowded than they would normally be had the wintry precipitation not arrived. Homeowners and shopkeepers would soon be out, here and there, to clear sidewalks and steps, and the roaring sounds of snow blowers and scrapes of shovels in driveways would interrupt the normal quiet.

At the Home Brew, one of the three coffee establishments in the downtown area, one by one the regular collection of faithful customers would soon be passing through the doors that opened at seven. The patterns of this populace would unfold pretty much as they had for years. Some customers would order their latte or espresso, complaining about the cold and the snow whose arrival confirmed the start of winter and dwindling daylight. Others would enter smiling, greet the servers by name, glance at the latest artwork hanging on the walls from local people hoping to make a sale, order their green tea or decaf, and extol the changing seasons or show the ebullience of the holidays soon to come. Some might buy a newspaper or a pastry and linger awhile at the small cozy tables near the plate glass windows overlooking the sidewalks outside and the colonial-looking city center beyond.

By eight, Sheriff Bertrand LaBounty walked in for a coffee and a quick break after having been on the job since five. He stamped his snowy shoes at the door and removed his black leather gloves as he walked towards the counter. "Good morning, Judy," he said to the proprietor. "Looks like a post card out there."

"Good morning, Bert," she replied, "and yes, it does; there are still some good things about living in New Hampshire." The stylish and trim Judy Cobble moved to the espresso machine, knowing that her friend would order the same drink he did almost every morning. The forty-something wore clean blue jeans and a colorful flannel shirt that highlighted her salt-and-pepper, shoulder-length hair.

"Will you be at the meeting tomorrow night?" she asked, bringing the man his small cup.

"The city council meeting, you mean? That's today?"

"No," she whispered so her other customers wouldn't hear, "our meeting."

"Yes, I'll be there. We've got a lot to talk about."

She brought him the morning *Observer* and pointed to a story outlining the evening's city council meeting and the matters the members would be discussing and acting on, assuming their deliberations were thoroughly concluded enough to vote. Judy pointed to the article so her friend wouldn't miss her silent message.

Besides the ordinary business like the approval of permits to install new metal detectors at the entrances to the local hospital, the newly renovated bed and breakfast some entrepreneurs from California were running, and the Mosque or other issues on the docket, others would be sure to make for a standing-room-only crowd in the audience: the purchase of six new drones for the police department and the demolition of the Mohawk Mills complex in the hopes of attracting new investors into some potentially desirable real estate.

"Yes," he said to her after skimming the article, "I'll be there. Both."

The day was uneventful for the Sheriff, but when he walked into the city council chambers for the evening meeting, the packed room signaled that this would be a contentious gathering. The room inside the Hallet Springs City Hall was formal and opulent. The mahogany paneling carried ornate moldings and a rich, deep maroon varnish that made the room feel regal. Each of the nine council members sat behind a bank of desks similarly adorned in intricate woodworking, their microphones protruding just slightly from their platforms that held their slim computer screens An American flag stood in the corner, and when the Mayor struck his gavel to signal the start of the meeting, everyone in attendance rose to face it and voice their pledge.

"This being the hour of six p.m., I hereby call the meeting of the Hallet Springs City Council to order," sixty-year-old Mayor Peter Haddad intoned, in the same formal manner that he had throughout his four terms as an elected official. He quickly dispatched with the customary formalities as the simple business items were brought up, politely discussed, motions moved, seconded, and voted on without much controversy.

"The next item," he said, addressing the council and the audience of residents who came to the meeting, "is the warrant article that permits the expenditure of city funds for the conveyance to the city by eminent domain the ownership of the abandoned Mohawk Mills property, Grand List register number 65599676, for the purpose of demolition and rehabilitation determined by the Office of Economic Development."

He introduced the issue by recapping previous discussions of this council about this major decision, the recommendations of the subcommittee working on this project for the last two years, and outlining the forecasted budget, which was illuminated on the wall monitor to his left. Members of the audience studied the numbers assiduously on their phones or tablets.

"The purpose of tonight's discussion is to hear comments from the general public, as required by law," he continued. "Those giving testimony are limited to three minutes; please come to the microphone in the order of the sign-in sheet."

First to arrive in the center of the room was Howard Conroy, owner of a small clothing store in downtown Hallet Springs. "Good evening," he began. "I am a small business owner and support the warrant article wholeheartedly. As the council knows, the Mills are a blight to our area and detract from economic advancement for everyone. Tourists arrive and get the impression that our community has fallen on hard times, that the best was found in some bygone day. The demolition of those buildings will revitalize commerce and prompt new interest in our city. God knows, we need that. We have exhausted all other options and our application to the government for status as a historic site is going nowhere; we can't wait any longer." Conroy spoke about how other similar-sized localities in New Hampshire had mounted redevelopment efforts, most with good success, and saw a rise in economic improvement for their communities.

After he thanked the council and went back to his seat, the next speaker was Susan Alvarez. "Good evening, council members and members of the public. I am a speaking in support of the warrant as well, but from the perspective of science. I am an environmental scientist at the University of New Hampshire and have studied the Mohawk Mills project for years. I want to point out that this property is called an 'orphaned site' by the Federal Environmental Protection agency; that means that it is not large enough or serious enough to be called a Super Fund site, and therefore eligible for money for clean up by the government. However, it is on their list of locations that are likely to have toxins and carcinogens in the soil. As you know, the Mills have had a variety of owners, tenants, and manufacturing uses over the decades. Preliminary soil tests are indicative of ground water pollution from a host of chemicals, some of which can put people who even walk on the property at risk of health problems. That's why, years ago, the city wisely fenced off the property to limit exposure. Still, the city can't rely on federal help for any mitigation of pollutants on those acres, and the cost estimates of that part of the project, in my opinion, are underestimated." The professor continued to elaborate on what particular chemicals are likely to be found in the buildings and land around them and what it might take to safely dispose of them once discovered.

A cadre of other speakers made their opinions known, most voicing strong support for the city's efforts to remove the complex of dilapidated buildings from the face of the earth. The only speaker who shared opposition was Millie Hargrove, the chair of the historical society, who argued that the Mills were an emblem of the area's once-thriving manufacturing history and that preservation was more attractive than destruction. "Our society has been imploring the U.S. Department of the Interior and the National Parks Service to designate the Mills as a site of historical significance," she testified. "You'd be surprised how important it once was. Even though our application has been in the works for years, we need to give them more time to decide." Her seventy-year-old voice was weak even with the microphone, and most who strained to hear her were polite but found her points unconvincing.

"But we really don't have time," the mayor announced sarcastically to the assembly as the lady returned to her seat. "Do we?"

Doreen Pierce followed Hargrove to the center of the room. A large lady with a quick and booming voice made her a stark contrast to her demure predecessor. As the wife of a former state senator, a past member of the school board, and current president of the Hallet Springs chamber of commerce, Pierce was well known to most in the room and, as the council members came to a posture of attention they had not displayed for Hargrove, the gallery of citizens quieted themselves as well. "Ladies and gentleman of the council," she began fervently. "I speak in favor of this project and know that the removal of the Mohawk Mills can only help the future of our community. While other speakers have pointed out the numerous economic and aesthetic benefits such a renewal will make, I wish for you to consider something else. Namely, that the Mills, in their current state, are a sanctuary for the homeless. They are a den for miscreants and mental defectives and allow people with not enough money to find shelter from the elements here in Hallet Springs. Nobody wants this, we can ill afford it, and we must rid our community of this social detritus. They are takers, not makers, and no one wants them here."

Most in the audience nodded, as did more than one council member. "These people who take refuge there," the woman continued, "can't probably afford a place to live, but that's their own fault, I guess. New Hampshire is generous in public assistance, in my view, and I did some research about this. These people are takers; they don't contribute. They are parasites. What we give to people taking public resources like this riff-raff has not changed since 2003. In other words, we have not given them one extra dime over the last few decades and that, council members, is something to be proud of. Maybe they'll finally get the message in their mentally ill brains—get a job."

"With the demolishing of the Mills, they will be displaced. That is the reality they should face; they can either move someplace else, get a job and pay their way, or expire; it's up to them. They should go to Vermont or Massachusetts or wherever; I don't really care. If you ask me, what's wrong in many places in the U.S. is that people can't stomach the fact that the weak have to perish. We should take a lesson from overcrowded countries like India or Somalia. Take care of yourself or die and spare the rest of us from the burden of giving you a free ride. Isn't that our State motto? Live free or die, it's all the same to us."

"The other problem is," she continued, "there are others in our state who offer them charity. That's not right. If you feed a feral cat, you end up with more feral cats. Take that nun at St. Teresa's, for example. She feeds 'em and makes our problem worse. But what do you expect from her kind?"

Pierce took a deep breath at the microphone so her passion for her sentiment would not give the impression of fanaticism in the minds of her listeners. "Thus," she calmly concluded, "I support the warrant regarding the removal of the property in question because of the economic, but more importantly the social improvement that will come to Hallet Springs. Thank you for the opportunity to speak on the matter."

At that, she got up and returned to her seat. As she walked back into the crowd along the narrow center aisle of the room, she saw smiles on the faces of almost everyone in the rows as if she had returned from scoring a winning point.

The last speaker of the evening was a member of the finance committee. He referred to a report previously given to the council that addressed a methodology for finding the revenue to defray the new costs the city would bear should the renewal project go ahead. He wanted to make sure that the audience understood that offsetting reductions would happen in the human services appropriations over a span of the next five years.

As both the public and the council members exited the room after Mayor Haddad adjourned the meeting, lively conversations broke out, the people smiling with confidence that when the council voted at the next meeting, the measure was sure to pass.

Frank Stringfellow was in the back of the room listening with attention to each speaker, passive on the outside but having a slow boil of emotions inside. As the crowd thinned, he had a clear sight of the sheriff still at the front of the meeting room, and the two locked eyes. Each knew without words that the other man concluded the same unfolding of events would now be inevitable.

Throughout the proceeding, Frank debated whether he should ask to be heard. He would say he was a new resident of Hallet Springs, working for a local farm, a veteran, and someone who thought that the decisions being debated here were a tell-tale sign that the country was headed in a dangerous direction. Knowing that most in the room would dismiss him as a flatlander—a non- native of upper New England—he pushed down this impulse. *I'm done with being brave*, he thought to himself. *Maybe it's not my fight.*

CHAPTER 10:
PANIC AND PROTECTION

AROUND THE SAME TIME ACROSS TOWN AT THE MILLS, THE usual cadre of acquaintances had just finished preparing a meal they all called dinner. By most standards, the modest stew was assembled by their free-will donations of whatever they could obtain from their own funds or the food pantry at St. Theresa's, or other less discussed methods.

Derek added a can of cooked carrots he shared from his ration of staples from the pantry earlier in the month. Tommy brought a can of potatoes. Mary and Brian contributed a package of hot dogs they obtained from the food distribution program at the Salvation Army, it being the tenth of the month, their assigned day to get any meat. They sliced them into one-inch pieces with a dull jackknife that Brian guarded as if it was his most prized possession. Derek, unable to stand in the food pantry line until later next week, scoffed some salt and pepper packets earlier in the day from the local McDonalds as he was adding some sugar to his coffee at the beverage station, careful to do so only when the teens at the order counter were busy with other customers. These he tore open and sprinkled into the pot with the other ingredients.

Like many others after him, Frank contributed his donation to the communal pot, a package of dried bacon bits and some macaroni intended for a salad rather than an impromptu stew. Bristol also shared something she could give, which tonight was one-half a package of dried barley from a brown paper bag.

"That'll take some time to cook," Frank announced to the group, "but we have time." He stirred the pot of food, waiting for the water in the pot on the open steel grate to boil over the open fire in the darkening machine shop at the Mills. The December evening that night was colder than the previous one.

The motley group assembled their chairs and up-ended milk crates in a circle around the fire and waited. Max Cherryfield and his dog King Charles were there too, and found an open place next to Bristol.

She sat on a dirty plastic Adirondack chair someone had found in the woods near the Mills. Its grimy slats had more than one tear, and jagged chinks made the armrests rough. She sat quietly, looking at the concrete at her feet, all the while keeping an ear open to ways she might be helpful to the group that was preparing for their meal.

As faithful as the sun, Charlie was happily wagging his broad tail, ever eager to follow his slow-moving master to whatever place or circumstance that man needed to traverse. The dog, like his friend, needed the warm water of a soothing soak and the shampoo that would give their skin, hair and spirits some welcome refreshing, but neither companion minded the scent of the other. Max pulled up a crate next to Bristol, and Charlie went right over to say hello.

"Do you like dogs?" Max asked the girl. As he expected, she offered no verbal reply but reached down to pat the canine's head, her hand slowly descending to his muzzle so her delicate fingers could give him a gentle scratch underneath his blue collar. The dog sat, encouraging the contact.

"Well, he likes you," Max offered, "that's for sure. He's a good judge of character."

Bristol smiled, briefly turning her head toward Max, and making a timid eye contact. She got off her chair and moved to the concrete, legs crossed, and stroked Charlie with both hands, ruffling her fingers beneath his ears, and then moving down his neck then along both his sides to his hind legs. After a minute or so, the dog got up and turned himself in a tight circle and lay down right against the girl's folded legs, almost in her lap. On one of his back legs, she found a few thistly tangles of hair bundled in tight knots. These she gently tried to loosen, but since the snarls were hopeless mats, she found herself wishing for a pair of scissors. Careful not to tug on his hair, she moved her fingers slowly.

The teen's interaction with Charlie made her think of her own dog, Shep, an energetic golden retriever she and her family raised as a pup, the dog being a gift from her father when she was eight years old. The girl and the dog, like Charlie and Max, were practically inseparable. Painfully shy, both her parents thought that an animal companion might do just the trick, and for a while, it did. Bristol and Shep bonded easily. She took fastidious care of the animal and particularly found his weekly baths in the family bathtub great fun. Charlie's soft fur reminded her of how silky Shep's coat was after that pampering.

Bristol thought about how much she grasped the dog on that frightening night when the government officials came to arrest and subsequently deport her father back to Central America. As if it was yesterday, she recalled the shouts, the tears and screams from her emotional mother when the immigration officers zip-tied her father and man-handled him into the back of their van, the piercing blue revolving lights on its roof cutting the darkness like a laser. Clinging to Shep in her bedroom as the seizure unfolded, she remembered hearing her mother crying out after her husband as they whisked him out the front door: "Miguel! I love you."

Max watched this patiently. "Did you ever have a dog?" he asked her. She didn't reply. "Yeah," he said, "I know what you mean." After a moment, Max said, "I think I know why God invented dogs."

Bristol turned to him, puzzled at the unique phrasing.

"It was probably at least two reasons," he continued, looking back at her. "Either it was because they never fail to love you, they stick with you through thick and thin, with even a little bit of kindness you give them, they adore you forever. He probably knew we needed that. Or, he knew they would make us happy. Well, as long as they're alive that is, and..."

Max grew suddenly pensive, his voice trailing off at his last phrase. Continuing her petting on Charlie's spine, she turned to the man, raised her brows, and looked at Max with a caring curiosity.

There was silence between them, which Bristol took to mean that Max wasn't ready to say anything more. She shifted her attention back to the spaniel whose eyes started to close as the girl's strokes slowed to a pace that was lulling the dog to sleep. Every so often, he would exhale a deep breath as if a sigh of peacefulness. Bristol herself felt more relaxation than she had felt all day.

"I don't think Charlie's well," Max said. "He's got no energy and he's not eating like he used to. Maybe he knows I can't afford more. Could that be true?"

Bristol nodded. She looked at Max and saw the exhausted, disheveled man almost in tears. She reached out her hand to him and, when he held out his in return, she cupped her grip around his knuckles, feeling the sandpaper-rough calluses on his palm. In that instant, her mind was a flood of memories about Shep and her life with her parents in Omaha, which seemed like a lifetime ago. She could vividly picture how the dog would bound through the fallen trees or scrub bushes like a gazelle when she had him off leash as they walked through the woods behind their rented ranch house just outside the city line. Walking with him, she felt a calm come over her, which was the perfect time to think about poetry, her schoolwork, or what life might bring to her in the future, the musings of any sensitive and curious teenager trying to make sense of a puzzling world coming into focus as her eyes and awareness matured.

Those peaceful memories were also seasoned with turbulent ones following the arrest of her father by the immigration police; how, soon after, her mother couldn't pay the rent on her waitress salary; the humiliation her classmates would have inflicted on her had they known she and her mom called their minivan home; and how food for Shep was derived from the restaurant waste that Louisa could sneak away when her boss wasn't looking.

She remembered how Shep was the only being she felt she could confide in, hoping that somehow his amazing canine brain could comprehend her messages via some mysterious verbal osmosis when they walked alone after school. She poured out her heart to the dog about everything, particularly her worries about the ever-increasing amounts of pills her mom seemed to be swallowing despite Bristol's concerned pleadings that she should get to the clinic in town and talk to a doctor.

Her last day with Shep destroyed her heart with the force of a nuclear bomb, the shock wave also taking out her paper-thin feeling of security in life, her motivation for school, any optimism for about the future, and her trust in others. There, holding Max's hand, she recalled the face of the nurse in the hospital that night of Louisa's overdose and how the woman's expression of sympathy was perfunctory and efficient. She remembered how, when the people from the state's child protection agency helped her retrieve her backpack from the van and saw Shep in the back, they phoned animal control to secure the dog, saying that minors under their custody now couldn't keep any pets in the temporary foster care she would be placed in that night. When she protested through her tears, they tried to assure her that the animal officers would try to have him adopted into a good home before the two-week deadline they followed before he was put down. As they muscled her into the back seat of their car, she could hear Shep barking out his emotions of panic and protection.

When Bristol saw Frank coming towards them with two bowls in his hand, she released Max's hand and her painful recollections.

"It's my turn to serve tonight," he said to the pair, handing them their portion of the meal.

"Thanks, Boss," Max said. Looking into his bowl, he saw chunks of cut hotdogs sitting in a watery broth of boiled vegetables. With his plastic spoon, he stirred the dish quickly and counted out the sections of hotdog it contained. He bent down next to Charlie and retrieved two of the four pieces, which he put in front of the dog. Bristol rose to her feet and looked at her dish. She stirred the mix and spooned out a few sliced carrots and a section of meat and added it to Charlie's meal. *One dog to another*, she thought to herself. Charlie got up to sniff them, paused to look up at his friend, and when Max nodded, he started to eat.

The group ate in silence, each lost in their own thoughts with no sound other than the crackle and steaming noise coming from the green wood on the campfire in front of them. Without warning, a clear crack sounded from the ceiling above, mostly caused by the cold outside air making the aged timbers of the roof contract. The pop made everyone look up but Bristol. To her, the sound confirmed something she'd wondered about in the last few weeks, her conviction that some places have auras or spiritual energies. She had the notion that ancient and unnamed spirits dwell in old architecture, as if the passage of time and the advent of decay invites the mysterious forces of the universe to inhabit the spots after most humans have forgotten them.

Someone's looking out for us, she thought to herself, *and they are happy with us.*

CHAPTER 11:

IF YOU HATE, THEY WIN

JUDY COBLE WAS GLAD SHE REMEMBERED TO BRING HER leather gloves with her as she walked out onto the sidewalk after locking the door to her coffee shop the next evening. Glancing at her storefront window, she took pride in the green artificial garland lining the perimeter of the glass inside as its multi-colored string of lights twinkled, thinking that the new Christmas decorations looked inviting. She adjusted the red bow on the evergreen wreath on the door and turned to leave. The thermometer on the bank across the street read twenty-five degrees, but the chilly wind and the darkness made it feel much colder. She zipped up her ski parka and pulled its collar up over her neck.

As she walked down Main Street, she exchanged a quick and pleasant greeting with the people she passed, provided that she knew them as customers or neighbors. Her telltale smile was visible, even with her fatigue from being on her feet all day and the financial stress of keeping her business afloat, particularly after the forecast of her accountant that she would likely need to lay off some part-timers in the next month after the holidays if January revenues fell short. Still, her worries weren't sufficient enough to tempt her to head for her cozy home in Lakeside, a border town to Hallet Springs some fifteen minutes away, so she could find some dinner and a glass of Merlot after she started a fire in the woodstove and collapsed on the couch with the novel she began the other day.

Instead of heading to her car in the parking lot near Main, she made a left turn onto Myrtle Street, past the many low-slung brick buildings erected almost a century ago, many with long empty storefronts, their huge, plate glass windows reflecting the glare of the streetlamps and plastered with paper posters advertising events that seemed a distant memory. Between a row of these places, she came upon a wooden door that desperately needed some attention, its peeling green paint revealing the cracked and dirty oak that lay beneath. In the window of the door, she found a small white decal about the size of someone's business card with nothing but the letter "W" printed modestly in the middle.

The inside of the dimly lit vestibule of the apartment building had a bank of mailboxes and doorbell buttons underneath each one. She found the one with what looked like "W" in the name slot and pressed it twice. A loud buzzer sounded, and then the door popped ajar; she opened it and climbed the familiar flight of stairs, unzipping her parka as she climbed.

Apartment ten was on the second floor at the end of a dingy hallway lighted only by a small, grimy wall sconce that looked like it hadn't been cleaned in years. She put two sharp knocks on the door and soon Sr. Isabel Gakunde bid her welcome, a quick smile flashing from her face.

Judy greeted the others there: Frank Stringfellow, Bert LaBounty, Estelle Ramirez, and Caspar Chen. They were sitting around a simple wooden table in the kitchen of the apartment, a place that fit with the cheap and dirty feel of the hallway. In the sitting room beyond, a scratched and cracked leather couch sat amidst some dark end-tables, one of which supported a small lamp that emitted the only weak light that could be seen from the street.

"Any word about your daughter, Bert?" his neighbor Estelle asked.

"Nope, not a thing," he answered glumly.

She had asked the sheriff this question, almost every month, for the last two years, ever since Bert's only child Clarice walked away from the apartment he kept for her and from her life in Hallet Springs. Estelle was a stocky gray-haired woman one might think should be retired and not running a sprawling dairy farm, one of the last of its kind in New Hampshire. After her husband died ten years ago, people thought she would surely sell off the property rather than work to keep the risky adventure afloat, but the tenacious widow kept it alive, saying that farming was the only type of life she knew.

Clarice's departure came when she was twenty-five and riddled with what any psychiatrist or therapist would label as delusions, which had crippled her young adult life since she started working in her first job after high school. Even with his contacts in law enforcement in other cities in New Hampshire, and even with the professional courtesy he received from counterparts in other states, he could not locate her. That meant only a few possibilities.

First, after having been subject to the "treatment" system the state delivered, she had reached the limits of her tolerance of the social control they imposed and fled. That would require her to dig out the tracking implant surgically inserted in her arm. That act brought the consequence of having no ability to get her measly government disability income or medication—no compliance with the rules, no help. This would force her to live by what weak wits she could muster in between the bouts of whatever delusions, irrational euphoria, or activity-stopping depression her bipolar disorder conjured up while the daily emotional upheaval coursed through her daily existence.

Second, she may have drifted from one place to another and died in some manner, either from the elements, from starvation, from her own actions, or from crime. Bert held out hope in the first possibility, since that was far better than the other. There was, of course, a third option—one he didn't think about much, given what he had learned about the mental health social service system in the U.S. these days—which was that she had received the right service from some agency, was free of her crippling symptoms and living a life of recovered health, and for whatever reason, choose to keep her life a mystery from her family.

Clarice hadn't vanished in anger; it wasn't after an argument or bad turn of fortunes. Just one day, after her dad became impatient with leaving phone and text messages to her, a visit to her Spartan apartment on Myrtle gave the man the stark feeling that she had fled.

Somewhere after the weeks turned into months of searching for her as best he could, Bert stumbled upon a clandestine network of non-federal or state people, informally collecting themselves underneath the official channels so as to avoid the narrow state restrictions designed for social control. It was called Via Verde. The members formed small and quiet groups all over the country, loosely affiliated with each other, so that if any state discovered their charity work in their cell and punished them with fines, arrests, or any pressures that forced them to disband, no one group would jeopardize the service of the other.

As best anyone knew, Via Verde's network extended from the Mexican to the Canadian border. Some members thought that the various nodes formed three "pathways of hope," one line along the states on the east coast, one up the Mississippi River Valley from the Gulf to Ontario, and one along the foothills of the western slopes of the Rockies to the panhandle of Idaho. No one knew for sure, since the various cells in one community to the next only communicated by personal associations or coded letters written in longhand.

After filing a missing person report with the FBI, Bert was exhausted from his search. Feeling a heartbreak that only people with depression know—the kind that sucks any scrap of energy, hope, positive thought, emotion, or act of self-care out of you—he felt as drained of strength as a drop of water vanishes from hot desert sands. By accident, a secretary at a New Jersey mental health system he once visited through the course of his search for Clarice, whispered to him something about an option that was trying to remain hidden from authorities. They were mission-bound to deliver what charitable efforts they could to people with mental illness, services that the government did not allow. She gave him a business card with what, at the time, only looked like it had the letter "W" printed on it. On the back, she wrote a phone number.

Soon after that, more than a few phone conversations took place between a man called Fred in the weeks that followed. Eventually, Fred agreed to meet Bert in the train station in New Haven, Connecticut, where the sheriff, after convincing Fred of his trustworthiness, learned that the man's real name was Simon St. John.

Simon explained that he was part of Via Verde and that the charity work they did was completely illegal in most states, including New Hampshire. What the man told him was that slowly over time, and almost imperceptibly to the voting public and some lawmakers, fewer and fewer acts of public or private support had been valued, continued, or funded by society. Even those from religious or civic organizations were considered to conflict from the fundamental unspoken aspiration that citizens either take care of themselves, move on to someplace else, or perish. This downward transformation of culture, some claimed, happened by accident when people were paying attention to their own affairs and not the public fabric of the American society. Others thought about the shift in more sinister ways, holding that some malicious anti-government effort was afoot, hiding in shadows over decades but manipulating politics away from a culture of caring that had been part of U.S. history since the Progressive era of the early 1900s. This group, non-violent but every bit as dangerous as a terrorist plot, had won, Simon explained.

His words rang true in Bert's experience, knowing what he had seen in his career as a public servant in New Hampshire. From what Simon knew, there was no group like it in the Granite State, putting the notion in Bert's head that he could organize one.

"It gives new meaning to the state motto," he said to Simon. "Live free or die really means live free of public help or die, it's all the same to us."

On the train ride back to Hallet Springs, Bert mentally mapped out how he could carefully organize a VV group in his area of the state. The meeting that evening in Clarice's apartment was their tenth assembling.

LaBounty wanted to change the subject quickly. "Congratulations on the news about your farm, Estelle. I read about it in the paper. Putting all that acreage into federal conservancy is very generous."

"It was a long time coming, Bert," she answered. "Now all I have to do is finalize the labor covenants with the feds that will assure the place will still be a dairy farm in perpetuity. All I have to do is show that it's still a working farm, which means I need to find the right people who can work it for me."

Like the other gatherings, the conversation that night was loosely structured and informal. It centered around sharing current news that might affect the needs of the disabled and marginalized people they were trying to support, while escaping any attention from law enforcement or other state authorities.

"Christmas will be here in a few weeks," Estelle said. "Frank, what does your group at the Mills want?"

"I asked about that last night," he answered, "and do you know what Tommy said? It was cold, you know, and I saw the holes in his jeans and his coat was way too thin for winter. But he said, 'do you suppose Santa could wrap up a few more cans of food? It would be good not to be so hungry.' Then he apologized to me for asking too much from

Santa. Max wanted a case of dog food for Charlie. Most wanted boots or gloves and warm hats."

"Tommy's right to be worried," Bert added. "Next month, there's another reduction in people's supplemental nutrition assistance program taking effect. I think it's about a ten-percent cut."

The group felt another collective blow, even though they had become all too accustomed to news like this. The holes weren't just in Tommy's jeans, but also in whatever remnant of the social service safety net was still in place.

"I hate them," Estelle yelled, her anger aimed at legislators and the heartless voters who elected them. "They say they don't have the money!" After a calming pause, she said, "maybe that's true."

"Never give in to hate, ever," Sister Isabel offered calmly, her first statement of the evening. "If you do, they win."

"Isabel," Judy asked as the meeting was drawing to a close, "are you feeling OK? You are awfully quiet tonight."

The nun looked at her friend and mustered a small smile, but the response not convincing enough for Judy to assume all was well. "What is it?" she asked her.

"I've had some bad news today," Isabel continued, "a letter from home. My adoption mother in Rwanda died last month. I didn't know about it. A letter from a friend came today."

Judy looked at her friend with sadness and sympathy. "I didn't know you were adopted," she said.

"Yes," Isabel replied quietly, "it was a month or two after my own mother was killed, and my brother, too." At this, Bert and Frank stopped their own conversation and turned their attention to the women, sensing that something important was being shared.

"You don't talk much about your childhood," Judy said, "even though we've known each other all these years. At that, the nun smiled, a genuine one this time.

"I don't share my memories of the genocide too often. It was a terrible time. I was ten, I think. I remember being trapped in our small apartment, my mother, brother, and me. Kilgali was going crazy then, the Hutu militia massacred Tutsis with impunity. My family is Tutsi. We knew we couldn't stay home because sooner or later, they would come to our building and kill us. Our only hope was to either run out and find the UN troops who were there or find a way to get to the cathedral in the city center because it was a place of sanctuary that the militia would not enter."

There was silence in the room as the nun told her story. Judy sat next to her and reached for her hand. Wordlessly encouraged to continue, Isabel took a deep breath and exhaled.

"That night, mother took what little money we had into her bag and told us to find our jackets. Yves was 13, older than me. I remember my mother leading us out the back door, away from the street, and we started to walk quickly. I wasn't sure where she was taking us, but I remember how scared she was; she held my hand so tight I thought she would break my bones."

"She said, 'you must follow close, keep silent, do whatever I tell you.'" The nun removed her hand from Judy and fumbled in her pocket for a tissue and, once finding it, wiped her tear-filled eyes.

"We walked from one side street to the other, looking for the UN trucks, but they must have been in another section of the city. It's big, you know. But after an hour of searching, mother said we had to find our way to the cathedral. We were all frightened. Then I remember, we heard voices of a group of men coming behind us. They were screaming when they saw us. Mother looked back and saw them. She released my hand and told me and Yves, 'run, run!' We did but we didn't want to leave her. After a half minute, my brother and I stopped to look back and see where she was. By then, the men had caught up with her. One of them raised his machete high, and with a quick slice, brought it down on my mother's back, from her left shoulder to her right hip. I saw her fall in pain, but she still yelled, 'Run!' The man struck her with the knife again when she was on the ground."

"Before I knew what to do next, Yves started to run back to mother. Another man slashed him across the stomach and killed him. That was 1994. Almost a million Rwandans were slaughtered like that in a few months' time."

"My God," Judy said, "how did you escape?"

"I'm not sure, to tell the truth. I remember that, where I stood, there was a high fence separating the street from someone's yard. I saw a small hole under there, probably made by a dog digging his way underneath. It was dark, maybe the men didn't see me, who knows? I crawled under the fence and ran, like my mother told me. Before long, I was too tired to run and I was walking, crying, wandering, scared to the bone. Suddenly, a soldier with a blue helmet ran up from behind me and scooped me into his arms. He said something I did not understand, but before I knew what was happening, he ran to a big white UN truck that was around the corner and put me in the back of it."

"Inside, underneath the canvas, there was a large group of women and children, some men too. All of them looked terrified; some of the kids were sobbing. One of the women sitting on the bench—she was young and had a baby with her—made some room for me and I sat next to her. I remember her big arm reaching around me as she pulled me close to her; I put my two arms around her waist and cried. The truck drove us to the cathedral."

"The soldier saved my life that night, and I don't even know his name. But I pray for him every day. The woman in the truck, Raffaella, she adopted me. She must have kept her cancer from me. That awful night, I lost one mother and received another; now I have none."

Her friends in the room said nothing and the silence fit the moment like a glove. Each seemed caught up in the story, their thoughts taking them to speculate how that sort of trauma might impact any young child, and how, their kind, gentle and loving associate led a life in stark contrast to the powers that must have fueled the genocide of her youth.

"If you hate," Isabel said, disrupting the quiet, "they win."

CHAPTER 12:
COLD, CRUEL, AND POWERFUL

AS THE GATHERING WAS ENDING, THE MEMBERS REACHED for their coats and casually made their way to the door. Bert graciously shook each hand as they got ready to leave, giving each person a warm embrace, a caring gaze, and supportive smile.

"Isabel," Frank called, "I'll walk you home."

"That would be nice, Frank, thank you," she replied quietly.

Alone in Clarice's apartment, Bert went to the kitchenette and arranged the two chairs at the small table nicely. He found a small dishtowel in a drawer and dusted off the counters. Moving to the sitting room, he dusted the few pieces of furniture, scanned the room to see if anyone had forgotten anything, and moved to the table lamp near the window. Looking at the wall outlet, he saw the timer-switch he bought for Clarice last fall, set the on/off time for the proper hours for winter, and then switched on the lamp. *There's someone home, waiting for you, Clarice,* he thought to himself, vainly hoping that somehow she would hear his plea.

Going back to the kitchen, he found the small plastic bag he'd brought to the meeting before the others arrived. Reaching inside, he removed a worn cloth Santa Claus toy that stood about ten inches high if you carefully and patiently propped it up. This family heirloom found its place on the LaBounty mantel every Christmas since Clarice was a toddler. Gently placing the toy in the center of his daughter's table, he hoped she would see it as soon as she walked in, if she ever did. At the wall pegs for coats, he put on his parka and took one more glance around the room before locking the door behind him.

* *

ANOTHER FATHER WAS THINKING ABOUT HIS FAMILY ALSO, but the Salvadoran was not worried about bundling himself up against the cold but looking for a section of floor in the gymnasium not occupied by many of his fellow *caminandos*—walkers—who were offered a place to stay out of the elements. Opening shelters where they could, many simple communities dotted the trek from Central America to the U.S. border, a journey they all believed was a migration from desperate poverty and violence to opportunity for income and safety. Miguel soon found a spot near a far corner next to a family with two small children who, he thought, should have been in school someplace, not joining this parade of hungry, searching, sad souls heading north.

Unrolling the sleeping mat given to him by an aide worker at the entrance, he dropped his backpack at the head of it and acknowledged his floor-mates next to him. "Hola," he said. They glanced back with a smile but offered no reply.

Meeting up with the marchers in Guatemala City, Miguel had no idea how many men, women and children were in this wave of migrants. Even when the roads were straight for a mile or two so he could see the throng ahead, there was no way of counting their number. All he knew was that this ragtag assembly, all tired and underfed, were also resolved with a motivation derived from desperation, their hopes and dreams carried in a backpack they kept in their heart every bit as real as the one they lugged with their meager possessions.

He took off his sneakers and sat down on the mat. Reaching into the plastic bag of items he, like everyone else, received outside the gym door, he saw that it contained a bottle of water, a wrapped sandwich, a small box of Band-Aids, a travel sized tube of toothpaste and a tiny brush, and an energy bar.

Despite the din of voices and commotion in the room—conversations in Spanish and English between the caminandos and the volunteers hustling here and there to assist them, the cries from hungry babies in their mothers' arms, the announcements on the public address system meant to orient the crowd to the available services found in the adjacent tents outside—his thoughts wandered to a place of reflection about the last few weeks of his trek. Even if he had friends or acquaintances joining him on the journey, it would be nearly impossible to keep together. Instead, he found himself conversing with whatever group of people that informally clustered together on their monotonous march that day.

Most were walking away from their poverty brought about by a collection of events beyond their control. For some, it was the ongoing ravages of climate change, which brought wild swings in precipitation and drought over the last few years such that the coffee bean industry in Central America was only about one-tenth of what it was just a decade ago. A blight called coffee rust, a browning of all the leaves on every plant from too much rainfall, was unstoppable; and as the bottom fell out of the agricultural sector, so too did fieldworkers, processors, truckers, and others see their livelihood dried to dust.

For others, it was the intimidation and violence that pushed them to leave. Like Miguel, the strength of the gangs that were in fierce and deadly competition for the illegal drug trade inversely matched the weakness of governments to protect their citizens. As one rose, the other declined. Better, they thought, to take their chances trying to get through the U.S. to Canada than to be a casualty of the murderers who mostly traveled around with impunity and bravado. Even people who were neither drawn to nor conscripted into these criminal groups were under their economic and social control, because no aspect of community life was spared from this all- encompassing pestilence.

As Miguel slowly relaxed on his makeshift bed, he knew that tomorrow would be an eventful day because the throng he was with was within one day's hike to the border town of Brownsville, Texas. A huge decision would have to be made; seek asylum or find a *marocha*, an unprotected hole in the barriers that separated Mexico from America. Unlike the boundary between Guatemala and Mexico, a transition he and the others accomplished with relative ease since the Mexican government was liberal and compassionate in issuing transit visas to migrants heading north, the crossing of the Rio Grande would be far less hospitable. The looming question was which course of action should he choose: the former would afford him some limited but lawful protection in the U.S. should it work, and the latter might afford him some degree of freedom to search for his wife and child outside of U.S. immigration officials' watchful eyes. For some immigrants, this group was remarkably like the gangs they were fleeing—cold, cruel, and powerful.

He reached into his backpack for a small pouch he used for important documents. In between his Salvadoran passport and birth certificate, he found a small photograph of Louisa and their daughter Maria, the small girl of eight years, happy on her mother's lap, both with infectious smiles that spoke volumes about their love for the man taking the picture. Miguel recalled that summer picnic when he snapped it, a day the three shared together that seemed too far distant from what life had become for him at that moment. He remembered the feeling he had at that instant that he was blessed to have such a fulfilled and happy life.

From weeks on the road, Miguel had learned how to shut out the noise and commotion of such a busy shelter as the gymnasium he was in that night. Putting the photograph back in its place, he tried to sleep. As he drifted off, he knew that the familiar worries that occupied his mind in almost every waking moment would be there in the morning as assuredly as the sunrise: where were Louisa and Maria now, why hadn't she been in contact, what was their fate?

Hundreds of miles to the north, his daughter was also sleeping on a cold floor behind her stack of pallets in her corner of a dingy, abandoned warehouse in New Hampshire, but without the kindness of strangers who were helping migrants on their travels. Her sleep was, like most every other night, a fitful oscillation between fleeting moments of rest and scary dreams that caused her legs to twitch and her body to sweat. Most of them had something to do with the man who raped her and some even carried the memory of the cologne he wore during her many violations. Like many other nights, she bolted awake when the shocking dreams and the sensations pulsing through her tired muscles were too much to experience.

She sat up from her sleeping bag with a gasp, breathing heavily as the beats of her heart raced in fear. Since she could not distinguish the dream-danger from waking-danger in that moment of fogginess, Maria's first reaction was to look through the slats of the pallets to the darkness beyond and scan for any intruder who may have walked into the huge room. She squinted her eyes with the seriousness of a hawk and reflexively tensed up her muscles, realizing in an instant that she might have to tie up the loose sneakers on her feet should she have to flee into the blackness and escape.

Listening, sensing, waiting…she sat there stock-still but ready to spring up in a burst of energy and motion. She turned her head slightly, trying to attune her ear to any noise or signal of threat. But after a minute of intense guardedness, she only heard the familiar sounds of the night breeze casually drifting through one of the broken windows above her. The wind stirred the trees outside gently and either the wooden floor or the ceiling timbers above creaked slightly, adjusting their mass to the change in ambient air. Listening more, Maria heard the comforting sound of the bird outside who offered her its familiar melody. The rhythmic flow of the river added another sound into her consciousness as her panic eased. Relieved, she laid back down to attempt sleep again, telling herself that there was, as usual, no one in the warehouse. *This is a good place*, she admitted to herself. She closed her eyes, but it would be some time before her body's fear-drenched reaction weakened enough to induce the unconsciousness she craved.

CHAPTER 13:
DON'T WORRY, I BROUGHT A SHOVEL

EARLY THE NEXT MORNING, THE SUNLIGHT FILLING THE GYM-
nasium cast a brightness into the space that roused the sleeping crowd
with renewed energy. Miguel assembled his belongings, laced up his
sneakers, and headed out to the tent he hoped would have some hot
coffee or something to eat.

That same sunshine fell on the woods behind the Hallet Springs
Recreation area where Frank Stringfellow was slowly making his way
through the trees and up a small hill where, hidden from view, he could
look down over the soccer field where a few police officers and other
men stood outside a white van about one hundred yards away. The area
had only about five inches of snow, so Frank found the walking easy.
Still, he was careful to feel for any covered sticks that might snap under
his feet, making an unfortunate noise that could carry to the men in
the distance.

It was just as Bert LaBounty described in the last meeting of
Via Verde group in his daughter's apartment. Representatives from
American Dynamics would be demonstrating their newest police
department drones to the Mayor, Public Safety Director, and watch
commander Jason Krebs from the police department. Bert told the
group that these new replacements for the remote flying surveillance
vehicles currently deployed over the streets of Hallet Springs would give

a new feeling of safety to the general taxpayer, and a new tool to authorities that could be used for making the lives of people deemed undesirable even more monitored. He was particularly worried, he told the group, that these new models would have, for the first time, the capability for more than remote video observation. They would have tactical intervention features and audio. If any suspect did not heed the audible orders spoken through the drone, each unit came equipped with taser capacity that could render a person immobile until an officer on the ground could arrive.

At the edge of the forest overlooking the field, Frank lay down in the cold snow and removed a pair of binoculars from his backpack. He focused on the van in the distance and counted ten men, one of them sitting at a small portable table that supported a laptop and a large joystick. He could see a large drone the size of a suitcase on the plowed road behind the van, its five helicopter-like fans starting and stopping, presumably at the bidding of the salesman pressing the keys of the computer. As he scanned the men, Frank saw someone he recognized: one of his former veterans, Jason Krebs, looking fit and trim as ever in his blue police uniform.

The cold snow beneath Frank's body was, unfortunately, a too-familiar feeling. Like many times before, some sensations or sounds would instantly catapult his mind and emotions back to his years as Lieutenant Stringfellow in one of his three tours of duty in Afghanistan. Most of his memories of the longest war in U.S. history riddled in a swirl of fear, trauma, camaraderie, and killing. That instant, lying prone in the snow, binoculars in hand, called him back to one morning in the mountains overlooking a small village beneath his position where Taliban fighters were regrouping. When he radioed his observations of the sunrise stirrings of the guards outside the target building and confirmed that the missile could be launched from the Predator unmanned aircraft above, he saw them leave. But it was too late.

A woman and six small children had just crossed the threshold of the house and stepped on to the rocky dirt road outside. "Shit," he called into the radio, "too many collaterals!" But before he could say the next word, the kids, the woman, the house, and the small yard beside it became a smoky crater of rubble, audibly announced by a deafening blast to the entire community and anyone in the majestic mountains that surrounded it.

Frank turned over on his back in horror of what he had just done. *Now I murder kids*, he thought to himself. As the echo of the explosion faded and the smoke and dust started to settle on the village below, and before Frank could even start to process his complicity in this violence, another blast erupted just twenty yards from where he and his squad of seven Rangers—Jason Krebs among them—were perched. The rocks they were hiding behind gave them some cover from the bomb, but they instantly realized they were exposed. Until that moment, they hadn't seen that a group of Taliban had taken up a position above them on a nearby ridge. As the soldiers were watching the village below, their enemies were watching them from higher ground.

A second mortar shell rocked the ground, this one much closer to the men than the first. Rifle fire from the Taliban filled the air, some finding their targets in three of the Americans huddling behind rocks that were insufficient to shield them. Frank turned and saw their exsanguination painting the ground in crimson. While the others returned fire, he quickly rolled to the private on his left to staunch the man's bleeding from the wound in his jaw, but he could see that the soldier was not breathing.

In the next seconds, a barrage of explosions from the Taliban fell upon the squad, either from mortars or rocket-propelled grenades. As his hearing slowly returned, Frank found a gap between the rocks around him, looked for a target above him, and started firing. He could hear his men doing the same, but the volume of noise from his group was far less than it was just moments ago.

Amidst the clamor and adrenalin of the firefight, Frank radioed back to the base that controlled the Predator above. Ducking behind his cover to hear the pilot's confirmation of their situation and the request, he turned to scan the position and number of his fellow soldiers firing back at their attackers, just in time to witness three more explosions land on the group, sending the bodies of two of his comrades flying in the air.

That was his last memory of his last day in combat in the cold mountains of a desolate country. In the base hospital in Kabul, he woke up to the crippling news that his right leg was mostly shattered, riddled with shrapnel and two bullet wounds; but more seriously, that he was only one of two survivors of the fight that day. Nearly all his entire recon squad of seven wonderful and dedicated Americans were going home as casualties of war. Lieutenant Stringfellow and Sargent Krebs, however, would soon go home too. Each would carry different scars.

In the avalanche of these memories, while Frank's eyes were still watching the police officers in the distance, his concentration was riveted back to his Army experience as if it was yesterday and not decades ago. Some laughter from the offices snapped his attention back to the present, which was just as well since his recollections and survivor's guilt, the consequence of his years of trauma in the war, would be back soon enough to once again haunt his waking consciousness. That's how it was for the man ever since his honorable discharge from the military and the aimlessness he felt as he desperately tried to recover his physical and emotional health; the years of depression, flashbacks, and self-loathing that dogged him no matter what state he traveled to or what small job or circle of acquaintances he'd acquired. It settled over his soul like a fog that never lifts, obscuring any marker of happiness.

The whirring noise from the drone also caught Frank's attention as it started to rise from the ground and hover about fifteen feet above the van. Though Frank was too far away from the group to hear their conversation, he could see that the officers were intently listening to the sales representative at the laptop controlling the drone.

"As you can see," he was telling them, "the display here shows status, coordinates, flight conditions and trim, RPM for each propeller, and remaining battery life. We have smart engineers at American Dynamics, and they have vastly improved the performance and utility of these units. They are only available to law-enforcement agencies."

"Municipalities that have converted their old models to this new AS1600 version tell us the changes are remarkable. They particularly like the increased speed, enhanced video and voice, and the new immobilizing capability that gives the pilot at operation command the ability to stop an individual should the need arise."

"Can you tell us more about that?" Lieutenant Baskar asked the man. "We think that will be really useful to us."

"The taser feature of the AS1600 allows the operator to render a non-lethal pulse of electricity, like the tasers you have now on your belts that have been standard issue for police for decades, from 20 feet between the drone and the target. A key command on the panel here lifts the cross- hairs on the video monitor, telling the pilot the unit is diverting battery power to the taser. What would we do without improved batteries? They've come a long way." The salesman shook his head in astonishment.

"When the operator is within range of the target—you can see the meter showing that here—and fires the pin, the wire tether from the drone delivers the shock, immobilizing most, if not all, adults who weigh three-hundred pounds or less. Quite a kick. Of course, the pilot should announce a warning to the suspect through the public address option to satisfy any legal stipulation a state might have."

"Can you demonstrate?" Baskar asked.

Frank was still looking through his binoculars while he lay at the base of a pine tree overlooking the field below. He saw one of the men walk around to the far side of the van and a few seconds later, come back into view now walking a large dog on a leash that looked none too pleased to be following the stranger, the animal straining on the leash, seemingly eager to escape. Frank did not grasp why a sales demonstration would involve a dog.

"Got this beast from the Hallet Springs pound. He's set to be put down anyway, so I bought him for this demonstration," the American Dynamic's rep explained. "The electroshock from the drone has been tested to deliver a non-fatal dose on most American adults, but we wouldn't want to demonstrate on a human subject anyway."

The salesman returned to his table and laptop and, with keystrokes, sent the drone higher into the morning sky. Turning to his assistant with the dog, he nodded his head and the hapless brown retriever was released. Quickly running towards the woods at the end of the field, the drone flew in hot pursuit, descending to about twelve feet off the ground and accelerating to close the distance between it and the animal.

Within seconds, the machine was only yards away from the dog. Frank could see that a flashing red light from the underside of the drone started to illuminate and, seconds later, it fired a large dart into the fleeing dog's neck that was tethered to the drone by a wire. From what Frank could see, it must have delivered an electric shock, which immediately made the animal falter, its head plunging to the dirt while its forward momentum launched its back end upward, so it somersaulted in a heap. Its task complete, the drone hovered over the twitching dog waiting for the next command from the pilot. It was just as the Sherriff described.

"There, see that?" the rep asked. "Simple as that. This will stop 'em."

Frank took it all in and saw enough. All that Bert told him about these new-model drones was true, though he never doubted his friend anyway. Still, the deployment of such devices was an alarming escalation in the municipality's unspoken war against its "undesirables," the vulnerable people trying to survive on their fragile wits and crushing poverty, like his many acquaintances hiding at the Mills just trying to stay alive.

He rolled over in the snow and returned his binoculars to his backpack. Crouching low, he retraced his steps through the forest to the dirt road that eventually led back to a residential part of Hallet Springs, then back towards downtown. *We'll have to get the rocks higher* he thought to himself.

How or when this personal mission to resist the state and help protect the people with any sort of mental or emotional or addiction challenge blossomed in Frank's being was hard to say. It was certain, however, that upon his discharge from the army and his struggles to overcome his injuries, his physical recovery—trying though it was—seemed far faster than his mental one. The plague of nightmares of combat, the recurrent memories of friends made and lost in firefights, and the constant fear and panic-laced vigilance he brought to every circumstance in civilian life, all fueled the restlessness and wanderings that took him from state to state, city to city, shelter to shelter, until he interpreted all he was witnessing as a call to action. What he saw was a nation that was slowly making hatred towards people with mental illness, addiction, or poverty socially accepted. The warrior in him knew when a direct assault was likely to be futile, as was the case now at home, but he felt that some other way of helping victims of this catastrophic social shift was what he could do. So, despite his own struggles with his trauma, he vowed to assist whatever vulnerable person or group of people he came upon in his travels. When he arrived in Hallet Springs years ago and was nearly arrested by Sheriff Bert LaBounty for homelessness, and when the two men, during their interactions, carefully disclosed to each other their common drive for a new justice, Frank decided to make his stand of service and protest here. His subsequent learning about Via Verde from Bert was the final confirmation.

Back at the van, the police officers who had viewed the drone's flight, targeting, and firing upon the dog through the video display window on the laptop, were smiling and complimenting the sales rep on the cool efficiency and ease the tool proved to have. He showed the group the "return" command, and a few key strokes signaled the drone to fly back to the landing coordinates where the demonstration began.

"What about the dog?" Lieutenant Baskar asked.

"Don't worry," the salesman replied. "I brought a shovel."

CHAPTER 14:
GET A JOB OR GET THE HELL OUT OF HERE

AS FRANK WALKED TOWARDS TOWN ON THE STILL-UN-cleared sidewalks, he eventually came to an intersection of Lincoln and Merriman streets when, waiting for the traffic light to stop the many cars criss-crossing the roads, he saw Tommy Hodges stepping into the flow seemingly oblivious to the danger.

Tommy's bulky weight and huge face might have been like a pro football linebacker had he been 20 years younger, but his untrimmed black beard, faded and ripped blue jeans, and dirty open jacket gave the unmistakable message that this was a man some history book would have called a hobo. His brown ankle-high work boots were, as usual, untied. While strangers may have thought that this lapse was yet another sign of the man's lazy or slovenly nature, people who knew him understood that a significant pain in his spine prevented him from bending; and his large extended belly didn't help either.

The morning had begun for Tommy like most other days. In his studio apartment above the bowling alley, he hauled his 350-pound body upright on the edge of his bed as the morning sun spilled through his only window. He looked around the room towards a small oak table and the two chairs beside it. As was always the case, Tommy saw the pieces as if they were made of wobbly rubber instead of wood. Any person without the challenge of schizophrenia would see simple, strong kitchen furniture that might have needed a good coat of polish, but Tommy saw something that no one would dare sit on, much less use for a meal. He always wondered whether the things were meant for display in some modern art museum instead of something practical.

As his slumber from sleep slowly faded, the voices in his head arrived as predictably as the dawn. *You're a piece of shit*, a craggy witch-like voice began, *you know that?* Then came the voice that sounded like one of his male high-school teachers he remembered in Boston: *Don't you think the world would be better without you?* Next came a series of sounds without words: crashes of pots and pans, an explosion, trumpets, a baby crying, someone giggling. What followed that was the voice of another woman yelling instructions to Tommy in a language he had never heard before.

The large man hoisted himself to his feet and went to the window. Looking out at the fresh snowfall from the night and the white blanket effect it created on the buildings and houses on the street below, he thought to himself, *just another day,* and tried to focus his mind on something other than the threatening chorus of the maelstrom in his head.

With focused efforts, Tommy found that he could push the voices to the back of his mind where they wouldn't overwhelm his thoughts and concentration, so that he could attend to whatever issue or task the moment required. Doing so at the window, he felt the pains his body signaled, not only from his back, but from his knees and feet as well. *New boots*, he thought to himself, *got to get some.*

Heading to the bathroom, he grabbed his toothbrush from the holder and put warm water on it from the sink. *You can't even afford toothpaste, you worthless shit.* It was a scolding female voice from his mind who he had come to call Brenda. Her messages and manner of

speaking seemed to be more constant than the other auditory hallucinations, and even though the voice was harsh, crude, and always accusa-
tory, Tommy found her sounds somehow comforting in their constancy,
somewhat like talk-radio without the radio playing in the background
of life in a way that only he could hear.

The voice of Brenda was demanding his attention as he lumbered
along the sidewalk towards Lincoln and Merriman, to his appointment
for his monthly trip to the State Office of Mental Illness Management
downtown for his "medication and money" service, or M&M as it was
colloquially called by those involved. Even with Brenda ranting, Tommy
was keenly thinking that if he missed this meeting or refused to allow
them to have a sample of his blood to judge the presence of the medications he was ordered to take, he would have no income for the rest of
the month. *So, I watched this movie last night*, Brenda explained. *It was
about an axe murderer; come to find out, it was you.*

"That wasn't me. It couldn't have been," Tommy protested aloud
to the voice no one else could hear, consumed and angry at the accusa-
tion. Fixed on the crosswalk in front of him, he stepped into the traffic
on Lincoln, not aware that it wasn't the right time to do so safely. A
black Mercedes 325i swerved to miss the man, the driver quick to spin
the car to the left while jamming the brakes. The screech of the tires and
the blast from the horn pushed Brenda into silence. Tommy halted and
looked up innocently.

A young college-age woman in a fur-collared ski jacket opened
her door and got out of her sports car. "Hey asshole," she shouted, "I
could have hit you!" Tommy looked at her sheepishly, holding up both
his hands showing her his open palms, hoping the gesture was both
calming and contrite.

"Sorry," he managed.

Her anger continuing, she said, "You people are all the same! If I
hit you, I might have dented my car."

"Sorry, lady. No harm done." Tommy resumed his crossing now that the other cars had stopped to take in the scene, many of them clogging the busy intersection.

"No one wants you people around here. Get a job or get the hell out of here; just don't keep sticking your hand out looking for help." She got back into her car and slammed the door. When her car crossed behind Tommy, she rolled down her window and shouted, "Get the fuck out of Hallet Springs, will ya?"

Witnessing this exchange as he crossed from the other side, Frank caught up to Tommy a few steps further in his walk. "Tommy," he called, "are you OK?"

"Oh hi, Boss, ya I'm fine. You?"

"That was close. I saw that car almost hit you."

"Ya, you know. Shit happens. I'm sorry to have troubled you, but look, I'm almost late for my M&M, so I can't talk now. See ya."

As Tommy continued, the voice of Brenda came back into his consciousness as the distraction of the near accident, and the brief interactions that followed it, passed. Brenda returned to her usual taunting. *You should have just decked that woman; what a bitch!* "I don't do that," he answered to no one. Brenda began to laugh, and another pandemonium of voices and noises resumed.

Amid this internal racket, Tommy thought about the injections he'd be required to receive in the next hour or so. One was, they told him, a medicine that was effective at removing auditory and visual hallucinations that come with schizophrenia. Tommy wondered when this therapeutic effect would happen, since he'd been on this particular chemical cocktail for about five years. When they asked him how he was doing and if the med was helping, he would nod and say, "OK." No one bothered to ask anything further.

The second injection was an assurance that he would not consume alcohol. To the treatment system of "services," the advent of this agent about ten years ago was a godsend. They could mandate through court order that a sufferer from a psychotic or bipolar illness or post-traumatic stress disorder, who showed an exacerbation of symptoms or social problems after they drank alcohol, would be required to "consent" to the medication. This drug was called a long-acting antagonist to alcohol. Should a person have both in their system, a distressing physical reaction would take place, making the person almost incapacitated with nausea, cramps, and lethargy almost like a bad flu.

Fortunately, Tommy never had the symptoms of alcoholism; but unfortunately, when he first was taken into the treatment service program at the state hospital in Concord some ten years ago, he had been trying to calm the torment of voices in his head with Jack Daniels, for nothing else seemed to help. As soon as blood tests revealed alcohol, he was tracked as a client in denial of a substance-abuse problem, given the medication regime that included the antagonist, and subsequently the link between his meager monthly income and compliance. His explanations about his pre-treatment coping strategies fell on deaf ears.

Thinking about all this, he wondered how his life had taken so many wrong turns. Was it the accidental missteps he'd made somewhere along the way, or the funny twists of fate that befall anyone, or his genetics, or merely the struggles of life anyone coped with in the impersonal, pressured, distrustful, and callous society the American culture had become? *I could sure use a beer,* Brenda said. *How about you?* As Tommy turned the corner onto Main Street near the front door of his destination, he thought to himself, *why do people hate me?*

CHAPTER 15:

OUTLAWS

"I'LL TAKE YOU AS FAR AS WICHITA," THE DRIVER OF THE SEMI told Miguel, riding shotgun in the cab, "then I'm headed east." His passenger nodded and smiled.

Miguel looked out the window at the stark countryside outside the moving truck as Route 16 passed through miles and miles of the south Texas plains. He was feeling how nice it was to find a trucker going north who stopped to help a hitchhiker and didn't ask many questions. It was good to sit and rest, even if the loud red cab of the Kenworth wasn't all that comfortable.

The crossing into the U.S. had gone more smoothly than the traveler anticipated. From hopping into the small dingy with the others getting across the Rio Grande in the middle of the night, to his crawl through the short passage underneath the wall, to the secluded and shaded outcroppings of vegetation he used to rest along his trek northward, life had presented far fewer obstacles for the Salvadoran than he feared. Far from confident, he knew that Omaha was still a long way off but, at least for the next two or three hours in the truck, he'd probably be OK.

"You know," the portly, unshaved driver said, "it's against the law for me to pick up hitchhikers anymore. I could lose my permits and get a fine." Miguel turned towards the man but didn't reply. "If somebody stops us, I'm tell'm that you're my brother. OK?" The passenger nodded.

"Know what I say?" he continued. "Screw 'em. I'll help someone if I want to. I'll pick up any damned hitchhiker I want to. What the hell sort of country are we turning into, anyway? It was never like this before." The driver launched into a tirade about how the United States had become a different nation than what he remembered over the last two or three decades. Even from behind the wheel of his traveling hulk of a semi, he witnessed the morphing of "the land of the free and the home of the brave" into the "culture of the callous and the gathering of the greedy." He lamented to his passenger his theory as to how this transformation happened, starting with the commonplace thoughts that profit comes before people, that freedom is decoupled from charity, that infrastructure everywhere was allowed to deteriorate, and that the idea of interpersonal connections, relationships, and associations—a social fabric essential to democracy—had become almost extinct. Pausing from his diatribe, he turned his eyes off the road for a second and looked at Miguel. "Where you headed, anyhow?" he asked. "What's your story, if you don't mind me ask'n'?"

Miguel told the man about his plan to find his wife and young daughter in Omaha and how he had been removed from them years ago. Sensing the trucker's sympathetic reactions to his story, he confided that the violence in his homeland made it much too dangerous for men of his age to stay, lest they are blackmailed into joining a gang and become a hapless pawn in their drug wars against rivals. He told him that his family in the states was the most important thing in his world, that getting reunited with them meant more to him than anything. He shared that he hadn't heard from his wife in over a year or so and that this silence was a painful form of heartbreak. For an unexplainable reason, Miguel recapped his entire sorry saga, and the summing up and sharing made him feel that the burden on his soul was a tiny bit lighter.

There were miles of quiet between the two in the truck after that. When the semi pulled into the travel center just outside the city and parked on the outskirts of the lot with the other rigs, Miguel zipped up his jacket and extended his hand to the driver to thank him. Reaching behind the seat, the driver said, "Here, take this gallon of water and these." He held out two apples.

"Gracias," Miguel replied. As he climbed down from the truck, the driver yelled, "Be safe, amigo. And remember, not all Americans are bad."

Before long, the afternoon sun was bright but the cool air along the road outside the small town of Furley made for a pleasant walk. Finding himself in the busier parts of the community, he thought it best not to try to hitchhike and draw attention to himself. As far as anyone could tell, he was just someone walking home or to work.

After an hour or two, he found himself on an isolated stretch of road bisecting farm fields on either side. The desolate countryside gave the Salvadoran plenty of time to get lost in these memories of the two most important people in his life that he'd not seen in years. Maria would be a teenager now. He started to consider how much the two would have to talk about. How does one catch up with your child after having been ripped from her life so suddenly? As to Louisa, what he longed for most was her embrace; talking through their separated years would come in time.

His peaceful silence didn't last for long. He heard the faint sound of a car far behind him and though he assumed it would zoom past soon enough like so many countless others in the last several weeks, it did not. He was tempted to turn around as the noise told him it was slowing but he thought better of it. When it pulled to a stop several yards behind him, Miguel knew he should halt as well, and he turned around.

The unmistakable markings of a police car met his eyes. He assumed the piercing stare from the driver would make the next few moments incredibly risky. What he didn't appreciate at the time was that, before the officer left the car, the dashcam was purposefully not engaged. The door opened and a female Kansas state trooper exited and brought with her what looked like a semi-automatic rifle. Her trim black uniform didn't even attempt to hide the bulletproof vest that hugged her torso.

"Good afternoon, sir," the officer said. "May I see some identification? Documentos, por favor."

Miguel assessed that the trooper was in her mid-thirties. Both her build and bearing told him she was no novice, an assumption confirmed by her business-like tone of voice.

The man retrieved a cloth wallet from his back pocket and silently removed his driver's license issued by the State of Nebraska that had expired about five years earlier. Wordlessly, he handed it to the officer, his body tensing and mind attending to every nuance of the moment of fear. Lt. Mia Hoffman took the ID and studied it for a moment. "Come into my car," she ordered, and he quietly obeyed.

She settled him into the back seat and returned to the front one where she could enter a few keystrokes on the laptop affixed to the dashboard. Miguel tried to see what was on the screen, but the wire mesh separating the two areas made it impossible. Like other police cars he'd been in, this one had no door handles on the inside. As the officer studied screen after screen on her computer, Miguel worried that the longer she took, the worse it might be for him.

Finally turning to her captive, she said, "You just left a truck that picked you up hitchhiking, didn't you? A Kenworth with a red cab, right? Verdad?"

Miguel tried to feign that he didn't understand her English.

"I know you speak English, sir, no need to pretend," she stated firmly.

Miguel tried to evaluate his options. But before he could corral his thoughts, the woman came closer to the metal grate. "Miguel," she continued, this time with a softer tone, "I know something about you, and I want to help."

"That trucker—big guy, baseball hat—who picked you up?" she continued, "He called my cell phone. Teddy's a friend of mine. We're in the same club, so to speak."

Miguel didn't know what to make of her sudden change of demeanor, nor the hint of kindness in her tone. From what he could see of her eyes, however, she seemed sincere.

"Here it is, Miguel," she explained. "What I'm about to say, and our meeting today, never happened. Got that? Teddy, the trucker, told me where I might find you and that you needed help. I will lose my job if my bosses find out."

The man looked stunned and still apprehensive. Sensing she needed to convince him, she asked, "What was the last thing the trucker said to you? He said, 'not all Americans are bad' didn't he?"

She handed him a small business card with two letters printed in the middle, "vv." On the back, she had written NAMI in ink. "You are an illegal and you are looking for your wife and daughter in Omaha. Don't, whatever you do, go to the authorities. When you get to Omaha, ask people where the NAMI office is—that's the National Alliance on Mental Illness. They have a missing person network, and they will help you and not ask too many questions."

Unsure what to make of this information, Miguel looked at her quizzically but sensed a feeling of relief washing over his awareness while his tense muscles relaxed just slightly. "Thank you," he said. "This is amazing."

"Then," she continued, "whatever comes next, keep an eye out for anything or anyone who shows you a symbol like that: two 'v's—that stands for Via Verde. We sometimes disguise the message, so it looks like the letter 'W.' Got it?"

"Si," he managed, still confused but grateful, "Via Verde."

"Right," the officer confirmed. "We do kindness, and that makes us outlaws."

PART 2

"We are each one of us parables."

– FRANK WILLIAM STRINGFELLOW (1925–1980)

CHAPTER 16:
THE LINE WILL BE SHORTER

THE AFTERNOON SUN WAS STRONGER THAN IT HAD BEEN the weeks before, but the cold air in the drafty rooms at the Mills didn't want to surrender. Those chilly, shaded spaces of the abandoned buildings wouldn't feel the seasonal warming of the indoor atmosphere until May. Outside, a foot or so of snow covered most of New England even though, by mid-February, most everyone wanted winter to be over.

The regulars who called the place home were biding the time together in the grimy workshop like they had been doing informally most every day around two p.m., tending the fire in the center of the room's concrete floor. Frank, Derek, and Margie were playing cards while Bristol sat in her usual place on a workbench where she could look out the cloudy window to the forest beyond the Mill's back parking lot. The pines, maples, and oaks were spared the weight of the snowfall due to the strengthening light.

Lost in her private thoughts, anyone looking at her might have thought she was daydreaming, but her mental machinery was much more purposeful and moving at a steady pace. *Spring,* she thought to herself, *that's the time to move again. But where?* It was a valid question, as the solitary teen felt she had no family, no home, and no security anywhere she could think of. As vast as she knew the world to be, as packed with people it all was, no one, she felt, had a place in their heart for her; no mother, a father God-knows-where in Central America, not even a bed to call her own. All the girl really wanted was a place where she wouldn't be afraid.

Tommy entered the room and scanned it as if taking attendance. "Sorry I'm late, everybody," he said cheerfully.

Derek looked at Margie and smiled victoriously. "There you are! What did I tell you? He'd apologize for just walking in the room. Knew it! Hand it over—we bet four bucks."

"You just cost me two smokes, you dumb ass," she shot back, looking at Tommy. "I shouldn't have taken that bet."

Frank looked squarely at the woman, his unapproving glance speaking louder than any reprimand.

"Sorry, Boss," she said. "Got it: respect. Sorry Tommy, sorry Derek, sorry Boss Frank, sorry cards, sorry floor, sorry Mills, sorry sky. Damn it! Now look, Tommy, you got me doing it."

Her sarcasm finished, she returned to her hand of cards and fired one on the table. "Let's play," she said. Tommy took a step closer to the game and, considering his options, walked away towards the workbench where Bris was sitting atop the flat surface. Tommy hoisted his large body up on the bench too, close, but not too close to the pensive teen. Perhaps it was the smell of gasoline on Tommy's grimy coat that pushed her thinking in a new direction.

"Hi Bris," he said to her, "mind if I sit here with you?"

Bristol smiled.

"Thanks. If I bother you, just let me know and I'll go." She didn't turn away and the two sat in silence for a minute.

Tommy's soiled tan coat looked like it hadn't seen a washing machine in years. His once black Wranglers were now gray with age, but they too looked and smelled like they were better suited to a trash bin. Still, the clothing was fitting to the bulky man in that his scruffy beard and matted hair were strangers to things like shampoo and combs.

What could be seen through the whiskers of the tan skin on his face show more wrinkles than would be typical of a man in his mid-thirties. The hobbling crush of poverty can weather a person every bit as much as living in the elements.

"Know why I apologize to people all the time?" he asked quietly, so only she would hear. Bristol gave no reply save for open eyes and the slightest turn of her head.

"OK then, since you asked politely, I'll tell you, but you have to swear not to tell anybody. OK?"

Tommy knew better than to wait for her agreement.

"A few years ago, when I turned thirty-three, I think I had a dream. It's hard to say, but it clearly wasn't real, and it wasn't voices or symptoms, and I know I was asleep. But the dream was stronger and more powerful than I ever experienced before. If it was a dream, it wasn't regular. It wasn't just symptoms neither, because this felt much different and better. Something powerful.

"I was in the big open place outside standing by myself on top of a hill. In every direction, you could see hill after gentle hill rolling off far into the horizon. It was all grassy and green, warm, and peaceful. Not far ahead of me, there was a big line of people standing shoulder to shoulder, all looking in the same direction; I knew somehow that they were waiting for me. The line had every sort of person you could imagine, and it went on and on, hill after hill, as far as the eye could see, all in a single row like a garland of people that went on for miles, just standing there waiting. There must have been thousands of silent people in that line.

"They were waiting for me. Somehow, I knew that I was supposed to start with the first person and go on down the line, stopping at each one, until I reached the horizon. My gut told me that that's where heaven was. God was there, waiting for me, at the end of the line.

"Then I had this conviction, see; my gut told me what I had to do. Somehow, I knew in my bones that I was supposed to start with the first guy and look him in the eye. Standing there, I would see all the man's pains; in time, I would feel them too and they'd become a part of me. His heartbreaks, his sorrows, his failings, his guilt. Turns out, each person in that big line would be someone I hurt or somebody I did wrong by in my life. For most of my life, I was an angry and mean asshole. But, looking at them face to face, I would see the fragile person inside just like God does. This wasn't a punishment for me, see, just an awakening. When I took on their pain, they would vanish, but my own heart would get a little crack in it.

"I'd go to the next person, stop and look them in the face, eye to eye. I'd understand how she'd suffer every day, what insults and hurt she carried. I'd *really* know and feel all the bad things everybody there had to handle. Then my heart would crack a little bit more, and I'd go to the next one, and the next, and the next. Hurt, hurt, hurt. Crack, crack, crack.

"By the time I was reaching the end of the line, my heart would be broken into a million tiny pieces, maybe just molecules where the flesh had been. Once that happened, I'd be ready to enter heaven and see God."

"So, I figure that if I can be gentle now, kind when I can, not hurtful to other people at least, that line of people will be shorter when I die. I don't want to be a mean son-of-a-bitch anymore."

Bristol's eyes were wide as she took in the story. Her face showed the kindness and empathy she felt in her soul, but went unexpressed with her voice. The fact that he trusted her with this intimate secret made her feel honored, which was a sensation she had never felt before.

As Tommy stopped, a grave and comfortable silence hung between the two and they both wanted to respect it. They both gazed at the gray floor beneath them. When the moment was right, Tommy said, "You can have a mental illness like I do and still have dreams, can't you?"

Bristol looked up at the man and nodded.

"They can't take away your dreams, can they?" he asked, knowing she wouldn't answer. *No, Tommy*, she thought, *they damn well can't.*

At that moment, a large bird that had been hiding in the rafters of the ceiling swooped across the workshop and found a new hiding spot in the timbers. It let out a call, the same owl-like hooting Bristol was fond of hearing almost every night, the five or six notes unmistakable.

"Looks like a mourning dove," said Tommy. "It must have come in one of the broken windows around here and she can't find her way back. They winter here in New England very successfully, and most people don't appreciate that."

Bristol looked at her friend with surprise at the confidence of his report.

"Its real name is Zenaida macoura," he continued, looking at her modestly. "I used to want to be an ornithologist. I even got into Cornell after high school. Couldn't afford it. Then the voices started and that was that."

After a moment, the bird repeated its cooing. Bristol looked up the high ceiling to try and find it, but the dove was well hidden. Realizing that this was the creature she'd come to appreciate for its comforting, gentle music each night, she thought about her belief that the Mills had a psychic energy flowing through it which even used animals to animate it. If that was the case, then, just maybe, things would eventually be OK.

CHAPTER 17:
MY TICKET

LATER THAT AFTERNOON, MOST OF THOSE GATHERED IN THE room started to disperse, each with their own destination and strategy for solving their unique problem of the moment, be it food, shelter, or respite from their emotional demons or mental struggles. Tommy left Bristol without a word, and while in some other setting a polite "good-bye" would have been the customary way of terminating a social encounter, his way of leaving was in keeping with the group's mores, too. Bristol could barely see the forest now as the dimming daylight signaled that she too should move and find a safe corner in the vast factory before it was too dark.

With the card game over, Frank left the workshop as well, but not before glancing at most of the people around him as if his wordless eye contact was enough to bid them some kindness. When his gaze fell on Bristol, she smiled and nodded.

Frank had time on his hands after Christmas because his seasonal job at the tree farm stand was over. They would put him back on the payroll when it came time for heating up the greenhouses to start sowing the seeds that would, by May, be tall enough to sell to the customers in Hallet Springs who wanted to plant the colorful annuals around the inside perimeter walls of their homes or the window boxes they would have here and there to make their sanctuaries cheerful and bright. He trudged through the snow to the small house he rented. It was nearly perfect for a veteran with new enemies: post-traumatic stress, guilt, and anger.

The cottage was on the outskirts of Hallet Springs where a mixture of older and newer dwellings were scattered about the area, each with a long driveway and some with gates, the large distances between them making any sort of communication between neighbors unlikely. Frank could not think of a time he had any sort of opportunity to meet them even though most could see him walking back and forth to work as they drove past him in their cars, staring but not acknowledging the man. In the first few months of his tenancy there, he did wave hello to the drivers whose cars he'd come to recognize; but after a few weeks without a wave back, he stopped the greeting.

As he unlocked the only door to the house, Frank felt grateful that the building fit his needs so well. The kitchen was tiny and without enough space for a table; the living room just big enough for two soft chairs and a few lamps; the bedroom sufficient for a full-size bed and dresser; and the bathroom even had a tub. What he liked best was the solitude and quiet.

After his dinner, he sat at a small desk in his living room and opened one of its side drawers. He removed the old revolver he'd discovered weeks ago at the Mills, returning to his task of restoring it. The Smith and Wesson looked remarkably better than it had when he accidentally found it, but whether he could get it to work was another matter entirely.

Reaching beneath the desk, he pulled up a cardboard box with the tools and supplies he had been using to restore the piece. Most of the aged grime came off well from the barrel, frame, and grips, but telltale signs of rough use were everywhere to the trained eye. It was clear to the Ranger that many screws were turned over the years by an improper driver and the scratches near each hole might indicate careless maintenance of the key moving parts inside, performed by a careless owner. Still, as Frank attended to the weapon over the last few weeks, he scrutinized, cleaned, and properly oiled each precisely engineered part so that it would carry out its function when the moment came.

Frank carefully removed one screw to remove the cylinder and ejector rod from the frame. He put solvent on a small patch of white rag and used the cleaning rod to force it through the barrel, and repeated this with all six chambers of the cylinder. Putting it back in place, he pulled the trigger to make sure the hammer, firing pin, and cylinder stop moved in harmony. *This will have to do*, he thought to himself.

Pulling open another drawer, he found the only bullet he found with the gun, and he wiped it clean with a rag. He set it down tip up next to the revolver and studied both.

My ticket, he thought, *but to where?* This would depend somewhat on the decision he knew he would be called to make someday. Pointed in one direction, the anger just short of rage inside his brain would, with the easy squeeze of the trigger, propel the bullet towards a target that would make the round his ticket to prison. Pointed in a different direction, say the roof of his mouth, the ticket would likely take him to hell but certainly not heaven. With only one shot, however, he'd have to make it good.

CHAPTER 18:
"HE'D NEVER BE ELECTED DOG CATCHER NOW"

WHILE THE OUTCASTS AT THE MILL PREPARED THEMSELVES TO head over to St Theresa's for dinner, the well-heeled residents of Hallet Springs and the county also were starting to arrive at a far more luxurious setting than the basement of a century-old, poor church. Here, there was no shortage of black tuxedos and elegant ball gowns as the invited guests entered the large banquet room at the Grand Mountain Country Club. The governor expressed regrets, but her representatives arrived in a dark limousine.

The occasion for the gathering was the retirement party of Sheriff Bertrand LaBounty. Anybody who was anybody wouldn't miss this, because the lawman's reputation and accomplishments were known throughout New Hampshire. He was a man with a storied career, praised by members of all political parties that passed through the legislature or executive branch, someone known as a "doer" who navigated the changing culture in the state and the country with style, integrity, and high marks from anyone above him. The voters thought so as well, accounting for his nearly forty years of service in his position.

Naturally, the assembly there that night wanted to honor him memorably, toast his entry into a well-deserved new chapter in his life, and hear his reflections on his decade's long role. Some might have considered this the premier social event of the new year.

The sheriff too, was bedecked in his finest dress uniform, looking every bit as the imposing, no-nonsense lawman whose presence seemed to command any room into which he entered. The new white shirt he wore looked like it hugged his muscular neck a little too tightly but any viewer's eyes were immediately drawn to the resplendent gold buttons of his blue coat and the array of medals to the left of his lapel. The jacket fit well enough to hide his service revolver, but he felt he didn't need it that night, given the pair of armed deputies standing in the back of the room or the police drone outside patrolling the parking lot and immediate neighborhood around the facility.

Despite his unmistakable military bearing, the broad smile on his face as he greeted and mingled with the guests put people at ease. As the throng found their name cards on the round tables impeccably arranged in the dining room, so too did the dignitaries take their places at the head table on the stage, flanking LaBounty and his wife seated in the center.

Champagne and vintage wines punctuated every course of the lavish meal and, by the time dessert was served, the master-of-ceremonies Mayor Peter Haddad set the agenda of speeches in motion. Close friends, colleagues in law enforcement, and state officials of various departments all extolled the contributions the Sheriff had made during his long tenure to the citizens of New Hampshire. Clyde Owens, Chief of Staff to Governor Esteguard, read a proclamation and narrated with an attempt at humor about how he and LaBounty often had respectful but heated disagreement on one matter or another. The guests laughed politely on cue.

When it was time for the honoree of the evening to speak, the guests rose to their feet in rousing applause as he walked to the microphone. Every ear was keen to listen, and every face showed a warm smile.

He had considered this moment for many weeks, torn as to whether he should seize the time or let it pass, respectfully, expectedly, graciously. In the end, he decided the matter, knowing his well-prepared remarks would be something of a surprise.

Like most retirees, he began by thanking his faithful wife, Margaret, all the people who donated to or supported his many campaigns, and his many coworkers and subordinates whose dedication was beyond question. He smiled with sincere humility, just like everyone there anticipated he would. Then his words turned decidedly serious.

"Tonight, as much as you have warmed my heart with this feast," he told the party-goers, "as I leave, the weather in my soul is cold and gray."

"This ought to be good," Owens whispered to his wife Patrice. "This old dinosaur should have retired years ago."

Her husband's quip was no surprise, as his private contempt for LaBounty was established ever since the attorney general expressed a worry to the governor that the sheriff was showing too much discretion in enforcing anti-vagrancy laws.

LaBounty continued. "Many of you don't know that I have been, among other things, a quiet observer and a student of history as I've done my job day in, day out. I see something grave. We are, my friends, in a struggle.

"On one side, there are many who believe that much more of our public resources and tax dollars should be devoted to stopping crime and the degradation of society that stems from people struggling with poverty. Disability, illness, addiction, that sort of thing. They expect the state to do more to shelter them from seeing hardship, blight, suffering, and the like. Not, mind you, to do anything about that, but just to keep it out of sight. New Hampshire, like other states in the U.S., has done much to deport—in effect—those populations of concern to other locations. Trouble is, other states are doing likewise, so the migration of this population, north to south, east to west, is now bidirectional. We move people out, and others move in.

"For those who hold this view, the question is, 'where is the path to greater safety?' They want protection from crime, illness, and the burden of any concern. This is their greatest motivation.

"On the other side, there are many who would rather we invest more in the technologies necessary to make everyone secure in their own digital and material bubble. What matters is that the promotion of individual life, made possible by every electronic or digital advance, take overarching preeminence over community life. As long as I can work from home, that my kids can learn remotely through an AI teacher available to them 24/7; as long as I can get everything I need delivered to my doorstep; as long as a strange person doesn't need anything from me; life is good. People like to believe that society exists to help individuals create their unique paradise on earth." He glanced up and saw many heads nodding in agreement.

"For those in this camp, the question is: 'How can I shore up the metaphorical moat I have built around the castle I call my life, and what can the state do to help me achieve that insulation?

Owens looked at his wife and said, loud enough for those around him to hear, "What the hell is he doing? Good thing he won't be looking for votes again," she nodded.

Looking out at his listeners, the sheriff now saw only grim faces where smiles and laughter had been just moments before. He instinctively knew that these patricians didn't expect to hear anything so serious, but he didn't care. For once in over forty years in public life, he felt he could speak his mind.

"But I want to offer a third alternative," the man said after a heavy pause. "It is this: What is the path of the greatest love?"

"He'd never be elected dog catcher now," Owens announced to his wife. "This is rich!" he chuckled.

"That is the question we all must answer," the sheriff said. I know it sounds radical and many of you have probably not ever heard it put this way, but I'm convinced beyond doubt. We've built a nation for ourselves that has forgotten one of the core truths of democracy, the idea that we are all in this together. Forget that, and we can forget everything: no earth, no freedom, no health, safety, prosperity, or happiness.

"What we have lost," he said with slow emphasis, "is the belief that hurt and hardship that falls on anyone, is hurt and hardship that falls on everyone."

The speaker paused, not knowing whether he should say more or not, and as he looked out to the frozen audience, he saw only puzzled looks. To the crowd's astonishment, the sheriff simply said, "Thank you," and headed back to his seat.

To that, a mild level of applause of polite response came from the seated guests in vast contrast to the adulation their clapping conveyed at the outset of his oration. Caught unawares by this bombshell of an indictment, the mayor returned to the mic to conclude the agenda, hastily giving the perfunctory congratulations to LaBounty and the community's best wishes for a long and happy retirement. The guests got up to leave, as did the people on stage at the event's top table.

Owens and his wife stood too, and he went over to the sheriff. He reached out to shake his hand and said with a smile, "I always knew you'd turn out to be a self-righteous jerk. Instead of giving that speech, you might as well have climbed onto the table here, dropped your pants, and taken a shit right in front of people. You would have had the same effect!"

He didn't wait for LaBounty's reply but turned to get back to Patrice. Taking her arm, he looked back at the sheriff and said, "And you can forget any help from the Governor about finding your daughter. She can't appear to be helping insurrectionists."

CHAPTER 19:

HAPPINESS, SAFETY, AND SELF

TWO DAYS AFTER THE BANQUET, REPORTER PAULA DAMASCUS opened the large glass doors at City Hall and passed effortlessly through the metal detector after the security guard next to it examined the contents of her shoulder bag. "You're here to see the mayor," he informed her after looking at the list of permitted visitors to enter the building. "Use this elevator up to the third floor. His secretary will greet you."

Once she was ushered into his office, Mayor Peter Haddad got up from his desk, a broad smile on his face that was ubiquitous whenever the politician met with the public or the press. Dressed in a gray suit and thin crimson necktie, he prided himself on being urbane and stylish, a tall and trim man with handsome features. He took great efforts to show himself to be a man of charm and grace, but feisty and forceful when making a decision of government. He was a skillful operator when he needed to persuade, aptly plying the levers of power when it was necessary, but charming enough for his prey not to realize they were being treated as a means to the mayor's ends.

"What a pleasure to talk with you, Ms. Damascus," Haddad began as he showed her to chair in front of his desk. "I'm always happy to give time to the *Observer*."

"Thank you for giving me some, Mr. Mayor," the reporter replied brightly, "and I know you are busy so let me begin." She removed a pad of paper from her bag and then placed a small recording device on his desk and looked to see if he had any objections, which, of course, he did not. "I'm following up on the small story about the sheriff's retirement speech. We covered his departure but not much about what he said on his way out. I was assigned to write about him a few weeks ago and I found his message to me then very"—she paused, searching for the word— "unusual, no, troubling. Half of what I wrote never made it into print, but that's another story. What did you think of his party?"

"Well, I'd say the party was great and the county did a topper job of the banquet. Too bad the sheriff didn't go gracefully, but I'm not worried about his opinions now, nor is anyone else. People won't pay it much heed, if you ask me." Haddad smiled dismissively. "There are far more important things to talk about, don't you agree?"

"Yes, true," she answered. "But what about his speech? What did you think?"

"Honestly, I was taken aback," he replied calmly. "I was surprised that he would be so ungrateful and give such an incendiary message. I guess he's entitled to his opinion, I just wish he'd gone out quietly."

"Do you think he's right?"

"You mean about a different path and all that? It doesn't really matter what I think about it; it matters if the people believe it. By my read, nobody does. People are content to be on the path we're on." Haddad folded his hands on his desk.

"And what would that be?" she asked.

"Advancement, prosperity, expanding your assets, investment, and the safety that comes from insularity. That's what everyone wants for their lives. Trust me."

Paula was writing a few notes as the mayor spoke. He gave her a moment before continuing. "But what would you say about the people who, for some reason, aren't able to be on such a path?"

"Let me explain. We live in a time that has regained an appreciation of the deep wisdom of social Darwinism. People survive if they are fit to do so; if not, it's nature's way that they don't. Many people believe that Americans should have taken a lesson from countries like Somalia, Bangladesh, or Pakistan years ago. We just didn't have the stomach to let people die. Today, the rebirth of Darwinism takes care of that hesitation, so we are all better off. It's another great Renaissance, if you ask me."

"You sound persuasive," she said, the complement landing square as Haddad smiled.

"The truth is persuasive, isn't it? It just makes sense. We should all work for the common good. That means, working so we can all make our own life better. After all, didn't the president get elected on the slogan, 'Making you great again'?"

"And is the city doing that?"

"Yes, indeed!" he answered emphatically. "For starters, after many years of deliberation, we're finally poised to put Hallet Springs on the map in a huge new way. We do have the festival that brings in a good flow of tourists one time each year, but we need more. Opening the prime real estate in Hallet Springs to new development is the key. I can't tell you how many inquiries I get from builders and businesses wanting that location if only the Mills weren't there. They are an eyesore in the area, and now we have the momentum to rehabilitate those acres. I can see vast new apartments, malls, restaurants, and new tech services springing up; we need that. With that economic boost, each citizen can better get what they want: more happiness, safety, and self."

"Don't the Mills have a lot of history?"

"Yes, I'm sure they do, but no one cares about that. Besides, capitalism pushes us beyond the past to new ways of prosperity. It's the American way of life. We have to take them out."

Glancing at her watch, Paula felt that she had to shift the conversation to a different topic, hoping she might be the first reporter to get the man's unequivocal statement. "Mr. Mayor, there's much speculation that you plan to seek a higher office. A run for governor, state senate perhaps? Care to comment?"

Haddad was coy. "There is that speculation, yes. I'll be holding a press conference in Concord very shortly, and I'll be sure to invite you. It's no secret that I've had an exploratory committee working for over a year. I have a strong message about social reform that the voters want in our beautiful state."

"I've heard that some would call your policies 'social de-form,' not re-form."

"That's because they don't know what they're talking about," he replied, shrugging off the critique.

Their interview continued with topics that ranged from the city's current preparations for the festival to national politics, to local safety improvements. Haddad was keen to tell her how the new police drones were turning out and how pleased he was that the Hallet Springs PD had the latest aerial hardware. "Another way we're getting on the map," he told her with pride.

The allotted time for her interview transpired, Damascus turned off the recorder and gathered her things. The Mayor came around his desk and shook her hand, thanking her politely.

At the door, Paula turned around to put one final question to the Mayor. "Ever heard of Via Verde?" she asked.

"No," he replied. "What's that?"

"Another story I'm working on; no matter. Another time, perhaps?"

CHAPTER 20:
LET'S NOT TALK ABOUT THE STACK

AS ONE WEEK ROLLED INTO ANOTHER IN HALLET SPRINGS and the snowy ground was slowly revealing patches of earth here and there, everyone was starting to feel the hope of spring that was not far away. This wasn't true for Maxwell Cherryfield, however, who hadn't left his cabin on the outskirts of town for several days.

Max's was one of a cluster of small buildings constructed decades ago when tourists came through the area looking for a night or two of lodging. Each wooden building, the size of a one-car garage if your vehicle was small, once must have had just enough room for a double bed, side chair, sink and tiny counter, and private bathroom with shower and plastic curtain. As the tourist industry melted away, so too did any effort to keep the structures intact, inside, or out. When one owner unloaded the property to the next, the sale price declined such that the only type of future for the collection of cabins was in long-term rentals to people of concern who had only the measly occupancy voucher from the Department of Housing and Urban Development. Next to the shack that Max and Charlie occupied were a dozen or so similar ones each about twenty paces apart, and each occupied by a single man or woman remanded to the State's Mental Illness Monitoring System.

Max stayed home, keeping a close eye on his ailing companion and confidante, King Charles, the now thin and frail spaniel who had been by his side for the last nine years, through good times and bad. For Max, the "good" time was a spell without the crippling symptoms of schizophrenia when, for some inexplicable reason, the auditory or visual hallucinations his illness conjured up would give his soul and entire being a peaceful respite. Needless to say, Charlie didn't experience or understand all that but, just like the mysteries of mental illness, some mysterious canine intelligence told the dog when his owner—his bosom friend—needed him most.

But today, it was Charlie who needed Max, and both beings knew why that was so. Charlie was dying.

Max bent down to pet his dog who lay on a ratty pillow in the corner of the ramshackle cabin that was his special spot on the planet, his home. The improvised bed came from the town landfill that Max and his counterparts would explore from time to time when no city employee was present. In his cabin, he covered the pillow with a tired fleece blanket for the dog and the spot smelled like a combination of sweaty canine and pee, the scent of which bothered Max not one whit. Charlie was breathing slowly and didn't move much when his friend stroked his side gently.

"How about some food now?" the man asked with as much tenderness as anyone could muster. "I know; let's celebrate and have some tuna. You like tuna," he reminded the small creature. "I'll be right back; stay here."

Moving swiftly to the metal cupboard near the sink, Max retrieved a can the size of a hockey puck wrapped in plain white paper bearing only the name of its contents and not much more. It was the type of commodity item that the government provided "people of concern" like Max at their once-per-month food ration available at the MIMS center downtown. Max was saving this precious fish for a special occasion, and sharing it now seemed appropriate. Cranking a hand opener, he pried the top and examined the contents, which looked like something most people in Hallet Springs would not feed their cat.

He brought the meal to Charlie and sat on the floor. Then he offered the dog a dab of the tuna on his index finger. A twitch of the nose was all Max could see in the dog's response. "OK," he said, "maybe later when you feel up to it."

Responding to a familiar awareness that materialized in his mind, Max turned around and saw her. Constanza was standing behind him in a white nurse's uniform, there plain as day, even though the three locks on Max's door were tightly securing his premises. "He looks about the same as yesterday," she observed with a tender voice.

"How do you know when to come and go?" Max replied.

"You know, Max," she answered, "hallucinations like me are all in your head."

Connie spoke the truth. The trim young lady with shoulder-length brown hair today, had a kindly face and the color of her scrubs seemed to highlight the deep blue of her eyes. Max saw and heard her in every bit the same way as he saw his failing dog, but had any other human being been present, the man would have appeared to be having a conversation with no one, his monologue sounding like only one side of a friendly chat.

"It won't be long now, I think. I bet he has cancer; a tumor the size of a football," Connie continued. "Just make him comfortable." Max pondered this, not registering that the dog himself was not much bigger than the object she suggested.

"Not sure how to do that," Max replied, turning back to Charlie. Then he got to his feet and walked over to the sink right through the space his apparition occupied. He took a dishcloth from the strainer and dampened it with tepid water from the tap that Max had come to appreciate as hot, a lukewarm temperature being the maximum the dilapidated dwelling could produce. He returned to Charlie and wiped the motionless dog's face.

"Maybe it's time to put him down," she continued, "you know, like we discussed. The stack."

Max knew that the visage in front of him in that moment referred to the towering smokestack at the Mohawk Mills. Like most factories built in previous century in New England, the energy used to power the enormous machines necessary for whatever process was being performed to make whatever good the plant was aiming to produce had something to do with combustion. By necessity, this required the venting of smoke or other pollutants into the sky and that required a chimney large enough to get the smelly gas high away from population. The stack at the Mills was well over 150 feet tall with a diameter at the bottom large enough to fit Max's entire cabin and the one next door. Unlike many others of its kind, the huge cylinder of brick in Hallet Springs had an eerily narrow black iron stairway and handrail snaking around it like a corkscrew so that workers could manage the periodic cleaning or inspection of such an important investment. In more recent times, one smaller tenant was a research arm linked to the University of New Hampshire that used the belching output at the top of the stack for an array of instruments that measured the carcinogens and particulates finding their way into the sky. Decades of neglect, however, left the twisting staircase precarious as the march of seasons made the metal rust and the mortar between the face of the deteriorating tan brick weak and weathered, especially on the north side of the aging column.

"He probably needs to be put down," Connie said sympathetically. "But you can't afford the vet bill, can you?"

"No, no way."

"Then, the stack is an option. At the top, he goes in. Euthanasia and burial in one simple toss. Easy-peezie."

Everyone in Max's group knew the lore connected with the stack, as did most of the populace in the local region. The tower was a place that people used to end their life when the crippling emotional pain of desperation and despair became too much, when the future held no relief, and when day after depression-filled day escalated into a decent towards death. The group would talk about it from time to time, speculating how many people might lie in the bottom of the structure that had stood purposeless for decades, save for being a vehicle of twisted comfort for those seeing it as such. In one such conversation, Margie speculated that those who jumped into the stack wanted their death to go unnoticed, quiet, and unremembered, as if that symbolized the tenor of their life. Others, she thought, jumped outside the gaping hole on the top, knowing that someone would eventually find their splattered remains and must speculate on an answer to an unanswerable question: Why? Those souls, she said, were sending a message.

Remembering that if he appeased the hallucination, Connie would sometimes go away, Max said calmly, "I know." Then, addressing Charlie, he asked, "how about if I tell you a story?"

Connie became indignant. "Not another goddam story to your dog! Let me guess, 'Charlie the wonder dog.'"

"Once upon a time," Max began with a slow tenderness, trying to ignore his hallucination, "there was a mighty and noble dog named Charlie. He was brave and strong, and everyone knew him as Charlie the wonder dog."

"OK; I'm out of here," an internal voice called. "I can't stand you sometimes. But I'll be back; count on it." Max turned around and didn't see anything. "Don't mind her, Charlie," he consoled the dog, "and let's not even talk about the stack."

CHAPTER 21:
JUST ENOUGH TO GO FORWARD

PEERING THROUGH THE RAIN-SPECKLED WINDOW OF THE large bus, Miguel took in the sight of something he had never seen before. His fellow travelers on the Greyhound perked up as well to view the expansive cityscape of New York City at night, lights as far as the eye could see illuminating the vast array of skyscrapers, bridges, docks, cars, and trains all pulsing with energy and movement even at that early hour. Despite his fatigue from the numerous hours in his seat and his sleepiness at three a.m., he sensed that many other passengers also seemed to stir when the bus barreled around a particular bend on the busy I-95 that afforded such a remarkable view.

It was not unusual for the Salvadoran to be robbed of sleep in the middle of the night, be he on a bus or in a bed. Peaceful rest and happy dreams are seldom found in anyone mentally processing the grief that comes with loss, especially the kind that arrives after tragedy and death. A fitful night's rest was all Miguel had experienced ever since being taken from his American wife and daughter years ago, but the turmoil in his mind now came with a double demon, the news that Louisa had died from an overdose of Fentanyl and that Maria was a runaway he was struggling to find. Looking out the window at that hour was nothing new.

It would have been difficult for anyone to fathom everything that Miguel had come to learn from his encounter with an assortment of people who made up the Via Verde group in Omaha, a cautious and clandestine introduction arranged by a particularly helpful volunteer at the city's chapter of the National Alliance on Mental Illness. He had forgotten all their names, unsure even if the names they gave him were true, but would never forget their resourcefulness and access to information that an illegal visitor to the U.S. could ever hope to get.

On the one hand, what the network gave Miguel was terrible news. From looking at public records and other databases, they were able to piece together the events of Louisa's downward spiral, made quicker by drugs in the years after her husband's deportation. They were able to trace Maria's path, too, starting with her being remanded to the State of Nebraska and the string of foster homes she was placed in, her numerous truancy reports and minor infractions with authorities, and eventually her flight from the Department of Youth Affairs and the resulting warrant for her detention.

Both events gave him a complicated sort of heartbreak that seemed paralyzing at times, perhaps because he was bone-tired after finally reaching Omaha following the hard and precarious journey from his two-room placa-walled home in Talnique. The thought of returning to his family in Nebraska propelled him, day after grueling day on his trek, and that goal was gone now like a sunset. His sadness at the news of Louisa's death, a grief mixed with guilt that he was not there for her, and the pain knowing that Maria was lost, probably frightened, and running who-knows-where, was a bitter cocktail of emotions that could become a poison in one's soul if he let it. But now he would have to rely on the same fuel that propelled him for months: love. He had to find Maria.

On the other hand, what the VV group gave him was both help and hope. First, they gave him some much-needed shelter and food, the essential ingredients to recharge his strength. Second, they gave him the sympathy he needed in that moment to fathom the loss of his wife and the near-crippling news about his daughter's escape from authorities, both of which would be a massive blow to any human being. Third, they trusted him with just enough information about the VV network he could rely on as he began his second risky journey to rescue Maria. From what they could determine from their contacts with access to police databases, the teen had a minor altercation at a homeless shelter in Greenfield, Massachusetts about a month ago. At least that was a clue he could explore.

Like a maelstrom, all this swirled around in his consciousness in those dark and early hours on the bus, scrambling his thoughts from one fleeting realization to the next. With every slip down the mental slope of sadness, Miguel also thought about how lucky he had been with stumbling into the kindness of strangers. From the first truck driver who picked him up in Texas, to the state trooper who first gave him the critical advice and guidance about Via Verde, to the network of safe places of refuge he used and the money he needed to traverse the miles between the Midwest and New England—all of which was unlawful and had to unfold in secrecy—he realized that his plight could be far worse. The tabulation of his gratitude offset his numerous losses and hardships such that his mental and emotional ledger was balanced, just enough to go forward, but not enough to be happy.

He would still have to trust in the future kind assistance from others if he was to complete the next chapter in his search because, when the bus deposited him at the New York terminal, he would have to find his way to the commuter train to New Haven, where his next VV contact was to meet him.

CHAPTER 22:
NO STOMACH FOR IT ANYMORE

THE COLD MARCH AIR BLOWING THROUGH HALLET SPRINGS at that late hour was as uncomfortable as any sunny day in January. Based on their military days when Jason Krebs was assigned to his unit, recalling the ardent fondness they both had for professional basketball, Frank made the informed assumption that he could find the police officer outside of the most popular sports bar the sleepy city offered, especially when it was game night. He envisioned the man sitting at the bar, a Celtics game on the TV, tossing back a few drafts, and pontificating on better plays he made in high school as a starting center for Hanover. Frank waited on the sidewalk across the street from the front door of the Laugh and Lager, hoping that he could find his old comrade, but he harbored no delusions that any close bond still existed between them. He pulled up the collar of his dirty coat and his black knit cap down, trying to move back and forth slightly to fight off the descending temperature. It was years since Frank cared about basketball.

As hoped, Krebs exited the bar and started walking towards a car parked curbside. Frank crossed the street quickly and was about ten yards behind him when he yelled, "Hey Jason."

Krebs turned and squinted to see if he could recognize the stranger in the dim light of the streetlamp. The voice seemed strangely familiar, something out of the past, but he couldn't place it at first. Frank stepped from the shadow.

"Frank Stringfellow?" Krebs asked with a smile of recognition. "Is that you?"

"Hello, Jason. Long time no see."

"What's it been? Twenty years or so? I'll be damned."

The men shook hands and only a few bits of small talk passed between them. "What are you doing here?" Krebs eventually asked his former platoon leader. Frank told the man about his life after his discharge from Walter Reed and the army, his years of travels from job to job in more states than he could recall, and that he'd taken a farm job in Hallet Springs just about a year ago. For his part, Krebs talked about going into law enforcement and that his job here held the promise of advancement. "Promotions are good," Frank said. "But leadership has a price."

"How many dead?" Krebs asked, referring to their fellow soldiers they witnessed who ended their young lives in one firefight or another in foreign countries or causes some politician thought worthy of their sacrifice. "Too many," Frank replied. "And not just soldiers."

The conversation between the two veterans was almost like a casual ping-pong of stories, reflections, and memories of their time as Rangers where the mix of good and bad experiences left indelible contours on their characters. Interspersed in that trading, Frank asked about Jason's family politely, but the other man did not ask the same of Frank, already knowing that his old lieutenant had no one left. Predictably, the conversation came back to their days in Afghanistan when Krebs eventually asked, "Think it was all worth it?"

"I haven't answered that yet," Frank said. "All I know is that what we have here now betrayed us all. Seems to me like there's a war over here and nobody knows it. Look around you, Jason; this is not the America we were fighting about. We're now slowly killing our own and we've got to stop. The country is going to hell, and people like you can do something about it."

"Yeah," he replied. "That's what I'm doing: get the bad guys."

"And that's the problem. Everybody thinks that 'bad' means anybody who needs help from somebody. What the hell happened?"

"Here we go again," Krebs said, raising his hands up in exasperation. "Lieutenant Saint Stringfellow, fighting like a Rambo on one day and helping out the people in the shit of the war on the next. You had to go back and try to rescue those girls from the Taliban in that godawful village, remember? How many guys did we lose that day? Or that old lady with the suicide vest? Remember her? You spent, what, thirty minutes trying to get it off her. How many damn soccer games with little kids did you play when we were off duty?"

"I seem to remember that you followed me most of the time, to the fight or not."

"Somebody had to watch your ass. We all felt that, 'cause some little kid or some old grandpa would have an AK or knife or grenade and you'd be dead."

The conversation paused as both men's minds conjured up the images and sensations of their experience of warfare, which for any soldier who is branded by the daily danger of death, are never too far from consciousness and often resurface despite valiant efforts to keep them at bay.

"I didn't come find you to swap war stories," Frank continued. "I came to ask you to do something."

"What now? Organize a soccer camp for poor kids?"

"No. Something harder. Start pushing back. Where you can, start complaining, start objecting; stop the city's war on poor people."

Jason looked down and shook his head. "Look, Frank. We're not doing anything different than any other city in the state or different than the whole damn country. Besides, I can't do much anyway."

"You can," Frank protested. "You have some authority that comes with your badge, and I'll bet, you're the guy who sets an example—you always were."

"Frank, I'm not the guy to buck the system. Besides, Wall Street is happy, which means everybody is happy. In another two months or so, I'll have enough to get that new Corvette I've wanted all my life. And even if I wanted to say something, it would mean the end of my career, and I can't afford that. You've always been the leader. Why me and not you?"

It was Frank's turn to look down while a silence came to the conversation. Then he looked up at Krebs, who saw a message in his old friend's face he had never seen in all their many years together in the Army. "That fuckin' war. It took all the fight I ever had in me. I got nothin'," Frank said, dejected and defeated. "I got no stomach for any fight anymore. Let's just say that courage and I are no longer on speaking terms."

"You don't know what you are asking me, Frank," Krebs replied. "It's cold. I'm out'a here. See ya around."

The policeman turned and walked over to his car. When he opened the door, he looked back at Frank and yelled, "Just so you know, I don't believe you." As he watched the car move down the street, Lieutenant Stringfellow put his hand back in his coat pocket to touch the Smith and Wesson nestled there.

CHAPTER 23:
CHANGING LIGHT AND PIGMENT

BY THE END OF MARCH, NEW ENGLANDERS START TO APPRE-ciate the tiniest hint that there might be an end to winter sometime soon, just like every season rolls on from start to finish. Then, the after-noon sun starts to feel a little brighter and the slightest bit stronger than just weeks ago.

That sun was present at largely empty St. Theresa's that Sunday as the few worshipers were leaving the building after a Lenten prayer ser-vice. Bristol sat alone in the last pew far away from the small collection of people at the front near the sanctuary that had gathered, a distance close enough to hear the readings and group reflections that Sr. Isabel Gakunde was leading, but far enough away to be safe and not expected to participate. She liked being in the building especially at that time of the day when the bright sky outside shone through the sooty stained-glass windows on the east and west walls. To her, the colors of the glazes needed the solar help to be appreciated and, just like the changing sea-sons, that illumination was time-bound but recurrent. An admirer of the art had to be there often to appreciate that little discussed-cycle, the unfolding interplay between light and pigment that changes the scene so magically as the sun and time pass.

Most important, no one bothered her there, either. The place was slightly warmer than the Mill and decidedly warmer than the 20 degrees outside, so the respite of the prayer service and the chance to rest was an appealing experience. As people exited down the aisle, no one acknowledged her or even smiled.

Her spiritual task over, Isabel walked down toward the exit also, not to leave but to greet the teen. "Ms. Bristol!" she said with a warm smile. "I'm so glad to see you. This is wonderful. Thank you for coming and being so thoughtful! You must have felt I wanted to see you."

The girl smiled back, and slid down the bench to make room for the nun. "How nice to sit here with you, child, for a little rest."

"I have something for you," Isabel continued, her African accent on full display, rich and resonant. "I know that Christmas has passed, but it is always that way in my heart. I have a gift. I'll be right back."

Bristol wasn't sure what to do next. In the same moment, the message from Isabel was both welcome and threatening. *Why would she do that?* the girl wondered, torn between the urge to bolt out the nearby door or stay and enjoy whatever the lady was offering. Just when her leg muscles tensed up to stand, the Sister returned to the pew and sat down with a thin wrapped package in her hands, the old bench creaking with her weight. Bristol's body relaxed.

"Here," she said, "this is for you from me. I hope you like it; open, open," she encouraged.

The teen looked at her with a mix of surprise and gratitude. Her smile continued as she took in the candy cane pattern on the wrapping, rubbing her palm on the surface as if motion helped her savor the gift more. She found the taped edge on the long flat item and started to slice the paper with her finger.

As the paper fell away, Bristol looked at the package on her lap: an amply supplied art kit wrapped in clear plastic that revealed rows of colored pencils, pastels, felt markers, and a string of watercolors with two brushes. Each family of media was a bright array of colors with subtle changes in shades. A pad of thick sketching paper was also tucked neatly in the pack.

Bristol looked up at Isabel and smiled.

"Let me tell you why this is for you," she told the teen. "I am so glad you come to see me once and a while. Weeks ago, I told you my story; do you remember?"

The girl nodded.

"When I was young, I watched how my brother and my mother were killed. I was alone and frightened, but I was rescued. As I child, I didn't know what to do, where to go, what would happen next. But, most important, I did not know why this was all happening to me. Why did I live when they did not? Today, I have a tiny answer, but I know there is more to learn."

"Miss Bristol," she continued, gently putting her hand on the girl's hand. "I don't know what happened to you. I don't even know your real name, but that is OK. I want to know your story, but you are not yet ready to tell me with words. That is OK, too. But, how about this? Tell me with pictures," she said, pointing to the kit.

Bristol looked at the gift and sat motionless, pondering the nun's invitation.

"You have a story; it must be a painful one, a terrible one, a private one. Do you know, some smart people think that if we human beings don't tell our stories, we die inside? Yes, it is true. We are all just animals who tell stories, and that makes us human. I think that if you don't tell your story, sooner or later you will explode. Not outside like a bomb. But your soul will explode inward and your heart of hearts will be scattered to pieces."

Isabel let silence hang between them. After a minute, she added: "Please tell me your story with no words, but with lines, and colors, and shapes, and all those things you have inside. It will be beautiful and strong and unique, just like you."

Bristol's thoughts and emotions were a frenzy in that moment in the pew, but not the whirlwind of anxiety and fear that dogged her most every day. If those inner awarenesses were shapes of color and light, they would be like a personal kaleidoscope, gently moving in a symmetry of beautiful arranging. She thought back to her last experience of getting a gift from anyone, and recalled that it was her sixth birthday party with her mom and dad in Omaha, the brand new bike and colorful dress for school being her most prized possessions at the time. Inexplicably, to that long-ago child, the subsequent years didn't offer much by way of gifts or happy times, as Louisa's addiction to pills and Miguel's deportation sealed the family's impoverishment. Her years in foster care offered no joy either.

Bristol was moved to thank Gakunde with her voice. She looked up at her and paused. So much of her wanted to ring out two simple words that expressed so much. Her courage was mounting like lava far in the earth, rising hot and powerful. She knew she still had this voice somewhere inside, but it hadn't been audibly present in the world for some time. The last time it blasted forth was the scream she made in the middle of her rape by her foster dad when she was just thirteen. Perhaps if someone had heard it then, the feeling mounting within her to move her dormant vocal cords and say "thank you" to the nun would be an easier thing to honor. However, the image of her attacker and the pain of her violation flooded in like a malevolent tidal wave that erased the happy feelings coloring her mind at that moment, obliterating the growing courage she was trying to summon to help her to speak.

Touched and grateful nonetheless, Bristol wept and reached out to hug Isabel, whose arms moved around the teen in a gentle reply.

CHAPTER 24:
IT WOULDN'T BE HEAVEN WITHOUT THEM

TWO WEEKS LATER, THE APRIL DAYS OF EARLY SPRING WERE bringing a renewed sense of life and activity to everyone in almost every place. Longer days of sunlight tend to do that, especially when heavy winter clothing can be dispatched to a closet, set aside for another three seasons.

The pair in the Flight Operations control room at the police station was enjoying their mid-morning coffee, and the two officers on duty there were casually watching the many monitors on the walls before them. It was a typically quiet day from their vantage point, being the six remote drones patrolling Hallet Springs on that clear and sunny early spring day.

"Catch the game last night?" one asked the other.

"Yep," she replied.

"What losers! So many errors. I couldn't believe it."

The conversation ended there, as the two didn't want their recorded voices to create the impression that they were inattentive to the situation portrayed on any one of the eight monitors they were assigned to study. One of them, in the upper right corner of the dark room, showed a group of people in a field outside the Mills walking toward the woods behind the factory.

"Check this out," the first man said to the other officer, "let's get a closer look."

What the drone spotted was a bedraggled funeral procession. Max Cherryfield held a bundle close to his chest the size of an infant completely covered in a green flannel blanket, the man clutching it such that his right hand appeared to be keeping the neck of the being within upright. From that height, however, the flying surveillance machine could not see the tears falling from his eyes.

"Looks like the regulars," the distant pilot at the station said casually to his co-worker. "Sooner or later, we're going to have to go in the Mills and get them out. Looks like one guy has a shovel."

An hour or so earlier, most of the regular members of the outcast community were in the workshop passing the time, as was their custom. Most talked about the problems of daily existence they were facing and the failures or successes they had in doing so. The serious atmosphere in the group that day was made worse when Max came in and announced that Charlie had died during the night, his halting voice weak and labored as his grief spilled out with every word and detail.

When the six people in the group made it to the edge of the forest and a sunny spot of scrub pine saplings, Derek said, "He was a good dog, Max; we'll all miss him." Then he started to dig.

"Dogs are the best," Frank added, as the group circled around to watch the excavation. "It's hard when they go." Max was only half listening as he cradled his cold companion in his arms. To him, the mourners there numbered seven, as Connie was there as well. She was talking over Frank's words of comfort and dressed in a formal black gown that looked too thin to match the chilly spring air. "We had Charlie for many years, Max," she said. "He stuck with us in good times and bad. Now it's just me and you, kid."

"I was always afraid of dogs," Margie added, "but not this one. He always made me calm when I patted him. I'll miss him, Max."

Bristol nodded in agreement; the silence that followed was only interrupted by the sound of Derek's spade piercing the ground. Connie came back into Max's head: "You could have spared us all this bother if you listened to me and brought him up the stairs to the stack. You could have said 'goodbye' to him while he was still alive. It would have been better—more humane—just a little toss." Her tone was gentle and consoling, a mismatch for her callous advice.

"I couldn't do it," Max answered aloud.

"Who you talk'n to?" Margie asked Max, whose unmoved gaze was on the deepening hole and his thoughts keenly involved elsewhere.

"His voices," Frank answered for the man. "It's OK."

Ever since his early twenties, Connie had been a recurrent apparition in Max's experience of life, a product of his illness that has baffled research and healthcare science for centuries. Something like a faithful friend, she would come and go unpredictably, her presence in his awareness sometimes distracting, sometimes moody and fickle, sometimes fun. Whether Max knew she wasn't real was anyone's guess. While the medicines he was required to take by the Mental Illness Monitoring regulations codified in state law were supposed to mollify such symptoms of schizophrenia, had anyone in the system bothered to ask Max if he still experienced any such phenomena, they would have discovered years ago that old and inexpensive drugs were having no effect. But the cogs in the monitoring system don't work well in Hallet Springs or anywhere else if something like individuality, consent, or personal medicine creates a problem. No one asked, so Max didn't offer.

Derek's handiwork completed, he speared the shovel into the mound of displaced dirt and reached up with both hands from where he stood, looking to transfer the corpse from Max's arms to the grave. Max slowly complied. Derek laid the bundle down carefully with the respect that everyone standing around the circle would have wanted. He stepped up out of the hole and waited.

Max said: "King Charles was the best friend, the only real friend, I ever had." As he said this, he could feel Connie taking his arm. "He died because of me. I didn't have enough to feed him, and I couldn't afford to take him to the vet when he was sick; it's my fault." He paused, and his colleagues offered no rebuttal. "He always wanted to be patted," Max continued, "now no one will ever touch him, and no one will ever touch me."

The group stood silently, seemingly trying to let the man's words sink in.

Then Bristol knelt on the ground and opened her art supply gift that Isabel had given her, her greatest possession, which never left her side. She opened her pad of art paper and grabbed a black marker from the case. She reached up and took Max's left wrist, tugging it downward as an invitation for him to join her. He did so, and when he was close, she plopped his open hand onto the white sheet and traced it with the Sharpie. Completing the outline, she removed the sheet from the pad and started to tear the palm print along the simple curving lines. The rips weren't very precise, and Max looked puzzled.

Margie was the first to realize Bristol's gesture. "Put your right hand down," she instructed Max, and he did so, still confused. Bristol separated his fingers so there was enough space to trace again and she repeated the outline.

"Here, Bristol, let me help," Margie said when the handprint was done. She retrieved a Swiss army knife from her pocket and withdrew the small scissors nestled in between the blades and other tools. Bristol gave her the sheet and extended her hand to Frank.

"I get it," he said. "Yes; perfect."

Frank knelt next to the artist and offered her his right open hand. She placed it on the next sheet in her pad and traced. His dark hand was much larger than Max's, so she arranged his fingers gently just so the Sharpie could wind its way along its edges. That one done, he offered her the other.

When the Boss stood up, she invited Derek to do the same; and when Margie was finished with her cutting, she also joined in. Tommy was next. Bristol then traced her own prints.

"Now what?" Max asked.

"Bristol?" Frank replied, anticipating what she had in mind.

Taking her cue, she collected all the handprints from the party and bent down to reach into Charlie's grave. She carefully unwrapped his green fleece shroud and arranged the paper hands on his body, as if each mourner was doing their part in holding the dog in their envelope of love. By luck, some of the paper fingers seemed to entwine themselves as if to suggest a symbolic bond.

Max began to cry. Margie reached around his back and, finding his shoulder, pulled him close to her. Bristol put the blanket back over the dog and stepped out of the hole. *Someone should say something now*, she thought to herself, her signature silence unwavering.

"We'll always remember Charlie," Frank offered after a while. "When I was a kid, I remember a Disney movie. Someone asked the question, 'do dogs go to heaven?' Then someone else said, 'of course; it wouldn't be heaven without them.'"

"Are they allowed to be back there?" one of the drone pilots back at the Hallet Springs police station asked his coworker, the two watching their monitors and the mourners vicariously through the surveillance drone's camera.

"Beats me," the other replied with a shrug. "Looks like they're trying to bury something; looks like a funeral."

One man moved the joystick he was manipulating so that the craft could circle the group so that each person's face, even from that high distance, could be scanned through their facial recognition database.

Instantly, the computers set to work scouring the massive files of personal information and photographs in the station's repository of data. Within seconds, a list of names appeared on the pilot's laptop.

"An animal, you think?" said the first officer. "A pet, maybe?"

The second man replied: "I don't think they're allowed to have pets." The man casually reached for his cell phone. "I forgot to put my grocery order in," he announced nonchalantly to his partner. "Rats." What he really did was send a text message to retired Sheriff Bert LaBounty that contained a snapshot of the names, including one Maria Mindaz.

Back on the ground, Tommy was the next one to talk. "What do you think happens when we die?" he asked.

"Nothing," Margie replied. "Things just turn to shit. Just like being alive, only different."

"That's not what the Hindus think," Derek offered. "They think your soul goes on and on. It jumps into another body, but maybe not a person. You come back as something better, if you've been good, and worse if you've been bad. You're stuck with this until you become perfect. Who knows?"

"That can't be right," Margie said. "Besides, feels like all of us are already dead, just buried above ground and still moving around."

I want to come back as a dog, Bristol thought to herself, *maybe then someone would care about me.* Max, still misty-eyed, was fixed upon the open grave and the green motionless bundle in the hole.

"I've seen a lot of people die," Frank said. "Some look like they have only pain on their face and others look kind of peaceful, especially if they are still able to look at you. Nobody should die alone, that's for sure."

"Max, you were there for Charlie; always," Tommy affirmed. "It wasn't your fault that he died. Everybody knows how much you loved him, and he you. Even I could see that."

"Hell ya," Margie added. Then she turned around to start walking back to the Mills. Frank soon did the same but not before putting his hand on Max's shoulder for a short while. Max did not acknowledge the gesture, remaining transfixed on the small open grave. Tommy walked closer to Max and said, "Sorry, so sorry, about Charlie and sorry if I said too much." After taking a few steps away to follow the others, he turned around and looked back at Max. "He was a great dog," he said.

Bristol started to gather her art papers to put them back into her pouch. Feeling tears welling up inside her, she also felt an urge to say the words that might capture her sorrow for Charlie and the wave of empathy she felt for Max. This was a different sort of sadness than the feeling she customarily carried each day, but she couldn't distinguish its distinctiveness. All she knew was that part of her wanted to go to Max, embrace him, and tell him through her crying and words how badly she felt at this loss. She took a short step towards the man to do just that. She opened her mouth to speak and, in a flash, the grief that moved her switched to fear. The teen swallowed hard, turned, and ran in the opposite direction from the others.

After a moment, Max turned to leave his companion for the last time. Connie strolled alongside Max, still tearful and looking only at the ground in front of him.

"Well," she said in a confident voice, "since you didn't toss Charlie in the stack, looks like you'll have to go in instead." The man gave no reply.

Back at Charlie's grave, Derek started to replace the dirt over the corpse. When the task was completed, he tamped the area with his shovel so that it formed a gentle little mound. Though the people heading back to the Mills paid no mind to the drones aloft, Frank did just the opposite.

CHAPTER 25:

YOU NEVER KNOW WHEN YOU HAVE TO THROW

ABOUT A WEEK LATER, A LARGER THAN USUAL GROUP OF life-weary people were hanging around the large workshop at the Mills, trying to revive a small fire, huddled in the center of the room. Some looked like they were quietly lost in their own thoughts, but others stood talking in a few small circles. Without much attention, Frank was unpacking a cardboard box he brought in, the contents of which was a dozen or so empty tin cans and plastic bottles from different rooms of the Mills or on the street outside.

At the far end of the workshop, he started removing an item and placed it on the floor near the wall. Before long, he arranged a line of them from one side of the room to the other, each rusty or dirty object spaced about two feet apart. He brought the box with him as he walked back to the center of the room. Derek came over to him.

"What's this, Boss?" he asked.

"Look," Frank replied, letting the title he made efforts to reject slip by. He showed Derek the remaining contents of the box, some thirty or more stones, each about the size of a tennis ball.

"What's up?" Derek questioned.

Without an answer, Frank gave Derek a stone and grabbed one for himself. He took his stone and threw it at one of the cans, missing it by only a few inches as it skidded by and struck the block wall behind the can with an audible crack like a billiard ball hitting hard. "You try," he said.

Derek hurled the rock towards a white milk jug and hit it squarely, both things careening loudly into the wall as well. Derek smiled. "Got it," he said with surprise. "I used to play center field in high school," he added proudly.

"I was a pitcher on my softball team," Margie said as she came up behind the men. "And I was damn good. What the hell are you guys doing?"

"Having fun," Frank answered. "Practicing." He offered her a rock from the box.

She took it, stepped aside, and cradled it with both hands together in front of her as she bent into a pitching stance. Her motion was natural. Picking out a target, her underhanded throw was as hard as the stone she let fly. Though it hit the concrete a few feet short, its path was true and the rock slid straight, knocking a soda bottle back like a candlepin at a bowling alley.

"Strike one," she announced with a smile.

The three took aim at the other objects in the row of trash, and soon the barrage of stones had scattered the cans and plastic in disarray. While Derek and Margie went to the wall to reset the targets and gather the rocks, Frank moved the remaining box of stones ten yards farther away. As he did so, several others joined him, their curiosity sparked by what appeared to be a loud and unusual game.

"Anybody seen Max?" Frank asked. Their shaking heads and blank looks gave him his answer. "Bristol?" he asked Tommy.

"Nope," Tommy said.

After they finished lining up the cans and bottles, they walked back to Frank and the group and saw the Boss offer a rock to anybody who wanted a go. "Alright," he said. "Let's see: you never know when you have to throw."

Some there declined, but others took their turn to see if they could knock some object down. More than once, the cache of rocks was depleted before several targets were still standing undisturbed. Together, the group collected the rocks and reset the trash, chatting and smiling at the fun.

"OK," Margie said when the group returned to the other end of the workshop, holding two rocks in her hands. "Let's all try all at once."

The barrage was mostly effective and thunderous in the empty room. Looking at the remaining Coke bottle that stood alone amongst its scattered counterparts, Margie chucked her last stone at it, catching it right at the neck, sending it careening backwards.

An unfamiliar voice came from behind the group: "Nice shot," reporter Paula Damascus said. Everyone turned to assess the young, neatly dressed lady, who looked to them about as out of place as a courtesan in a coal mine.

CHAPTER 26:
I JUST WANT TO LISTEN

AN UNCOMFORTABLE SILENCE FILLED THE WORKSHOP, AS the presence of any outsider was always greeted with apprehension. But since the stranger was alone and outnumbered, the people there were not fearful. Aware of these social atmospherics, Damascus knew she had to put people at ease if she was ever going to get their story.

"I'm with the *Observer*," she began. "My name is Paula Damascus; I'm a reporter. I was hoping to talk with you about the city's idea for the Mills."

No one moved nor answered, either because they still were trying to take in the measure of the smiling interloper or because life had taught them that most every stranger—even a petite female with a curious mind—was not to be trusted, at least not at first.

Damascus brought with her a cloth satchel, well-seasoned, with a long shoulder strap, and put it on the floor. She unzipped her light green windbreaker as if ready to make herself comfortable.

"I'm writing a story about the Mayor's plans for these old buildings. I heard that people have no place to live but here, and I wanted to find them. I snuck in through a hole in the fence and have been walking around for almost an hour or so until I heard your voices and the noise you were making. Looks like a cool game, by the way."

Though her tone was friendly and seemingly sincere, she saw only impassive and stoic faces in front of her. They taught her quite a bit about how to engage a source during her studies at American University, but book learning only goes so far when a journalist is no longer a student but a working professional. Internships at Politico and National Public Radio were helpful, but her first job after graduation was with the simple and struggling *Observer* in quaint but backwater Fontaigne County. She had never tried to interview homeless people before, knowing that the paper's readership, according to her editor, was just not interested.

"Is it true, what people say?" she asked, "Do some of you live here?"

No one appeared ready to answer as their study of the woman continued. Paula sensed that she had to say more.

"Let me tell you what I'm thinking," she continued. "Then you can decide if you want to talk to me. A few months ago, I interviewed Sheriff LaBounty before his retirement. Has anybody heard of him?"

Frank chose not to answer.

"He said that the country lost something over the years, something nobody saw coming, and it's bad, maybe even dangerous. He said that we just don't care about people anymore, we just care about the money we make and the things it gets us. That's it. I want to write about that, and I want to know what you think. I'm not with the police or the city; I just want to listen."

"I'll talk with you," Margie said firmly. "I've always wanted to give those fuckers a piece of my mind, lot of good it'll do. Come over here." Margie pointed to a corner of the workshop where some grimy plastic lawn furniture was scattered about. When they settled in there and the reporter booted up her laptop, a few other of Margie's friends—Derek, Tommy, and Frank among them—stood around close to watch and listen. Frank still held a rock in his hand.

"What do you want to know?" Margie asked, getting right to the point.

"Do you sleep here? Who lives here? How many people? Why here?"

Margie shot her a frustrated look, signaling that the question was naive. "Of course," she replied, "where else? Look around. Most everybody you see lives here, but not all." Damascus scanned the room and realized that even beyond the small group of men near them, most of the twenty or so other people were eyeing the meeting as well.

"How'd you end up here?" the reporter asked.

Margie rolled up the sleeve of her left arm and showed Paula her arm. She showed her a small bump the size of a dime slightly protruding from her skin. "The goddam system put me here, but they'd never cop to it. It pushed us all here."

"What's the bump?" she asked.

"The tracker they shove in your arm. Everybody here, mostly, got one. When I was a kid, they used to only do that with dogs. Then some asshole had the idea that they could put microchips in people and control 'em. So, if you are sick or poor or messed up and need help, they give you a few dollars a month and some worthless meds in your veins, a tracker in your arm, and if you let 'em, a chain around your soul. You can't get a job or go to school and the money is not enough to rent an apartment or eat more than once a day. That's how I got here; same as the rest." She looked up at her colleagues and made sure the reporter noticed.

"Don't you have any family? Any other place to go?"

Margie considered the question carefully. "I'm from Idaho, and my parents are dead. Know what the system told me there? They said that New Hampshire is a better state for people like me. They gave me a bus ticket and here I am, in the fuckin' Granite State. It means where they have rocks for brains. My life is worse here than back home."

"Why not head back?" Paula asked.

"Because." Margie answered, her eyes glancing at the floor. "Because."

Paula scanned the group close by them to see if anyone had anything to offer. Tommy stepped forward toward the reporter and his intimidating size made her somewhat anxious. "Can I talk to you?" he asked gently. Paula reached to her side and pulled over an empty plastic chair and welcomed him to sit.

"I got a one-room apartment over on Pilgrim Avenue. I used to have a job in a warehouse, but that was years ago. I've had depression all my life, and my work was the best thing. It helped better than any medication. I felt proud, people liked me, I worked hard. I was one of the only people they kept on after the robots came in. Then I hurt my back on the job and they dumped me and got more machines."

"The money I have now all goes to rent. Pretty much nothing left for food. I come here because staying in my room alone all day isn't good for me. My friends are here. Sorry; I took too much of your time."

"No, not at all," Paula answered. "You told me a lot, thank you."

Before she could turn around, Derek spoke up. "I was in sales, computer equipment like servers and hardware. Because I got addicted to oxy, I lost everything: wife, home, job, kids—all gone. I've been clean for eighteen years, three months, and four days. I've been unemployed for, maybe, twenty-one years. Know why? 'Cause nobody is allowed to hire somebody that's been in jail. Know what I miss the most? Voting. They don't let you vote, see, if you've got a record. Bastards."

"I didn't know that, any of that," Paula replied.

Unlike the young reporter, Frank did know all that and more. Throughout his rootlessness and wanderings since his discharge from the Army, he had come upon people with stories like these as he traveled from state to state, job to job. It wasn't as if he looked for them, but more that he was some sort of magnet who drew out these tales of trials and suffering, sooner or later, in the people he encountered. By the time he arrived in Hallet Springs, the weight of all of them was a burden moving him to actions he hadn't really considered. While the soldier in him was accustomed to conflict, the leader in him knew decisiveness. Yet, he told himself that the trauma he carried dried up any remnant of courage he may have once had.

As Damascus was listening to each person in the workshop, Frank paced back and forth on the outskirts of the conversation but taking in every word. He knew that the outrage and anger he felt towards the present American way of life wouldn't be bottled up much longer.

"What will you all do when the city tears down these Mills?" Paula asked the group. "Where will you all go?"

It was a question the people there didn't want to hear, for which they didn't have any answer.

"Good thing it's spring," Margie said finally, "there's always the woods."

Frank stopped his pacing. Looking at one of the large windows high on the wall across from him with its three rows of three panes in each opening—a tic tac toe board of glass—he tossed upward the rock he was holding in his right hand a few times and hurled it at the center pane. The force made a perfect hole, dead center.

CHAPTER 27:
ISABEL MIGHT KNOW

THE MOHAWK MILLS ONCE EMPLOYED THREE SHIFTS OF workers during the war years of the 1940s. Hundreds of people passed through the gates each day feeling proud that they were contributing, at least through their tiny part, to the effort that citizens knew would bring victory over hatred, imperialism, and dictatorship in Europe and Asia. They also felt happy knowing that the paychecks in their pocket were vastly better than the money had in the decade before the conflict. Most couldn't define the word "totalitarianism" if you asked them, but they would tell you that Hitler and Hirohito were bad and that we had to do all we could to defeat them.

Bristol wasn't aware of that historical fact as she explored the now-decaying Hallet Springs landmark that had been left unused and unwanted for decades. Had she been a student of the arc of that expanse of years, the teen would have naturally asked why all that community disappeared.

She enjoyed walking alone through building after building, each with its own unique size and layout, but similar in the wide and dirty wooden floorboards, the dust and dank air throughout, the grime and pigeon droppings on nearly every windowsill and beam, and the chipping paint on every wall. Where the roof was leaking, the damp floor beneath had green mold in various stages of development.

She climbed up a set of stairs in the main building, the old oak treads creaking as she ascended. It was a fair distance from the workshop out back where the group gathered for their meal and the warmth of the campfire they would build on the concrete floor. She was headed to her favorite room, discovered a few weeks earlier on one of her walks, knowing that it would be a good time to be there, the afternoon sunlight coming in the large windows being strong enough to warm the chilly, ambient air within.

Bristol turned a familiar corner in one of the hallways and entered a series of rooms, the first of which looked like a waiting room of a once-elegant office suite. It was encircled by a horseshoe of small rooms that were in about the same sorry condition as the factory buildings throughout the Mills. She headed straight for one that had large windows on two sides of the main building overlooking the main parking lot, which could still be seen through the cloudy gray grime on the glass. The room must have had a library of books, but the empty shelves now held only fragments of trash or old yellowing newspapers and magazines. It also had a large desk and rickety wooden swivel chair. Bristol pulled it closer to the tabletop as she sat down, its rusty wheels squeaking.

The girl removed the pad of artist sketch paper from the gift that Isabel gave her a few weeks before. She tore a sheet of paper from the pad, retrieved a black pencil from her kit, and started to write:

Dear Dad:

I'm not even sure how to get this letter to you, or where you are, but I had this urge to try to write in the hope that someday, even far away in the future, you'll get this note and the message of love I hope it sends. I miss you and mom so much, I'm not sure I can stand it anymore. I know that you may not be able to help me but that's OK. I think I'm learning how the world works and I don't blame you.

Not sure why it took me so long to get these words out to you. Let me tell you what happened—not sure how much you know because the last few years have been so crazy.

Bristol stopped, considering what would be the most important thing to tell her father and what she wanted, or needed, to share. Looking out the window and remembering fondly what a gentle man her father was, she feared that telling him every detail would break his heart.

Shortly after you were deported, mom took more and more drugs. You know she had her struggles, that's no secret; when they took you, she simply fell apart and we became homeless. It took a while and she tried her best, but we survived driving from place to place, scraping by with day jobs and handouts. It wasn't good. When she died, the police told me there was a dangerous batch of some drug (it began with an "F") out on the streets and people didn't know they were injecting a lethal poison in their veins. I hope she didn't suffer.

If I was old enough to drive then, I would have jumped into our car and run before they could catch me. Not knowing where you were or how to contact you (I don't think they really ever tried), they told me I had to live with a foster family since I was too young. The first family was creepy—nobody cared much or talked with me. The house was warm, at least, and the TV dinners were OK.

Seems like I went from place to place after that family was kicked out of the Youth Service system in Omaha. I don't recall how many homes but all I do remember was how sad I was. I started to understand why drugs look so good; at least your spacey mind takes a break from the pain and shit you have around you.

Dad, I have been running. Not exercise. Safety, I guess. I'm not sure where I am headed, but I know for certain that I have to keep moving, keep traveling. I feel better this way and, besides, it will be harder for them to find me and slam me back in some detention hole. Maybe I'm running away from all that's happened to me. Too much to talk about now, but maybe in person someday. For now, this is what I want you to know.

At my third foster home, the husband in the family (I don't even remember his name; Samuel, I think), somewhere in some shit town in Nebraska, he hurt me. Bad. Every day for weeks. Not with his fists or a weapon, but—you know—he went inside me. A lot. When I saw my chance to bolt, that's what I did.

I have never told anyone about this. Maybe it's OK for me to write it here because you will probably never get this. I can't just send it to El Salvador. I'm sure they need a better address than that. There's only one person around here (New Hampshire) who might help. She gave me a present the other day—art supplies.

Just so you know, I've been running ever since and I'm exhausted. But I know I can't stop. I've heard Canada is nice, so maybe that will have to do for now. Canada can't be that big—do you think you can find me somehow?

She stopped again, considering carefully if she should disclose more or finish the message. Somewhere in the distance, she heard a dog barking.

Do you remember Shep? I was thinking of him the other day when a guy I know had to bury his best friend, a cuddly dog named Charley, or really, King Charles. I know what he's going through. The man looked like his heart just disintegrated. I feel that every day. Nobody left to be your friend or give a shit if you live or die.

Know what? I learned a lot from being on the run. I learned that the world we live in is some sort of backwards fireworks display. Poor people like me are just the stuff you put in a cannon. People watch as we get shot into the sky at night, only instead of being colorful, we just explode in black sparks that nobody sees. And the crowd watching? They don't smile and get happy like normal fireworks—they just become lesser themselves, sadder maybe, and they don't even know it. Remember the Death Star in

"Star Wars?" I feel my soul has exploded like that but there isn't any light. I'm living out some real-life bad dream. I'm awake, but it's always a life of darkness before sunrise, and the sunrise never comes.

I do know, Dad, that you care. I have no doubt that you love me. I hope you know that I have oceans of love and longing for you. I want to be back with you more than ever. I hope you are safe. Ask my grandmother (what did you say that was? Abuela?) to pray for me.

All my love,

Maria

Her letter finished, she folded it in thirds and contemplated where she might find a way to post it. *I bet Isabel might know,* she thought to herself.

CHAPTER 28:
I DON'T EVEN HAVE A CUP

IN HIS DARK CABIN, MAX SAT ALONE AT HIS KITCHEN TABLE, silent and sullen as wave after wave of sadness flooded into his soul like a high tide that was never offset by a low one. The whistle of his teakettle had been sounding for several minutes, but the physical effort it would take to walk the few steps towards it seemed like a herculean task. A few minutes earlier, he thought that a warm cup of black tea would be sufficient for his lunch, but now that the water was ready, he wasn't sure. Slowly, he got up to silence the kettle. He looked into the blue cup on the counter that had yesterday's soggy lump of teabag and doused it with a half cup of boiling water. Each bag had to be used twice so that his precious allotment would last the month.

Today, the tenor of his thoughts was neither about economizing nor surviving until the next day, never mind the next month. He took his hot cup as he lumbered across the cabin and crouched down in a corner, placing the tea on the floor beside him. Looking up vacantly, Max noticed a ray of sunlight sneaking into his space through the small slit in the drawn plastic window shade, the shaft of light catching the many flakes of dust suspended in the air around him. The specks, he thought, were like the people he knew, floating chaotically, insignificant in the room, each gliding along on some random flight path, eventually destined to settle somewhere no one knew about or cared about with a

crash heard only by its counterparts. He felt he was one of these insignificant specks, but only if each could sense the unfathomable, soul-crip-
pling pain that filled his being.

Though Max was no stranger to emotional pain, the despair he
felt that day was reaching a whole new level of hurt. At this point, the
downward spiral of his thoughts and emotions would have been hard
for him to put into words because the mental storm underway in the
atmosphere of his brain had successfully and predictably knocked out
the rational thinking required for logical thought, problem solving or
verbal expression. All these require some brain power that wasn't there,
these essential capacities rendered impotent by the tornado-like maelstrom in his head that only he could face or feel. This devilish adversary
came not with sound and fury however, but with a persistent gnawing
away at any vestige of self-esteem, hope, happiness, or drive to live.

As Max sat motionless in the corner, the fleeting moment of
physical rest soon blended with the unsettling feeling of agitation, like
ants crawling around in his muscles. They were calmed when he moved,
but that required a strength he didn't think he could muster. This expe-
riential trap meant that, though he felt that he needed to sit someplace
to rest, he felt more comfortable when his body was in motion. Sleep
wasn't much of a respite from this ever-present struggle, as each nap or
night only brought him an hour or so of reprieve. Whether he was more
physically or mentally exhausted, no one could say.

He got up from his corner and went back to the table, leaving
his cup of tea behind. No sooner had he sat down, but he got up again
and paced over to a different corner and crouched down again. Though
he didn't plan on it, the spot he picked was near a pile of tattered notebooks stacked on the floor for want of a shelf. He casually considered
the coiled metal spirals on their spines and he reached over to pick one
up. He put it on his lap but didn't have the strength to open it. No matter; he knew what he had written in each one anyway.

Max had been writing journals for years, even before the mental illness called schizophrenia exploded in his life like a tornado, wiping out all semblance of normalcy, self-respect, and standing. Unlike a real twister whereby the severe devastation had an eventual ending, the storm in Max's life seemed to go on and on, year after painful year.

He looked at the collection of notebooks and remembered the nurse who first introduced the idea of using writing as a tool for therapy. Her name was Charlene, a counselor he encountered after his first episode of psychosis decades ago who was part of his aftercare plan from the state hospital. She thought that Max's scholarly bent and academic abilities might be a source of strength, a penchant for words suited to the task of journaling, so that the constructive effort of composition might serve as the infrastructure for his recovery of health. But that sort of creative intervention, the presence of a supportive therapist, an aftercare plan, and a hospitalization for psychiatric injury was no longer part of Max's life nor any other sufferer from mental illness in the present world.

The contents of these pages were a chronicle of sorts, but not a diary devoted to personal insights or anything like happy-go-lucky posts on Facebook. Max knew them to be something akin to a Satanic conveyor belt of loss, dumping into his life a recurrent bundle of factors that insidiously stripped away whatever was good. It clearly started with his illness that sucked away rational thinking, then came the loss of his wife Delia, then job, house, car, friends, income, savings, shelter, and food. As the belt delivered one reduction, there was precious little time for his brain to recuperate before the next loss arrived. The narratives in his journals told the story that he had come to see that this conveyor belt was more like a disassembly line; as time moved along, more and more good things that make for health and happiness were taken away. The loss of his dog was the most recent delivery of sorrow. In his fleeting moments of clarity, Max had come to understand that that was exactly what most people in the world wanted for him and others like him.

Max tossed the notebook back on the stack. He struggled to get up, retraced his steps to his small counter, and switched on the electric teakettle. He moved back to the table to look for his cup, which was still on the floor where he left it. *Figures*, he said to himself, *I don't even have a cup.*

For some unknown reason, when Max's mind was at a level of desperation like it was that day, Constanza was nowhere to be experienced. He realized this and concluded that at the times when he was completely depleted of hope and strength, when the internal pain was omnipotent and unrelenting, when he felt utter contempt and shame for what his life had become, when he felt both groundless and friendless, were the times he was thinking clearly. Were he lost in some vast ocean miles and miles from any source of rescue, he'd be keenly aware that his life raft was sinking. Perhaps that image was where his fearful agitation came from, those thoughts and emotions that stirred up such self-loathing, guilt and morbid thinking that was as natural to him as breathing. From these sensations, there was no escape.

Remembering Margie's words at Charlie's grave, Max knew in his bones what others at this point of depression know, namely that they felt as good as dead already, just buried above ground and still moving. He also knew that, someday, his life would end by suicide. For the last decade or so, he fought off the blistering assaults his mind was waging on his soul, but through the hours of weeping and exhaustion, he knew he was losing this war inside him. At some point, he concluded, when the perpetual conveyor of problems and failures dumped one more crippling hardship into his narrow life, he would run out of room and the endurance to handle it. *Besides*, he told himself, *no one will care.* Had Charlie still been alive, the dog might have innocently arrested the

black and bleak free-fall his master was on, but now that was a hope not
worth holding.

CHAPTER 29:
IN THAT TINY SPOT OF LIGHT

THERE WERE TULIPS RISING OUT OF THE WEED-TANGLED flower beds on each side of the door to the community kitchen housed in the basement of St. Theresa's Church, and the long line of people waiting to get in were mostly still dressed in winter coats, even though the warmer days of the early spring spoke of lighter clothing. A fleece jacket or thick hoodie may have been sufficient, but for some people struggling with a consuming babble of voices or the roller coaster of intense emotions that accompany many forms of untreated mental illness, switching the internal gears of comfortable habits with the changing season takes some time. Tommy and Derek were ahead of Bristol in the line, but it moved quickly once Sr. Isabel unlocked the door to welcome her many guests. As she did so, a police drone zipped by overhead causing some in the group to look upwards but for most, the customary object a hundred or so feet above their heads wasn't all that unusual nor interesting.

Like all dinner nights, the attendees were respectful, polite, and mostly quiet. People who knew one another used familiar greetings and gave each other some form of friendly recognition. On occasion, someone's louder voice carried through the room, but this was mostly after some joke or convivial teasing that happens when strangers see one another at the same place and the regularity of it all makes them feel less like strangers.

To a person, the group looked disheveled and shell shocked, a collection of souls who had just come into a place of shelter for a modest meal and a clean place to sit, rest, and eat. They looked like a small, tired, disorganized, and nearly defeated company of soldiers pausing from some battle for which they were ill-equipped but compelled to wage. One look at their dirty, tattered, and well-worn clothing would tell any bystander that their enemy was likely poverty, homelessness, illness, or some other grave obstacle seeking to rob them of health. In fact, the foe they were dealing with was something akin to a dangerous black hole in outer space that sucks in all light, matter, and stars into a vacuum of oblivion. The phenomenon wasn't celestial, however, it was very much earth-bound in the culture of uncaring that dominated most every aspect of American life, from sea to shining sea.

The guests knew the drill: form a queue that moved slowly to some steam tables donated to the Church in some previous century; pick a plastic tray from the pile, a paper plate, and a cheap set of utensils from the bins next to them; slide your tray down the stainless-steel rack in front of the table; and tell the smiling, and two or three friendly, volunteers what offering you would like to have, not that there were many choices. Without failure, Frank Stringfellow was one of them at the other side of the table, who, like the other servers, dished up whatever there was with a smile and polite respect, just like Isabel modeled and expected.

Attendees could count on a hot entree most of the time, some form of starch, and a vegetable, usually something from a freezer or a small salad of iceberg lettuce with shavings of carrots and usually one cherry tomato that had lost its flavor weeks ago. None of the guests realized what the nun had to do each week to find the provisions and the volunteers to keep her vital ministry of a humble meal running each week, but by some form of grace or luck she managed to do just that. For people who frequented the Mills during the day, this was just like an oasis or aide station somewhat away from the fight, and that was the conviction that kept the kitchen open as the cluster of volunteers scrambled from one problem to the next. Only Isabel and Frank were part of the Via Verde network.

Presiding over the event, the chubby nun made it a point to always greet every one of her guests with a warm interaction someone might witness at a family holiday meal. Measured and soft, her words seemed to find the right window with each entrant, not too brief to be perfunctory, and not too extensive or flattering as to be viewed as fake. Clearly, the woman's message to each guest stemmed from her own genuineness as it lodged in some spot of safety in the listener.

When the serving was done and group was settled and seated at the long rows of plastic folding tables, Isabel would move between the rows to see if anyone needed another napkin or an extra cookie or a refill of the watery juice or occasional cup of coffee, if they were able to manage one that night. "You are a guardian angel," Tommy Hodges called out to her from the end of one table.

As the troupe talked with one another at the end of the meal, almost on cue they each started to make for the door, knowing that it was soon time for Isabel and her volunteers to lock up and leave. Bristol seemed to hang back and made eye contact with Isabel, who was carrying some pots to the sink. She put them down and walked over to the girl, the puzzled look on whose young face seemed to be asking a question. When Isabel arrived, she found a folding chair next to the teen.

"It feels so good to sit down," the nun said. "I haven't sat all day," she confessed with a chuckle. "How are you, my lovely Miss Bristol?"

The girl smiled back but made no verbal reply. Isabel knew better than to wait for any words. She asked: "Did you have enough to eat?"

Bristol reached down to the floor and picked up the art supply case that Isabel had given her weeks ago. She placed it on the table in front of them and unclasped the front panel. She presented Isabel with a white sheet of paper folded in thirds, the unmistakable way a letter would be.

"Is this for me?" the nun asked. Bristol shook her head.

"May I open it?" The girl nodded.

Isabel took a moment and stopped after she read the first paragraph of Maria's letter to her dad, and looked up at her friend. "A letter to your father?"

The girl nodded again, and then was asked, "Do you want me to read it all?"

Another gentle nod.

The penmanship in the note was flowing, artistically proportionate and graceful; the seemingly effortless curls of the pen made Isabel's eyes feel like she was watching a dance. As she read, she felt those same eyes tearing up. Wiping them causally, she said. "Maria. Your name is Maria. Is that right?" The teen made no motion, but merely looked at the Sister with a searching gaze.

"Do you know where your father is now?" Maria shook her head and looked down.

"Any ideas where he went? You have a grandmother? El Salvador?"

Maria took the letter and folded it back up along the creases. She took a pencil from her pack and wrote "Miguel Mindaz, Talnique, El Salvador" on the panel. Then she gave the letter back to Isabel.

"You'd like me to mail it?"

Maria nodded.

"I will try." Then she added: "And thank you for the honor and trust you put in me to allow me to read it and to entrust this message to me."

Maria then returned to her art supplies and removed the sketchpad. Flipping open the sheets, she found a completed drawing, tore it from the pad, and present it to Isabel.

"Is this for me?" the nun asked.

Another nod came from the girl.

Isabel studied the drawing closely and, at first, she didn't grasp what she saw. The sheet contained what must have been thousands of points of color, each like a dot made by a felt-tipped marker. Some, however, were rendered by a colored pencil, still others by the slightest touch of a watercolor brush, and some areas had a background shaded by a rub of gray pastel. The depiction was abstract, at first glance, moving in a diagonal flow from the bottom left of the page to the upper right. Using dark colors of every shade, the artist chose deep blacks and browns, crimson, and cobalt blue. Deep green dots blended in and were split by the tiniest lines of white and yellow that swirled in concentric circles, blending there with brighter specks of blue, to light blue, to yellow to more white gathered in a tighter circle. The work made Isabel sense a brooding, desperate plea.

The nun gave the page back to Maria and said, "Here, hold it like this." Then she got up from her chair and walked a few steps away, still looking at the picture. "I thought so," she announced confidently.

Moving back to her chair, she took the rendering back from Maria and put it on the table in front of them. "My talented child," she added, looking squarely at the teen. "You are an Impressionist, I'd say. Did you know that? I studied art in college in London when I was young. Your work is called Pointilism—just little dots of color. An artist named Georges Seurat invented this technique. It was about 1900, I think. Most often, you must stand back away from the work to judge its true message. I did that with this."

Isabel stopped and waited for Maria to look at her. "Do you know what I see here?" the nun asked the girl. "This shows me someone like a diver in a deep ocean where it is cold, dark, and frightening. There in the depths, there is constriction and pain. The diver is looking up at the surface where there is warmth and air. In that tiny spot of light," she continued, pointing to the circle of white, "there is safety and salvation, maybe." Maria sat motionless. "I will cherish this gift always," Isabel said.

"Speaking of college," the nun continued, "when I was there the most fashionable thing was to have blue jeans like yours; if there were rips in them or holes in the knees, everyone thought you were high class and stylish. Isn't that silly? Look at yours, will you. Those rips would have been the best thing back then."

"Today, here in the cold, not so much," she continued. Come. Let's see what there is over there, at my J. C. Penney store."

Isabel got up and Maria took the cue as the nun pointed to the section of the church basement devoted to used clothing that was available to anyone who needed another pair of pants, or a shirt or a coat. The few racks did have blue jeans and a small table had shoes and sneakers nicely arranged by size.

A large sign hung over the collection. It contained two words first, "Jesus Christ," followed by a circle with a line through it, then the word "pennies." A line with smaller letters beneath this stated the message: Jesus Christ doesn't want your pennies, just your heart.

CHAPTER 30:
A MERE FLICK OF THE SWITCH

"THANK YOU FOR COMING, LADIES AND GENTLEMEN. I'M happy that this project is heading into the final stages." Mayor Peter Haddad sat at the head of a large oak conference table in his stately office at Hallet Springs City Hall and started the meeting with a confident message. "Does everyone know one another?"

"I'm not sure I do," said Police Chief Jason Krebs.

"Introductions, then," Haddad instructed. "Ladies first."

A thin middle-aged woman in a business suit spoke up. "Mary Cantfield, Chief Engineer with Dorchester Demolition." Her boss went next: "William Holloway, CEO, Dorchester." Next to him was the mayor's secretary, Victor Moore; then came Public Works Director, Samuel Neuveu. Then, attending the progress meeting for the first time in his new post, Krebs.

"Yes, welcome Chief Krebs," said the mayor, "and congratulations on your new appointment. I know that the people of Hallet Springs will be pleased with your service in the years ahead." The chief smiled as the engineer rolled out a large series of blueprints on the table.

"Gentlemen: In keeping with the City's phased plan for the removal of all structures on the Mohawk Mills property, our plan for the final part looks like this." Cantfield spread both her hands on the prints and extended them outwards so the intricate drawing of the buildings and their surroundings would be in full view. "After studying the design, building materials, age, and expanse of the factory, we are confident that the carefully timed series of explosions will bring them each down all within about thirty to forty-five seconds. These symbols on the drawings show you where each charge is placed, and the different colors indicate the sequence of the initiation of each cluster of charges. Dorchester Demolition was awarded this contract by the city because of our track record of success with terminations of this type, and we are glad that you've selected us to do this work for you."

"We have accomplished many projects like this," she continued. "Factories, ten-story hotels, small empty psychiatric hospitals, old schools—you name it. When we're done and all the rubble removed, you'll have thirty-five acres of prime real estate on your hands and a very attractive asset indeed."

"As you can see," added Holloway, pointing to the prints, "before any explosion, heavy equipment will have already demolished some of the smaller structures on the edges of the main cluster." He pointed to a few squares on the blueprint and continued. "On down day, the first charges will go off on what's called the weaving building, then the front office area, then the shipping and receiving warehouse; all this will fill the interior assembly building. Then, the smokestack descends last. The finale for the spectators. This will provide the most excitement for the media and the large crowd of citizens we expect to view the event from this safe gallery area here." The executive pointed to a remote parking lot on the south side of the campus and said, "The television trucks we expect from Manchester and Burlington, maybe even Boston, will be here as well; no doubt you'll want as much coverage as possible."

"We did a similar project with the old paper Mills in Berlin; you might remember that—it was just about six years ago. People drove from as far away as New York to see the spectacle. It was really successful," added Cantfield.

"Looks good to me," Haddad responded confidently. "How long?"

"First ignition to last, if all goes well, about sixty seconds," Cantfield answered. "And it will go well, we can assure you."

"Good," said the mayor, "But this is phase four. Let's review from the top. Chief Krebs, please."

Even though Krebs had only been in the top job for a few months, he'd made it a point to plan out all the unusual events that would be happening in Hallet Springs that year. The removal of the Mills and the renewal project it would inaugurate was perhaps the largest and most unique for the small community. Since planners were keen to link the yearly summer "Craft and Gem Festival" to the factory's demise, he knew that his resources would be highly taxed during those critical weeks when scores of tourists, merchants and mineral collectors would descend on the city from all over New England.

"Phase one pertains to entering the Mills with sufficient drones and officers to evict, arrest, or otherwise remove any vagrant or person-of-concern who might be using the Mills buildings for shelter or whatever. Our surveillance shows that this could be anywhere from twenty or more homeless individuals, drifters, illegals, or locals. We'll try first with the new taser-equipped drones, but the numerous buildings and many floors in each will make that difficult. Sooner or later, we will need human assets to find and remove those trespassers. We are prepared to immobilize many of them."

He scanned the table looking for questions or reactions, but the stoic people at the meeting offered neither.

"In phase two, the contractor can take over the site and prepare all wiring and the charges; you'll have total responsibility for your people and equipment. The police will use drones to monitor the property at night, and occasional patrols will review the perimeter security fence."

"Phase three is the period between the last preparations for implosion and the exact day for the detonation. To me, this is the most troublesome phase because all those charges are embedded in the structures and our offices must divert their attention and resources to the festival. Since the Mills come down at the end of the festival, a finale of a 'crowd pleaser,' if you will, the Public Safety department has to redeploy to assist with the influx of tourists, venders, campers, tents, and all the security prep work at the fairgrounds. We can use drones from time to time to patrol the Mills, but during this phase, my staff will be stretched pretty thin. We're talking about two to three weeks' time, I'd say."

Krebs looked at the mayor, wondering if he would use the time to comment on the formal request that he sent the city's personnel office for additional temporary officers. Since the mayor was silent, the chief concluded his report: "Phase four, as we just heard, is 'implosion day,' which takes place on the morning of the last day of the festival."

"Perfect," the mayor announced with confidence. "I think this will make it the best festival Hallet Springs ever had, and besides, bringing down the Mills is a campaign promise I made so the City's renewal project can move forward. Make no mistake: I need us to shatter every brick and beam and bolt holding up that old eyesore so there's nothing left but rubble."

"You'll get that," confirmed Holloway, "no worries there."

The meeting started to break up as planned, and the polite conversation at its conclusion involved everyone there but Krebs, who smiled politely as people started to leave the conference room but kept his attention on the blueprints that Holloway and Cantfield left behind. When the others had left, he asked Haddad to remain.

"Peter, I'm worried about phase three. We'll evict the vagrants, the demo people will set and wire the charges, then we go support and secure the festival. I'm pretty sure this will give all those squatters and homeless types the opportunity to come back in. What then? Another sweep?"

"Vagrants?" the mayor asked. "Don't you mean 'vermin'? Jason, I checked with legal and with insurance; if there are casualties during the implosion with this group, we're covered—the city is in the clear; don't worry. Besides, euthanasia and burial with a mere flick of the switch. What could be better?"

Judging from the expression on his chief's face, Haddad could read the apprehension or question that was going to come to him in the lawman's next statement. Preemptively, he said, "Jason, look. The city council and I awarded you this job because we knew you would not be squeamish about this sort of thing. Besides, this is happening all over the place. Think of it this way: We hatch two birds from one egg. We remove the blight from the landscape of Hallet Springs and some of the blight we have in the unwanted population. I call that a win-win."

CHAPTER 31:
THAT'S HOW WE SURVIVE

THE OAK BENCHES AT UNION STATION IN NEW HAVEN were sturdy and broad. Miguel sat in the third one, facing the large clock on the wall, just as his Via Verde helpers in Philadelphia instructed. Since Amtrak's Northeast Regional was late, he wondered if the man he was supposed to meet didn't stick around, but he decided to sit to rest anyway. He spent time studying the encased model trains that were on display between each bench and wondered whether people in the United States still had time to craft such meticulous replicas.

Miguel noticed two police officers walking around the large ornate hall, looking over everyone from a casual distance, but their scrutiny on him was pointed and unmistakable. He bent down and retrieved a book from his backpack on the floor between his legs so that his gaze would be on a random page instead of their blue uniforms. The ruse, however, didn't work and soon he heard and felt the two men coming toward him.

"Good afternoon," one of the officers greeted him suspiciously. "Do you have any identification?"

Miguel looked up and then leaned forward on the bench to reach for his wallet in the back pocket of his jeans. From somewhere behind the officers, a stranger came up behind the lawmen and said, "Esteban!

I'm so sorry I'm late. I couldn't find a place to park. Welcome to Yale." The greeting was loud, jovial, and enthusiastic.

The officers turned around to see someone they recognized from the newspapers, the President of Yale University, Doctor Simon St. John.

"Esteban," St. John continued, reaching for the Salvadoran's hand, a beaming smile on his face. "I'm so sorry I wasn't able to meet you at JFK. Welcome to the United States. I hope your flight was OK."

For his part, Miguel wasn't sure what was happening nor what to answer. Look at this smiling stranger, he simply said: "Si, Señor; todo bien." St. John handed Miguel a small white business card, embossed with the Yale logo on the front and the man's name printed in rich dark letters. Miguel instinctively turned the card over to find the blank side where he saw VV lightly marked in pencil.

Turning to the policemen, St. John said: "Officers, I am pleased to introduce to you the poet laureate of Argentina, Señor Esteban Velasquez. He is here for a series of lectures about the place of cadence in modern verse; its roots in Mayan celestial reckoning." He waited for the officers to reply, but they both looked puzzled. "Thank you, Sir," one of them finally said. "Have a nice day."

"My wife couldn't find a place to park so she's driving around the block," St John continued loud enough so the retreating policeman could hear. "Let's go."

Miguel picked up his backpack and the two turned for the exit. Outside, a dark blue Tesla arrived silently curbside and St John opened the rear door and the two men got in. The woman behind the wheel navigated the car toward the highway and soon entered the ramp headed north.

"Miguel?" St John asked his passenger. "Glad we are meeting. This is Margaret, my secretary. We are driving you to Greenfield."

"Thank you, sir," the Salvadoran answered, still a bit puzzled. "I didn't know what to think when you started talking back there." Miguel started to feel safe with these new acquaintances.

"The officers were only doing what they were trained to do," St John said. "Not all Americans are like that, as I'm sure you have seen, in the last few weeks, I mean."

Miguel studied the man carefully. His gray hair and trimmed beard, brown tweed coat, and polished shoes gave the man the appearance of wealth, while the soft tone of his voice spoke of a down-to-earth gentleness that was unmistakable. Glancing around at the leather appointments in the automobile, he wondered if he had ever ridden in so luxurious a car.

"I know," Miguel answered. "I have been helped by many good people; I'm incredibly grateful to you all. The Via had been a lifeline for me."

"I have been involved for nearly five years now, but to tell you the truth, I know it's grown and grown since then. We keep things quiet, as you can imagine, but I know this movement is more powerful than it was just a short time ago. We're not in the open—we can't be—but the things we do are helping thousands of people every day; I'm sure of it."

With the traffic thinning at this point, Margaret gained speed and the Tesla purred up the highway towards Hartford in the passing lane. "Considering all the Via people I met in the last days," Miguel asked, "I never heard anyone tell me how this all came about. Can you explain?"

"Yes, I will tell you what I know. We don't keep official records, nor do we have one specific leader. What I do understand is around about 2018 or so, some people in the United States were considering all the political restrictions and selfish nature that our country was adopting, not just in our states and communities, but in our view of our role in the world as well. They didn't like what they saw but progressive movements at the time found little traction, or votes, to accomplish anything.

"On top of this, economic forces in the country were conspiring to sequester more and more wealth into the hands of the very top elite multi-billionaires who, as a natural outcome of the greed that is at the root of unrestricted capitalism, believed the more they could acquire through commerce, the better for them. Somehow, they were able to advance the idea that charity was anathema to progress, financial progress that is; so, with the political clout they had they could impose more and more limits on things like public funding for social services, faith groups, and nonprofits and the like, so that the people in need facing poverty or hardships would eventually dwindle down to the very fewest possible number. What they did was to mock affliction of any sort. It was a massive stroke of media marketing and manipulation—a propaganda machine like the world had never seen before.

"Soon, a variety of tech companies saw a market advantage in all this. They thought their production might fuel the consumer demand for things that kept them removed from interacting with, feeling for, or thinking about anybody in need who faced any kind of challenge, particularly poverty. We've been a nation of walled-up selfish introverts ever since, happy to power up a type of social Darwinism that leaves the weak to their own peril."

"I have seen this in my country, too," Miguel said. "But in El Salvador, it's been mostly about the drug trade and the corruption needed to bring it to America. This has destroyed my life. But, please, where did Via Verde come from?"

St John's face shifted from confidence to uncertainty, and he shook his head. "I don't know, honestly," he replied. "No one knows for sure. Some say that we were started by a small group of wealthy, civic-minded people who knew that the country had to change but couldn't yet make their intentions public. Probably because they knew they would risk too much. Others think it was started by one silent, influential political leader who moves behind the scenes like some ghost of a chess player, moving pieces on the board of U.S. culture in some high-stakes game for the future. This person saw the writing on the wall, to use a cliché, that the path the country is on will only lead to ruin. I don't know who or how this was set in motion, but to be sure, I'm glad he or she or they did it. So, I'd say that our network was a reaction to Trumpism that started round 2020."

As the car speed up I-91 north and crossed into Massachusetts, Miguel looked out the left window to see the Basketball Hall of Fame, its giant four-story sphere on the façade of the building just starting to become illuminated by the tiny lights lining its curves. "I'm a Knick's fan," Miguel added, breaking the silence. "Someday, I want to see a game in person."

"They're playing the Celtics in Boston this weekend," Margaret said. "I hope you do get to a game one day."

"Yes," the president affirmed. "You will, Miguel; never lose hope. You will find your daughter, you will find safety somewhere, you will go to basketball games and walk in the woods, and picnics, and sleep in a bed, a happy life with your family."

"How can you be so sure? Faith?"

"Faith, yes, but more than that. Before becoming the president of Yale, my academic career was in anthropology. I have studied civilizations all my life, all types of civilizations. What I have come to understand is that sooner or later, cultures come to realize that human beings are designed to work together; that's how we survive. Oftentimes, cultures try every alternative to that first, but they come to see that their future depends upon cooperation and altruism. Whether you are wealthy or poor, Miguel, remember that everyone must work together and give something to others."

CHAPTER 32:
IDENTIFICATION, PLEASE

AS MARGARET GUIDED THE TESLA OVER THE FRENCH KING
Bridge in Gill, Miguel looked out over the railing at the flowing
Connecticut River below and the springtime greens of the various trees
on both of its banks. The height of the modest span was more than sufficient for any crosser to look out over the hillsides, bifurcated by the blue
water, and see the season beautifully bringing out new vegetation once
again, as if the warming temperatures were breathing new life into the
dormant trunks and twigs that slept all winter. Each oak, maple, birch;
each privet, boxwood, or laurel shrub; seemed to have its own shade of
green life, so typical a blend evident this time of year in New England.
The diverse palette of jade, avocado, lime, emerald, or khaki unfolded
on its own mysterious timetable, all influenced imperceptibly by the
strengthening daylight and the cocktail of rain and nutrients waking up
their roots as the earth around them slowly thawed. This fleeting picture of leafy magic is similar to, but distinct from, the brilliance of the
autumn array familiar to everyone in this corner of the country.

The no-frills lodge selected by St. John for Miguel's rendezvous
with the next member of the Via Verde network was uncreatively
named the French King Motel, in the area at the outskirts of Greenfield,
Massachusetts named by French explorers sometime during the
mid-seventeenth century in honor of King Louis the XIV. As Margaret

turned the corner to climb up the short driveway to the parking lot, it was clear that the clean but Spartan appearance of the instantly forgettable string of rooms and restaurant was the opposite of any palace that any king would call home.

St. John reached into a briefcase and gave a large white envelope to his passenger. "This is what you need for now," he told Miguel. "Inside, you'll find a Connecticut driver's license with your photo with the name Jorge Bergoglio, a small amount of cash, only about two hundred dollars, a map of the city of Greenfield so you can find your way to the library and Bureau of Public Records, and a cell phone with about sixty minutes of air-time or so. When you register, they will tell you that the room has already been paid for one night. We use this place because the proprietors don't check the SSA database on their guests, as far as we still know; if they do, you're out of luck.

Tomorrow morning, have breakfast in the restaurant here, and at eight-thirty walk over the bridge to the picnic area across the street where you can see the falls and the city. Your next contact is someone I met quite a while ago, a retired sheriff from New Hampshire. He will find you then. There aren't many police drones in Erving, but in case one flies by, just keep your head down and walk slowly."

Miguel took the envelope and quickly looked inside. He found the fake ID and glanced back at the president. "You gave me the name of the old Pope?"

"Yes," St John replied. "Ironic isn't it? Some people think he's the one who started Via Verde, but I don't believe that."

"How do you all make this happen? I can't imagine."

"You would be surprised," the man answered. "From what I know, the network of people helping anybody like you is a vast but secret power. When the right mix of legislation, politicians and cabinet members, wealthy industrialists and philanthropists, faith groups and grass roots foot soldiers like me are in place, we will go public and reclaim

America. Until then, we help one person at a time; each cell, one person each day."

The next morning, Miguel followed his instructions and made the walk across the bridge after breakfast. He found the picnic area and chose a table overlooking the vista on the other side of the road as the motel where the confluence of the Connecticut and Millers rivers made for a torrent of water flowing over a quick descent of rocks towards Turners Falls and then the east edge of Greenfield. As this stretch of normally quiet river turns from tame to torturous every spring, these class III rapids would soon test the skills of many a venturous whitewater paddler in the next few hours, drawn to the area by the challenge of the unique topography. Had they started that day, Miguel would have been in a perfect spot to see the colorful kayaks try to negotiate the wet swirly passages around the rocks and drops.

The acre or so of parking lot and scatted tables was a quiet rest area at that hour, so when a large old brown pickup truck turned in, Miguel turned with a start. Creaking open the rusty door on the driver's side, Bert LaBounty got out. He walked toward the front of his truck and took a cell phone from his pocket as he leaned against the hood.

A second or so later, the phone that St John had given the traveler sounded a chime that a text message had arrived. Miguel read: "Jorge? Brown Ford."

As Miguel walked toward the Ford, LaBounty got back in the driver's seat and reached to unlock the passenger door. The Salvadoran got in.

"Bergoglio?" Bert asked. Miguel nodded.

Turning back onto the roadway, it was Bert who began the conversation. "I understand that you need help; I'm the next person to do that. What I know is that you've come a long way and are looking for your daughter. The people who helped you so far contacted me two days ago; they said you would need to get into the library and public records database. That's all I know."

"Si, Señor. Thank you. Everyone has been—incredible. I can't thank you all enough."

Bert used a few back roads through the sleepy town of Turner's Falls, and crossed over a bridge to downtown Greenfield. He found the parking lot of the public library and found a spot. As he turned off the motor, he turned to his passenger and asked, "Maybe if you tell me what you're after, I'd be better able to help you."

Miguel paused to consider his options. For some reason, he recalled a brief conversation he had with a VV representative helping him outside of Philadelphia. She told him that she wondered if their network of humanitarians had been compromised, and that he should be cautious in disclosing too much to strangers, even those vetted by someone in VV as trustworthy; that he should only offer the bare minimum of information should the person in front of him be a spy for the groups seeking to unearth and unravel the charitable network. Ever since hearing that advice, Miguel wondered if, sooner or later, his luck would run out and he'd be arrested and imprisoned as an illegal. He wondered if the old man driving the old truck was authentic or someone under cover, working with a group of authorities to monitor, infiltrate, and then arrest anyone in the network.

As his internal amalgam of reasoning and emotions churned, the man scanned the interior of the vehicle and then whatever he could see through the windshield, looking for some sign that might afford confidence in his next decision and the statements that followed. If there was such an omen, he missed it.

"My daughter is missing too," Bert said, sensing his passenger's hesitation to say anything. "She has a mental illness; she vanished many years ago and my wife and I have been searching and grieving ever since. No luck. She's thirty-one years old. I know what it's like to lose someone."

Taking this as the signal he hunted for, Miguel said: "My daughter didn't run away, but they took me away from my family after someone reported me as illegal. I had to go back to El Salvador, and it's taken me seven years to get back here to find them. I made it to Omaha, and found out that my wife overdosed, and that Maria was bounced around in foster care until she started running. It was dumb luck that got me in touch with the Via people. They found out that Maria had almost been arrested in Greenfield a few months ago, so they helped me get here. She's 16 now."

"You've come a long way," Bert acknowledged, "and so has your daughter. Both of you must have plenty of guts. Let's go inside."

After opening the library door, the men walked through the metal detectors with ease. Looking for the typical array of computer monitors, they found a few tucked away near the start of the stacks of books and materials. Shortly after they sat down to boot up the machine, a middle-aged clerk came up and stood over them. "Identification, please," he asked.

Bert got up from his chair slowly, his size and height looming over the well-intended clerk like a mountain. As he reached for his back pocket, he brushed aside his unzipped jacket so the library employee could see his black side-arm firmly resting in its holster. When he showed his badge and ID to the clerk, he conveniently covered up the word "Retired" after his name, and when he flicked closed the leather case with his photo, the clerk retreated in silence, not even stopping to ask Miguel anything.

"I'm glad he didn't ask why an out-of-state cop was doing in a public library," the sheriff told his new friend.

"Me too," Miguel replied as they both returned to study the computer screen in front of them.

After a few hours of looking at articles from the local paper, police reports from the last month, and records supplied by the local homeless shelters and hospitals, the two men were not finding much about Miguel's young daughter. The Salvadoran would have struggled mightily had not Bert been with him. The Sheriff could scan documents quickly and decipher the illusive abbreviations and alphabet-soup of acronyms used in the criminal justice system. Besides the records from the Midwest, the best they could find was that Maria Mindaz was stopped by police outside a homeless shelter in Greenfield three months ago. The officers failed to check the SSI database, but then, when their oversight was discovered by their supervisor, a bulletin throughout New England was issued that the teen was a fugitive from the Department of Youth Services in Nebraska and that she should be detained.

"Maria Mindaz," Bert said quietly. "Why does that name sound familiar? I know I've seen it before, but I can't remember where."

Miguel felt defeated and stared out the window pondering what his next step might be, disappointed that this new lead about his daughter's whereabouts was turning cold. He glanced at his new contact who was busy punching the button of his smartphone and swiping his finger across its screen.

"Got it," he said excitedly. "What dumb luck, my friend! I think I know where she is, or where she was a week ago. Let's go."

Back in the pickup, Bert left the parking lot and quickly found the northbound entrance ramp to I-91. Miguel read the green sign that Brattleboro, Vermont was twenty miles away, and Hallet Springs, New Hampshire was forty-five.

"I used to work as the sheriff of LaFontaine County in New Hampshire," he told his passenger. "I still have friends on the force. The other week, I got a text message from one of them. Before I retired, I asked him to keep me informed of homeless people using the old Mill there for shelter. People with mental illness go there too, either because they don't have a place to live or because they have nothing to do during the day but wander. The officer knows I'm looking for my daughter; he could lose his job over this. Anyhow, a group was spotted outside, and the drones were close enough to get facial recognition. They think that Maria was with them."

CHAPTER 33:
THE UNITED STATES OF SCROOGE

BACK IN HALLET SPRINGS ON THAT SAME BRIGHT SPRING morning, the Home Brew seemed busier than ever, and owner Judy Coble was pleased. Frank was sipping a coffee and reading the morning edition of the *Observer* when the tinkle of the bell at the door made him glance up to see Sr. Isabel Gakunde enter. She looked uneasy and worried, and Frank couldn't tell whether it was because she was not a customer at Judy Coble's coffee shop or for some other reason.

She spotted Frank and walked over to his small table.

"Isabel, good morning," he greeted. "Please sit. Surprised to see you."

"Good morning, Frank," she answered as she moved a chair back. She sat and let out a deep breath. "I'm looking for Max. Have you seen him lately?"

"No. Not for a few days, in fact. People are getting concerned."

The nun nodded. "Yes, that's why I'm looking for him. Derek came to talk with me after the Kitchen closed. He asked me to check on Max because he bumped into him at the cabins and thought Max was in trouble. Derek said he'd never seen him so depressed. Derek said that Max wanted to give him the rest of his food cards and his journals. Whatever went on, Derek was scared. I can't find Max. There was no answer when I knocked on his door."

"I'll go there after work today. We'll find him."

"Frank," Isabel said, her tone shifting slower and a notch more serious. "I got some news yesterday too. St. Theresa's must close, and I have been reassigned to our house in Boston."

The message was a gut punch. "Why?" he asked his friend. "This is bad."

"Yes," she replied. "It is bad. Seems like there is a new state law that now prohibits religious groups from doing social ministry like our food kitchen or clothing store. It says that any such things must be done by the local municipality, in the interest of public health, better quality control, and all that. They will still let us nurture the soul, I guess, but not the body."

Frank didn't reply while the impact and repercussions of this news was filling his mind. He knew that for some of his down-trodden friends back at the Mills, and those like Max living at the poverty-pervasive margins of the community, the closure of an oasis like St. Theresa's would make their fragile existence much more precarious and unbearable.

As he was thinking, Judy Coble brought a hot coffee over to the table and sat down. "Here, Isabel. On the house."

The nun smiled graciously. Frank told Judy the news and as the words he used came into his consciousness, more anger mounted within him. He could feel his muscles tensing like compressed springs and the calming breaths he tried to take at the end of his message helped only a little.

"I'm stunned," she said, taking in the thrust of the new law. "But why do you have to leave, Isabel?"

"I'm not sure, but I think that the Superior General of our Order knows that my ministry is mostly about poor people—the outcasts, homeless, street people, you know. That's what I do; now, I can't do that here, at least not in a public way." Then she leaned closer to her friends and whispered, "But your meetings must continue without me." She looked directly at Frank, her gaze remaining until his eyes met hers.

"None of this surprises me," Frank said. "This is just one more nail in the coffin for the community. It's what I've been talking about all along. Slowly but surely, we've squandered what our country was supposed to be. Years ago, I fought against an enemy who took dignity and freedom from the weaker people, different people, people who didn't act or think like them. Now, the whole freakn' system here is exactly that same enemy. It ain't right."

Isabel looked at him again. "I understand your anger, Frank, but don't let it get the best of you. Channel it. Run for office, maybe?" He didn't reply, but looked down at the table and took one more sip of his now-tepid coffee.

Judy said: "Closing the kitchen. You know what this reminds me of? There's a line in *The Christmas Carol*, after some solicitors ask Scrooge for a donation to help the poor. They tell him that some would rather die than go to the workhouses. Scrooge says, 'well then they better do it and reduce the surplus population.' We are turning into the United States of Scrooge and the ghosts haven't arrived yet to teach us a lesson."

"When they tear down the Mills," Isabel added, "where will our people go? No shelter, no food. Now they'll be not only homeless but hungry, too."

"The mayor was in here yesterday," Judy said. "He was grinning from ear to ear, talking about that a good day it was. He was telling everybody that the demolition project was starting today. He was beaming. Let's get Bert and the others together as soon as we can. I'll call him this morning and set it up."

Finishing their drinks, Frank and Isabel got up to leave. They each embraced Judy, and none of the three smiled their goodbye. "We have to look for Max," Isabel reminded Frank as they exited. Frank nodded as he and the nun parted. While his thoughts went to the next steps he could take to find their missing friend, they also centered on his restored revolver tucked into his belt, wondering if he could somehow find a way to purchase more bullets, since one might not be enough.

CHAPTER 34:
RUN TOWARD THE BARKING DOG

FRANK LEFT THE COFFEE SHOP AND STARTED WALKING toward Blueberry Farm, knowing that he would arrive just in time to punch in. Ordinarily, the walk to work was a time he would organize the tasks he had there, like today's project of reroofing one of the barns. Instead, the conversation with Isabel and Judy turned in his head but, surprisingly, as the facts and implications of their discussion arranged themselves in his mind, the emotional product was not anger but resolve.

Out of the blue, a memory of a long-ago experience in a VA rehabilitation hospital surfaced, something he hadn't recalled until that moment. It might have been a class on meditation, or martial arts, or Zen Buddhism, but that didn't matter. What did register in that instance was a message from the instructor that, at the time, didn't sound like much. Inexplicably, though, Frank experienced the assent of awareness that gives a new light of meaning to one's being. The mediation phrase the instructor offered the class was that facing fears is sometimes essential for happiness: "The monk runs toward the barking dog."

Frank took a few more paces down the sidewalk and stopped, turned around, and headed back towards the Mills.

The veteran made a call to his employer to say that he had a family emergency and would be absent from work. A man of honesty, he felt that his use of the word "family" wasn't too far a stretch of the truth because, in the months he'd been experiencing a closer connection to the castaways at the Mills, more and more did he feel that his relationship to each in the group was some sort of bond. It was the same comradeship he felt towards his fellow soldiers in his many tours of duty in the dusty, dour, and depleted landscape of Afghanistan. People who fight together, come together. The higher the stakes, the stronger the ties.

As he hurried south down Main Street, he soon noticed Bristol walking north, both hands in the pockets of her brown jacket. A small smile came to her face as she got closer to the man and she stopped eight feet apart from him. Frank slowed his pace and approached her slowly, knowing from the past that this was the best way to start an encounter with the consistently fearful teen.

"Bris," he said seriously. "I really need your help. Max is in trouble. No one can find him. Can you go to his place as see if he's there?"

Sensing the urgency and concern in her friend's voice, the girl nodded and waited.

"If he's there, if he lets you in, see if you can bring him to the Mills." Frank made sure she looked him in the eye. He paused for a moment and ventured a message that, in that moment, was worth the risk. "I get that it's hard for you to talk, but I'm guessing you can. It's time to let it go. If there ever was a time someone needs you to speak, it's now. Max is not safe."

Bristol kept her stare on Frank. He put his open hands together and in front of her, inviting her to take them. She took her hands from her pockets that were each grasping two baseball-sized stones. His massive hands surrounded hers. "Please," he said. His seriousness was unmistakable. Glancing at the rocks she held, he said, "If you can't find him, come to the top floor at the Mills. The left wing, the corridor with the windows, overlooking the shipping docks."

Bristol turned and hurried across the street, knowing the quickest way to get to Max's cabin. Frank headed towards downtown and the Mental Illness Monitoring service office, thinking that someone there might have seen Max. With any luck, he may have found a sympathetic worker who might be persuaded to use the GPS locator on Max's tracker, but the odds of this happening, Frank knew, were slim even if he did convince the person that Max might be in some sort of emergency.

Luck was not with Frank that day, in more ways than one. Getting nowhere downtown, he picked up his phone and sent a text to Isabel. No message came back as Frank hurried to the Mills.

As she started to jog to Max's place, Bristol thought more about Frank's words. He wanted her to let something go, but what did that mean? Her silence perhaps? Born out of both necessity and self-protection, maybe wordlessness no longer served a purpose. *But,* she thought to herself, *what do I have to say, and who cares to listen anyway?* Yet, what she was not ready to understand in his message was something much deeper than speech.

CHAPTER 35:
A GOOD DAY

SEVERAL BLOCKS AWAY, MAYOR PETER HADDAD WAS GET-ting out of his car at the police station. Walking towards the building, he spotted Paula Damascus sitting on a granite bench near the circular entrance of the place, colorfully decorated with beds and cement plant-ers filled with bright petunias of red, white, and blue. A central flagpole was the dominant feature of the spot where the stars and stripes flapped proudly in the wind.

As he got closer to the entryway, the bubbly and smiling reporter stood up and greeted him. "Good morning, Mayor Haddad. Do you have a few minutes for some questions?"

"Well, Ms. Damascus. Good morning," he replied excitedly. "I always have time for my favorite reporter. In fact, this is fortuitous. How about joining me inside with Chief Krebs because we're about to begin phase I of the most important city renewal project in the last few decades. You'll have a bird's-eye view."

He held the door to the station open for her as she graciously accepted the man's invitation. There, the security guard ushered them around the metal detector and past the reception room door where a clerk led them to the chief's office.

"Jason," Haddad announced as he sat down. "This is Paula, she's from *the Observer*. I asked her to join us and report on our operation today. OK with you?"

"Whatever you say, Mr. Mayor," Krebs replied. "Hello, Miss."

"Paula Damascus. Good to meet you, Chief," she responded.

"Here's the situation, Mayor," Krebs began. "We're just about ready to begin phase I, the eviction and potential arrest of the vagrants at the Mills, but two groups of our staff on the ground are now tied up with a semi break down on Pleasant Street snarling up the morning traffic and a fire alarm at the Safeway that we're assisting. No matter, however. The drones will start the operation, and it's a good day, plenty of visibility."

"Sounds like you have things well in hand, then," the Mayor congratulated.

"Yes. As a matter of fact, the pilots are so impressed with the new drones that they feel they can fly one into the buildings, navigate room to room, and facilitate the extrication. We can even test the taser capability if necessary. They're eager to do that. Should we move to the control room and watch?"

CHAPTER 36:
KEEP HER SAFE

THE DISTANCE BETWEEN GREENFIELD AND HALLET SPRINGS
is not ordinarily a long ride; the picturesque and uncrowded highway
mostly following the Vermont side of the Connecticut River is usually
problem free and easy on the driver. But, when the occupants of the
car are uncomfortable with anticipation arising from the soon-at-hand
attainment of a monumental goal that concludes a herculean journey,
the body will produce a special form of adrenalin, or at least that's what
it feels like.

That hormone was pulsing through Miguel's being as Bert drove
him up the farm-dotted interstate. As one village blended into the other
after crossing the state line, Miguel received a postcard vision of the
splendor of the New Hampshire hillsides and White Mountains in the
distance to his right, and the sprawling farms and picturesque valleys of
the Vermont countryside on his left replete with their ubiquitous white
churches and New England style town commons.

Bert's pulse was quickening too, as he felt that if his theory
proved true and if they were lucky, he would soon be helping reunite a
father and daughter who had not seen one another in many years. His
thoughts also drew him to think with sadness and worry about his own
child, Clarice, whose whereabouts remained unclear.

"To be able to live in a place like this," Miguel said, interrupting the silence between the two men. "It must be a blessing. This looks like home to me, but without our volcano."

It wasn't clear when Bert had first thought about doing something he'd never contemplated before, but perhaps out of sympathy or empathy for Miguel and Maria, he started to formulate an idea that just might bring the family to some sort of safe life together. Hearing Miguel's observation, Bert felt comfortable introducing his notion.

"What do you know about cows?" he asked Miguel.

Miguel found the question odd. He looked at Bert, confused. "Vacas?" he asked. "Not much, but I like working with animals."

"I have an idea, and it just might work. Let's make a call."

Bert announced to his voice-activated cell phone to dial Estelle Ramirez, his neighbor and fellow Via Verde conspirator. The dial tone rang a few times and the lady recognized Bert's number.

"Hi Bert," she answered, "you just caught me back in from the barn. It takes me awhile to get to the phone these days; sorry it took long."

"Estelle," the Sherriff said, "do you remember a meeting or two ago when Frank told us about a runaway kid at the Mills who didn't talk, a teenager?" His tone was not the usual friendly one he would customarily use when talking to his friend, but the seriousness of the issues brought him straight to the point. "I think I found her father; it's a long story but we're almost in Hallet Springs."

While on speakerphone, Bert told Estelle all he knew about Miguel's family tragedy and his travels up from San Salvador, searching for his daughter. Miguel spoke when she asked him some gentle questions, he but couldn't have noted the catch in her throat when he said to her "all I want to do is find Maria and keep her safe."

"Miguel," she said, "a few months back, I put my dairy farm into something called Federal Conservancy. It's a long story, but they tell me that as long as I keep it running as a farm, they'll let me hire anybody I want to. This even means work visas. Would you and your daughter be interested? I have rooms here where you can stay, but I would want her to go to school. Maybe Bert can bring you both around later today and we can talk it through."

Miguel wasn't sure what to make of this offer at that instant, but the smile on his face spoke volumes. He looked at Bert, who nodded approvingly. "Gracias," he answered Estelle. "Muchos gracias."

Bert ended the call after he made a plan with Estelle. "Now," he said to his passenger, "let's go get Maria."

CHAPTER 37:
THEY'RE COMING TODAY

LIKE HER ALLY FRANK, BRISTOL DIDN'T HAVE MUCH LUCK FIND-
ing Max. Her loud raps on his cabin door went unanswered and when
she looked into every window, she saw that the place was empty. It was
as sparse and tidy as always. She noticed Charlie's makeshift bed undisturbed, still in the corner.

The uneasiness in her mind was growing. She had no first-hand
inkling that Max was on the brink of harming himself, but it may have
been Frank's urgent plea for help in finding the man that gave her such
a strong feeling. Over the years of living on the road by her wits and
snippets of luck, she had come to trust her gut feelings, which more
than once proved reliable and maybe even providential. Max had always
been kind to her, so if he was in trouble, she would do what she could
to help him.

Bristol started to jog toward the center of town, thinking perhaps
that Max was walking around the Common. She knew he would always
bring Charlie there for a walk around midday where the two would stroll
around the park-like green, the leashed dog eager to sniff around every
flower bed and shrub, inhaling information about things only dogs
appreciate, and leaving urinary messages for those who came after him.
For his part, Max happily indulged his bouncy and curious companion.

She didn't see him anywhere as she turned the corner onto Main Street where she could scan the Common and the sidewalks surrounding it. Somewhat out of breath, she recalled that Frank wanted her to meet him at the Mills, so that became her next destination.

Frank had arrived there about fifteen minutes earlier. He went straight to the workshop only to learn that none of the regulars there had seen him for the past few days either. "They're coming today," Frank announced.

"Those fuckers," Margie replied, getting up from the old milk crate that served as her chair. "Let's go. Upstairs everybody." As the group slowly got up to comply, they moved towards the nearest staircase. At the doorway, Frank repeated an instruction he'd given them a few days earlier: "Remember, before they announce."

CHAPTER 38:
KEEP TO THE PLAN

CHIEF KREBS ESCORTED THE MAYOR AND THE REPORTER down the hall to the drone control room where two officers seemed glued to the many monitors hanging on the wall in front of their long desk-like console. One man was slowly moving the joystick in a circular motion with one hand and typing on a keyboard with the other. The men only looked up at their visitors for a second but when Krebs raised his hand to them, they knew it meant he wanted them to keep their focus on their duties.

"The screens here show us what the drone cameras see," Krebs started to explain to Damascus. "Hallet Springs has six new operational models and two older versions for backup."

"Yes, I know," the reporter said. "Some months ago, I interviewed Sherriff LaBounty on this very spot."

At this, Haddad said nothing but shook his head.

Turning to his officers, Krebs said, "OK guys, what do we have?"

"We got three in the air right now, chief," one man said. "They're each moving to the Mills from different directions. They're on monitors five, seven, and eight."

"Where are the patrols?"

"Still with the truck accident and the fire department, but it looks like they're wrapping up soon," replied the other officer.

"Good," the chief responded. "When the first unit gets to the area, circle around the perimeter and show me the parking lot and grounds before you make the first insertion."

"Roger that, sir."

"This is a tremendous day," the Mayor added happily, as if he was on the brink of a victory. "It will be a new day for Hallet Springs!"

"Let's hope they leave peacefully," Krebs added seriously.

"No matter," the mayor answered, "I'm sure your people will remove them one way or the other."

Haddad's cell phone rang in his pocket, making him glance away from the busy array of monitors. He instantly recognized the caller's number and smiled. "Senator MacKenzie," he told the room proudly. "Calling us from Washington to congratulate, no doubt." The mayor turned and answered it, walking a few paces away from the others to take the call.

On the ground at the Mills, Max walked through the woods to the clearing out back where Charlie's grave was. The ground had settled somewhat, but certainly not long enough for any vegetation to fill in the bare earth of the small spot. Max hadn't been there since the dog's burial so it was the first time that he saw the large rock that Derek must have found to mark the spot. Max smiled to himself at the gesture, but that act of thoughtfulness neither lifted nor altered the daggers of depression he felt were shredding his heart. After a minute, he turned from the grave and started to walk to the stack.

At the other end of the complex, Bristol knew the slit in the high chain-link fence that surrounded the Mills very well. She bent and wiggled her thin body around the rusty mesh as she pushed the seam wider, a motion as familiar to her as opening the front door of a familiar apartment, not that she had known one for most of her young life. Getting herself upright again, she started to run towards one of the broken doors to the building and then moved along the first-floor hallways as quickly as she could, scanning left and right into one empty space after another, searching both for Max and for any of the others, but especially for Frank, wondering if he had any news about their friend. Her footfalls on the old plank floor, particularly when she had to jump over any of the detritus of broken furniture or metal machine parts strewn about, were the only sound filling her ears as she charged down the halls.

Not finding anyone, she entered one room and went to the window that overlooked the rear of the Mills and looked through the grimy glass. From that view, she could see the workshop building to her far left and the incineration wing to her far right with its huge cylindrical chimney aimed at the sky like a rocket pointing to the heavens. At its base, she saw Max heading towards the black iron staircase that wrapped around and around the structure all the way to the top.

Shit! she thought to herself, *he's gonna jump.* She bolted from the room and tried to get her bearings so that she could find the closest door out to the stack. What she didn't realize was that Frank and the others were two floors above her, opening any of the windows they could that overlooked the loading docks. In that bustle of activity, Frank saw Max walking to the stairs also.

Back at the control room, Haddad's face was growing more serious by the minute as he continued his phone call with the senator. While his expression was grim, his words to her were flowery. "This *is* news, senator," he said, trying to sound happy. "Thank you for all you've done on our behalf. I'm sure you have a busy job in Washington these days, so we appreciate all your work on this. Goodbye."

An angry mayor turned to Krebs and Damascus. "Damn it," he said. "After years, they finally did it."

"What's that, Mr. Mayor?" the reporter asked.

"After years of work from the Historical Society," he replied, frustration coloring every word. "The National Parks Service finally decided that our Mohawk Mills now have status as a National Historic Site. I bet that ass MacKenzie had something to do with it."

The reported smiled at this unanticipated news, feeling like she was privy to a front-page news story that only she could write. "How did that happen, Mr. Mayor?" she asked.

"Seems like, somewhere in the 1960s, the first research on air pollution was done here by the University of New Hampshire. You know that huge smokestack out back? That was the place they had all their instruments. The research that came from here became the basis of the Clean Air Act. This will change all our plans; we can't touch those buildings."

Haddad was not happy. He looked at the floor and paced. After a minute of silence, Chief Krebs said, "I'll tell the guys to cancel the operation."

"Hell no; not so fast," the mayor shot back, his voice tinged with anger. "We still need those bums out of there. Just because the Mills have to remain, it doesn't mean that the vagrants have to. We can still complete phase one and instead of the demolition crew, the feds will help us rehab the place. We still need those vermin out. Keep to the plan."

Krebs walked over to the console and stood between the two pilots so he could look over their shoulders at the screens before them. He studied the images that each drone was sending back, and he focused on the unit closest to the factory, which was approaching the front main gate and the imposing fencing that, still padlocked shut, prevented any automobile traffic from entering the desolate parking lot. The drone glided high above and over the barricade with ease and, at the instruction of the pilot, moved left so the scan of the perimeter could begin.

"Looks good, sir," the pilot reported. "Nobody outside, at least."

"I bet they're inside, then," the chief replied. "Keep moving towards the back. I think that the best place to enter will be through the large doors on the loading docks out back."

Paula walked to get closer to Krebs to share his vantage point, but not so close as she might be seen as interrupting the police at work. The mayor also moved closer too, and found his place right next to the chief.

CHAPTER 39:
BUT NOT TODAY

WHILE THE MOHAWK MILLS WAS A SPRAWLING COMPLEX OF brick buildings, to say that its layout was well-designed or deliberate would be a deception. The many years since its construction in the 1830s saw the addition of one new structure after the other as the unfolding years of manufacturing growth required more people, machines, and resources. As some owner's economic fortunes waxed and waned, so too did the tide of additions here, and renovations there, continue until there was no business left to do at the aging structures. Eventually, the money rolled out and the neglect rolled in to stay.

In its day, the place produced all sort of products under one owner or another, from bicycles to blankets, machine parts to milled goods, tires to toys. Only the local historians cared about the place anymore, and through their diligent research, put forth the data that one tenant at the Mills was once a respected scientific company that saw a future in air-pollution-measuring devices. Although they occupied only a small area in the massive cluster of buildings, their main testing guinea pig was the huge smokestack that still belched out all sorts of nasty particulates that would help them field test their creations in a real-world setting. It was the historic records of their studies that made the case for the U.S. government to have a keen interest in the entire jumble of buildings.

Not far from the old smokestack in the rear of the campus was the main and massive loading dock to which the daily parade of trucks would back up to be filled with whatever output the Mills made. Five oversized doors separated the dock from the warehouse and made an easy gateway for the forklifts that had to scurry back and forth from the trucks with their pallets of products. On the left and the right of the docks, two buildings rose three stories tall and seemed grafted onto the central warehouse and main building like afterthoughts. Together, these wings from the central building made for an interesting canyon, with the docks on the ground level right in the middle. Like everything else with the deteriorating buildings, one door had caved in from the battering of time and weather. It was through this passage that Chief Krebs planned to insert one of the city's new drones so it could snake its way through the maze of rooms and tell any squatter there that unless they left the premises immediately, verified by the craft's camera, they would be arrested, charged with vagrancy, and likely jailed.

From the control room, the chief and his two pilots were glued to the monitor receiving the images from the closest drone that was gliding in on the loading dock door, as calm as a summer breeze. With a sharp eye out for people on the ground and the large open door as their focus, neither the pilots nor the observers in the control room noticed the group of people on the third floor of the left wing look down at the drone as it slowly approached.

Frank watched it also, feeling relieved that his predictions about how the police would try to breech the building were accurate. Had he been in Krebs' shoes, he might have made the same plan, considering the objective and the tool at his disposal.

"What did I tell you guys," he said to the group, not expecting a reply. "See, just as I thought."

"Those bastards," Margie added defiantly. "But not today."

From their third-floor vantage point, she looked down along the row of windows and saw eight of her friends, her fellow homeless people made hapless by the callous system that cast them aside, standing ready to defend the only home they managed to have.

Fortunately, the architects of old New England factory buildings needed to bring in as much sunlight into their workspaces as possible, given the fact that conveniences like electric lighting wouldn't brighten the work areas for many decades. Margie and her colleagues stood in front of windows that stretched nearly floor-to-ceiling. They stood a pace or two away from the broken and missing panes, but with sufficient view that they could spot the approaching drone.

Back at the control room, the mayor took his eyes off the monitors and seemed to be lost in thought. He turned to the reporter, distracting her from her riveting look at the huge loading dock door dead center in the monitor, and said, "This is great! We can still put Hallet Springs on the map, but now it'll be all around the renovated Mills. There will be a museum, restaurants, shops, maybe even condos, and a theater. We can do this! We'll get superfund money or development funds from the Feds; people will love it!"

By then, the drone was right beneath them. "Ready?" Frank asked the group. No reply was given; none was necessary.

"Now!" he said.

At that, the group standing there threw rocks at the oncoming drone beneath them. The barrage was something that harkened back to the Middle Ages, brave knights atop high walls hurling whatever mortal objects they could make from the ramparts down upon attackers laying siege on their castle.

"What was that?" one of the pilots called out to the other as he saw a blip of motion directly ahead of the drone, passing from left to right in a flash. Before the other could answer, the image on their screen wobbled. "We lost one propeller" the other announced frantically as the craft started to dip downward.

Within a moment, many of the flying rocks found their mark and the drone plunged downward; as more stones hit it, two of its five arms were severed from the housing, sealing the fate of the instrument that would fly no more. It hit the ground hard like the many stones that pursued it.

"What the hell?" one of the pilots called out in surprise.

"The unit's down," the other replied. "Shit."

"Where's the next one?" Krebs shouted. "Get it there now. What's the status of the cruisers?"

"Ten minutes out," one man answered.

The chief immediately drew his radio from this belt to reach his officers in their patrol vehicles. He barked out the situation they'd just witnessed on their monitors and issued orders to engage any trespasser at the Mills with all force necessary.

At that instant, Frank caught a glimpse of a figure climbing the stairway of the smokestack almost midway up the twisting spiral. The person looked like Max and wore the same color coat. Then from a doorway near the loading dock, he saw Bristol racing toward the towering stack as fast as she could.

Frank's heart raced as he concluded that the man on the stairs must be Max. He turned to the group and said, "You know what we discussed. The cops will be here any minute so we all have to leave. Grab what you can: tarps, food, tools, whatever we can carry. Meet in the woods at Goose Pond." He then bolted for the exit, descended the stairs, and dashed out the building to run after the teen.

Krebs silenced his radio and asked his pilots: "You did announce the drone as a police vehicle, didn't you?"

Both officers were silent.

CHAPTER 40:
I'LL STOP YOUR FALL

AS MAX CLIMBED HIGHER AND HIGHER UP THE NARROW, open iron stairs that twisted up the tall brick smokestack, it wasn't until he cut himself on the old, rusty handrail that he felt some physical pain. Never having climbed to the top before, he wouldn't have noticed how the aging metal had become more and more deteriorated and jagged the farther up it went. Even if his awareness wasn't consumed by thoughts of death, he might not have noticed how on some sides of the stack, the corroded metal bolts tying the stair treads to the brick were pencil-thin and weak from decades of weather and the predictable march of seasons. But then again, it mattered little to the man whether he died by his own actions or by accident; it was all the same to him.

While each steep step up the twisting, dizzying stairway was an effort, Max's thoughts were remarkably relaxed. Connie was nowhere to be heard in his consciousness and the impressive view from the elevation revealed a 360-degree look at Hallet Springs, the green forests, and farmlands beyond, and the southern ranges of the White Mountains far in the distance. Though the sun seemed brighter as he ascended, the air seemed colder, particularly when the turns of the stairway brought him to the side where the bricks were shaded. In much of his life, the experience of nature—the sight and smell of it—gave him a calm he could muster to quiet the raging voices like Connie in his head and then distract him from the intense emotional pain he always felt inside. But this was not the case today, as he slowly climbed step by step to the top and the moment of his suicide.

As he kept rounding the narrowing tower about three quarters of the way up, he lost sight of the entrance to the stairway where Bristol had just jumped to the first step and started racing up. Glancing around, Max saw one of the police drones not too far away but paid it little heed.

Max, the teen thought to herself as she ran, *don't do this!*

Finally, at the top, he found a spot on the circular platform that curled around the very last rows of brick about three or four feet from the opening. He sat down to reflect and catch his breath. The rim of the massive tower still held steel brackets from the many instruments once used to measure the pollutants and smoke billowing up from the fires inside, but such fancy gear had been stripped away long ago. Reaching for one of these supports, Max peered into the sooty, cavernous cylinder, and saw not the slightest speck of light nor the bottom that he was sure to experience soon enough. The jet-black dust from centuries of smoke that caked the inside walls of the stack now colored his hands. He leaned over and when he looked away to the landscapes around him, he instinctively wiped them on his jeans. *I want clean hands when I die,* he thought to himself. He wondered if he should pray, whether there was such a thing as God, and if what they said was true, why was his life so filled with so much suffering from an illness he neither caused nor wanted.

Being so slender, Bristol's weight didn't cause much of a sound as she charged up the narrow spiral and the rustle of a passing breeze drowned out the creaking noise made by the growing fractures in the iron treads that were unaccustomed to the strain of people using them after all these years. Just like Max, as she rounded turn after turn up the curving stairs, she lost sight of the entrance, so she didn't see Frank starting to climb up after her.

As she moved around the final twist, the sight startled her friend sitting on the rim of the stack. "Bristol," he announced firmly, "you shouldn't be up here. Why did you follow me?"

At the question, the girl froze but looked intently at the man. Breathing heavily, she crouched down on the edge of the platform and stayed silent. Max thought her presence there would, at least temporarily, interrupt his decision-making and the courage he was building to jump into the black abyss of the massive chimney. He tried to conjure up some message that would send her back down to safety without him so he could finish what he came to this perch to do. It was not his plan to have anyone witness his death, much less a teenage girl with a lot of living to do if she could ever find a safe patch of earth to do it in. Since no ruse bubbled forth in his mind, he decided upon something honest but creative.

"It's time for me to retire, Bristol," he said, looking at her like a kindly uncle. "They say that you make a decision to retire when you have enough, and when you've had enough. Charlie was the last thing. Now that he's gone, I can check both boxes and go." He turned from her and looked at the round black hole just in front of him. "And it's not just Charlie," he added dejectedly, "I'm fed up with the whole thing. They make life too hard."

For her part, the young girl saw through this. He was trying to be compassionate, even at this end, so he was sidestepping his desperation with a true but muted message that she might understand. She moved herself just a little closer to Max.

Turning back to her, he said: "you should go down now. Be careful not to trip and lean against the bricks so you don't look down."

"What are those two doing up there?" the pilot of the drone at the police station asked his coworker in the flight control room, scanning the monitor on the wall. "Let's see if I can get a closer look." He skillfully turned a dial on the panel to his left, and then gave a slight flex on the joystick his right hand was moving. The camera on the drone quickly zoomed in and captured a sharp image of the two people on the stack, but it hadn't yet seen Frank, who was about halfway up.

Bristol's gaze did not move off Max. To her, he looked more depressed and downcast than ever, and while there was a halt to the talk between them, Max was listening to the voice of Connie that he heard as clear as ever. "Hey Max," she beckoned cheerfully, "come on down; it's beautiful in here" as if she was floating in some luxurious swimming pool. After a while, he looked at Bristol and said, "I miss Charlie, you know."

Moved by the moment but without much hesitation, Bristol made a mental jump of faith: "Have I ever told you about my dog Shep?" the girl asked.

Max opened his eyes in surprise, as hearing her child-like voice after all these months was like a brand-new sound in the universe. He felt honored, thinking that he might be the first one on earth to hear it. "Bristol," he said, "you're talking!"

She smiled. "My name is Maria,"

"Maria; that's a pretty name, much better than Bristol. Where's Shep?"

"Shep was my best friend back home in Omaha. They took him away when my mom died, and I had to go into foster care. I don't know what happened to him, but I miss him every day. After my dad was taken away, he was just about the only solid thing in my life."

Like other pet owners who opened their lives and souls to cats or canines, Max and Maria slowly swapped stories of the companionship and antics their animals added to their daily routine and the passing of time. In the process, Max's thoughts were retreating away from death, even though the loss of Charlie and Shep was a heavy, evident theme in the words shared, as if the grief was never far beneath the surface. Whether it was the connection unfolding between them through their mutual emotional connection to their dogs, or the fact that the long-silent Maria was offering so much, some internal drive for self-destruction was melting in Max's mind.

"I almost forgot something," Maria said. She reached into the pocket of her sweatshirt and presented Max with a piece of white paper, folded into quarters like a greeting card. He turned it over and saw a pencil sketch of a King Charles Cavalier Spaniel looking out at the viewer, full faced and wide eyed—bright, alert, and eager. The resemblance to Charlie unmistakable. Max opened the card and found a poem:

> *If tears could be my staircase or memories make my lane,*
> *I'd point them both to heaven*
> *and ask God to take away this pain.*
> *He knows how much we loved you and all you added to our life.*
> *Now sadness fills our spirits*
> *And the grief cuts like a knife.*
> *Yet crying makes no structures and remembrance no magic way,*
> *so be the Lord's good friend in heaven*
> *until we meet again someday.*

"I feel sad about Charlie; he was always a happy dog," she continued. "I know you miss him just as much as I miss Shep. I think I know why you came up here. Why not let Charlie play with God a bit more before you arrive and interrupt them?"

Max was silent. Then he asked, "Did you make this card for me?"

Maria nodded.

"I can't recall the last time someone gave me a card, much less made one for me themselves."

It was her turn to be silent. Then she said, "I think I might want to stay around here. And I have to figure out how to find my dad. Maybe, could you help me find a place and maybe get another dog?"

"I bet I could," Max answered. "Maybe."

"Could we go down now?" she asked, "I'm getting cold up here." She held out her hand to the man.

"OK then," he replied, "that would be nice. I think I want to go home anyhow."

"I envy you," she answered.

The pair stood up on the platform and took one last look at the beautiful vistas they could see all around them. They saw the sun dip behind one of the many passing clouds, their massive white cotton-like ephemeral mountains majestically moving against the azure blue sky. As it did, yellow beams of light shot past the darkening edges of the snowy mass making the picture fantastic, a theophany that might even give an ardent atheist pause. Maria was smiling while Max still looked stoic and revealing nothing by his face. "Let me go first," he said. "that way, if you trip, I'll stop your fall."

CHAPTER 41:
YOU CAN DO THIS!

MAX CAREFULLY MOVED AROUND MARIA AND TOOK THE first steps of the long climb down the steep stairway. Pausing a few seconds to soak up the last images of the countryside from the platform, Maria followed him. He turned around towards her and asked: "So you think I'll get to heaven and interrupt them someday?"

"Yes, Max, you will someday. But not yet." The girl could not have realized how wrong she was.

The curve of the wall on her right only allowed her to see the left side of Max's body as he descended but the next sound was unmistakable. Like the collapse of a sliver of glacier, the metal treads under Max's feet cracked, taking the steps, the handrail, and a huge chuck of brick from the stack, all of which, including the man, plummeted to the ground below. As loud as she could, Maria screamed, "Max!" Some of the debris narrowly missed Frank, who was a twist beneath them.

"Did you see that?" one of the pilots said to the other in the control room, taking it all in through the camera on their drone. "Looks to me like she pushed him," the officer replied. "Announce the warning."

"What the hell just happened?" Krebs shouted. "How far away are the patrols?"

"Five minutes, sir," one pilot answered.

"Krebs grabbed his radio and dispatched an ambulance, then ordered his officers in the field to get to the escalating emergency at the Mills much faster than they were. Both the mayor and the reporter were riveted to the monitors.

What no one knew at the time was that retired Sheriff Bert LaBounty and Miguel were listening to the police scanner in his truck, just arriving at the outskirts of Hallet Springs. A volunteer on the local Emergency Medical Technician squad, Bert switched on the hazard lights on his Ford and accelerated down the country road leading to the Mills.

The first pilot clicked the microphone on his headset. "You on the tower, this is the Hallet Springs Police Department. Do not move. Look at the drone and place both your hands on the rail where we can see them."

Maria was frozen in horror from witnessing her friend vanish right in front of her and not because of the officer's instructions. In fact, she had little awareness that the craft was hovering in the air not far from her, because the public address system the police employed was not operating.

"She's not responding. Maybe she's a jumper," the first pilot said to his coworker. "Juice up the taser; she's breaking the law anyway." The message was quick and stressed.

At that, the man keyed a few strokes on the console giving the command to the drone to transfer the proper amount of battery charge to the dart. "Just enough for one shot," he answered.

From his vantage point, Frank looked over the rail and saw Max's lifeless body on the ground below, alongside jagged pieces of iron stairs and bricks strewn around it. Turning upward, he could see the red warning light on the underside of the drone glow, and he remembered the demonstration he saw months ago at the soccer field. From the height of the drone, he could tell that its target was Bristol, an innocent teenager he had now put in danger.

As the drone was hovering carefully but slowly closer to the stack, Frank reached into the pocket of his jacket and removed the handgun he'd been painstakingly restoring the past few months. In an instant, he considered whether this was the moment he would spend his only bullet, whether the weapon would work as he hoped, and whether this next act would define him for the foreseeable future. He took aim at the drone and fired.

It dropped from the sky in the same way Max had fallen, a predictable and inescapable consequence of gravity once a life force had been disrupted.

"What happened?" the pilot shouted to his colleague.

"We lost number three!" the other answered, staring at the blank screen on the wall that just seconds ago had Maria in its crosshairs.

"Malfunction; looks like it's down," the other man answered. "Number six is close—I'll bring that in."

"What the hell just happened?" Haddad shouted at Krebs. The chief didn't answer but took a step closer to the pilots and looked over their shoulders at the screens, dials, and indicators on their console.

"Do it fast," Krebs sternly ordered the pilots.

Frank climbed up the remaining stairs and came upon the section that had given way under Max's weight, a gap of seven feet or more. The two treads before him looked none too sturdy as the bolts holding them to the bricks were protruding from their anchors in the brick. He looked up around the curve of the stack on his left and saw Bristol edging down the remaining steps on the other side of the missing stairway.

"Bristol," he shouted, "you have to jump. Quickly. I'll get you." Frank didn't expect a reply and his surprise wouldn't register until later.

"I can't!" she screamed in a panic. "I'll never make it."

"You can do this. You're one of the strongest people I've ever met! Come on!" he shot back.

The bending wall of the stack made the leap she would have to take even more risky than it would if the stairway had been straight, and the look on Frank's face made Maria believe that he knew that as well. Frank stretched out his arm over the handrail and opened his hand.

"Don't aim for me, aim for my hand," he instructed. "I'll get you." He no sooner yelled that when several more rows of bricks on the collapsed wall beneath them tumbled down and bounced off the stairs below and onto the ground.

Maria looked at him and hesitated. Over his right shoulder she could see a drone coming towards them and the red light glowing on its belly. "What if I can't?" she called back. "What if it's not worth it?"

"You can, and it is. Trust me!"

She studied her goal, a black muscular palm pointing outward over the open air and the perilous fall that would happen because of missing it. She rocked back and forth on her feet as if to summon both her courage to her soul and blood flow to her legs. Hearing the creaking of the treads as they wiggled with her, she leapt.

CHAPTER 42:

I TRIED TO GET MAX

IN MID-FLIGHT, MARIA THREW OUT HER RIGHT ARM TO CATCH Frank's one below her. As her hand crashed into his, her grip was not fast enough or strong enough to capture his and it skidded off the target but upwards towards his elbow. Frank curled his arm to hook hers and brought his left hand over to grab her right just as the girl bent her hooking arm around his, like some mid-air square dancers. The dynamic force of the acrobatic motion twirled her onto the stairs just below Frank's feet. She slammed into the brick of the stack and gashed her forehead. The momentum of her arc pulled Frank off balance so that he lost his precarious footing on the stairs, sending him tumbling down on top of then over her. As his superior weight sent him down the stairway, Maria grabbed the iron step with her free hand above her where Frank stood just seconds ago and, their arms still curled, held on tight.

With a long exhale, the man gazed down the winding stairway beneath him, a combination of relief and gratitude flooding his mind. If he felt pain in his shoulder from snatching Maria in her descent, it didn't register. His body was telling him something much more important than a strained muscle.

He turned to the girl above him on the stairs. "You're speaking to me," he said quietly. "Wow."

"I tried to get Max, like you asked," she replied, breathing heavily, the words filled with grief and defeat. "Instead, you had to save me."

Frank looked down to see if he could spot Max, assuming that a fall from that height was not survivable. From his vantage point, he could only see part of the lifeless body far below, face down on the ground, some yellow bricks of the stacks strewn on and around his friend.

Back in the control room, an angry Chief Krebs demanded, "Get closer to those two," instructing the pilot moving the last drone closer to the stack. The officer complied and tilted the joystick in front of him gently forward with his right hand, while simultaneously moving his left to a large round red button on the console with his left. His index finger hovered over it.

"What's your real name?" Frank asked the teen, looking up at her on the stairs above.

"Maria."

"Maria," he replied, feeling as if an elusive answer had finally surfaced. He looked at her, smiled, and gently said, "Let's get down; it's not safe."

As the pair slowly got to their feet, Frank retrieved a handkerchief from this pocket and handed it to Maria to wipe the blue and bloody bruise on her forehead. She did so and looked at the deep red stains it made on the clean white cloth.

He twisted himself to begin their descent and saw the drone coming towards them. He instantly sensed what might come next. As Maria started to take a few steps closer to him, he put his arm downward behind him and said, "Get behind me." The girl crouched low.

In the control room, both pilot's eyes were as fixed on their monitors as were those of Chief Krebs, the image clear and focused. A large Black man standing defiant on the high stairs was staring back. Frank unzipped his green barn coat and broadened his shoulders.

"Sir?" one pilot questioned, waiting for permission. Krebs looked at the monitor and recognized his comrade, Lieutenant Stringfellow, dead center and still.

Krebs was silent.

"For God's sake!" Haddad shouted. "Just do it." At that, he reached for the firing button, pushing the chief aside, and pressed it. The projectile from the drone, true to its function, launched like lightening from the craft, its speed making it imperceptible to those watching. Its consequences, however, were unmistakable.

The pin-like-round hit Frank in the squarely in the chest and a blow of electricity surged through the big man's body like a tempest.

In the first applications of this purportedly non-lethal technology decades earlier, a hand-held taser delivered fifty-thousand volts to the target's body, sufficient to cause a temporary disconnection between a person's muscles and the magnificent human brain that controlled them. The theory was that this disruption caused all of someone's 650 muscles to act uncontrollably, unleashing pain sensations as long as the operator—typically 20 or so yards away—dispensed the charge. The fifteen seconds of the additional electricity rampaging through the body was thought to be sufficient to incapacitate any violent actor threatening law enforcement or any individual in psychiatric distress, called "lunatics" in the medical journals of the day.

Over the years, however, as the voices from groups like Amnesty International or the American Civil Liberties Union were slowly silenced and as the chorus from civic authorities grew louder, Taser Inc. increased the voltage and modified the devices to fit into domestic drones made by American Dynamics through their sole-sourced contract with the U.S. government. Touting their advances as the next generation in crime-fighting, the company was clear to market that the threat-stopping, neuromuscular paralysis was just under the amount of electricity thought to cause ventricular fibrillation, but strong enough to incapacitate anyone amped up on methamphetamines or whatever hallucinogen was prowling the streets of America.

What they didn't advertise was the legal protections the government afforded the company that creatively shielded it from wrongful death lawsuits, nor their disclaimers about how many health conditions the target carried were beyond the scope of their testing. Included in that long list of risk factors they made no guarantees about was traumatic brain injuries like battlefield concussions.

Frank grabbed the handrail of the staircase with both hands when a tidal wave of pain in his heart overwhelmed his awareness of anything else. His eyes had difficulty keeping focus until all he saw was a bright yellow light. The muscles in his hands seized, and then relaxed, as did those in his legs. Just before losing consciousness, he felt like he was suffocating while his heart felt as it was on fire. Then he fell, tumbling down the stairs like a lifeless corpse where a robust person had been standing.

Krebs watched his old friend and fellow veteran from their years of military service together drop lifelessly. The control room was silent as Frank's electrified body tumbled down the curving stairway, the momentum of gravity forcing the unconscious man to roll downward.

"You wanted us on the map, mayor?" he asked, turning to Haddad. "I can see the headline now: Hallet Springs PD kills unarmed Medal of Honor winner, Lieutenant. Frank William Stringfellow." His sarcasm was clear and caustic. Turning to the reporter, he added, "Here's your headline: Trigger-Happy Mayor Files Fatal Shot."

"Now that's a story," Paula Damascus replied.

Maria grabbed the handrail and moved as fast as she could down the stairs. Since Frank's body followed the path around the curving wall, she had to traverse many steps, and the time before she caught up with him seemed interminable. Eventually, she found him as one of his legs luckily hooked itself around a baluster. Frank's motionless body blocked the stairs. He was on his back, head below and feet above, upside down and still, eyes closed and face scratched from the fall.

Maria did not know what do to and her heart pounded. Yet again, he protected her and yet again life robbed her of something good. Her mind raced with a cocktail of anger and sadness. Had someone been close to her, she knew she would summon whatever strength that remained in her and beat them to death. In a flash, those feelings vanished and when heartbreak set in, she crouched down and cried.

CHAPTER 43:
IN THE BROWN TRUCK

THE RUSTY CHAIN AND PADLOCK BINDING THE TWO ARMS of the chain link gate at the front entrance of the Mills was no match for the police cruiser's formidable bumper. The car smashed through the weak barrier with ease as it raced into the parking lot, its lights flashing and siren wailing. As it tore around the side roadway to the rear, Bert's pick-up passed through the open gate just in time to see the lawmen speeding away.

As the police came to the back, they could see Max's lifeless body on the ground at the base of the stack. They screeched to a halt and radioed back to the chief. Before they exited their vehicle, Bert's Ford skidded to a halt. Taking in the scene and then turning to Miguel, he commanded, "Stay here. Don't follow me." He quickly bolted out of his truck, grabbing his paramedic bag from behind the front seat. An instant later, the three men were crouched over Max.

"No breath sounds; no response," Bert said to the policemen as he picked his head up from the dead man's chest. One of the policemen looked up at the top of the structure, and then calmly addressed the two others: "Unsurvivable," he said.

From that spot, the three men could not see Maria on the spiraling stairway high above on the other side of the stack, still looking at the motionless Frank and frozen with fear. Looking at her friend, her protector, her big-brother ally there sprawled out beneath her, help-less, injured and possibly dead—right on the heels of Max's tragic fall and her own courageous leap—the teen felt the combination of shock, pain, and grief known only to those whose soul seems instantly crippled and spirit instantly crushed. She let out a wail, loud and strong like a wounded animal speared through the heart, moments before expiring.

On the ground, Bert heard the emotion-filled sound.

In that instant, Chief Krebs' voice came over the two policemen's radio: "There's a girl on the stack above you. Possibly another victim as well," it informed the men.

Bert grabbed his bag and ran to the base of the stairway. He shot a worried glance at his passenger in his truck close by. Miguel looked back intently, fighting the impulse to jump out and offer any untrained help he could. One of the policemen followed the sheriff.

Bert climbed the stairs as fast as his aging legs and heart would allow. He came around a turn and saw Frank's body lying in the passage like a corpse and the young girl at his feet above him. "Was he tazed?" he asked her.

Maria, tears in her eyes, nodded.

"Are you Maria?" Bert asked.

Another slow nod.

"Come on," Bert said. "Let's get you down."

He extended his left hand out against the wall and, with his right, pointed to an exposed stair tread just between Frank's hip and shoulder. "Put one foot there and come to me," he instructed.

The thought of being close to a stranger made her cringe with fear but she knew she had little choice. Maria complied and was soon competing for a perch on the same step that Bert was using. He moved his body toward the railing so she could squeeze by. "Help her down," he called to the officer several steps below. As she passed, he bent his head close to her ear and whispered, "Your dad is in the brown truck down there."

Another shock went through her being, this time a powerfully positive one. Reflexively, she looked up at the breathless stranger, an old man with a kind face now helping her like some guardian angel, with bright eyes. Moving down behind him, she saw the policeman a few steps below who turned and started walking slowly down.

Maria's legs moved slowly as the adrenaline fueling them in the last few minutes started to recede. Her thoughts, however, were still racing, but now with questions, doubts, and misgivings. Could the message Bert whispered be true? More likely, some mysterious person in the callous system known as American society made some cruel mistake and this would soon prove to be another heartbreak. Worse still, perhaps her first impression of the stranger was mistaken. Maybe this was a trick, she thought, so that when she approached the pick-up, she'd be apprehended by Youth Services and detained as an escapee. The closer to the bottom, the more she considered how, in her hard-lived life on the road, hope could be a fickle friend. Knowing that there were only a few steps to go, she considered that her safest bet might be to summon her remaining reserves of energy and bolt for the woods.

The camera on the drone aloft gave the pilots and the others in the control room an aerial view of these unfolding activities. Krebs ordered the officer manipulating the craft to circumnavigate the stack, since they could already see Bert assessing the immobile Frank. He wanted a better view of the department's other assets arriving on scene. What he saw was another police cruiser and the city's ambulance speeding in and taking up a position next to the other vehicles. A patrolman came out of the car and ran to join the other who was still examining the location of Max's body, while two paramedics from the ambulance jumped out and retrieved their gear and a gurney.

When the patrolman escorting Maria reached the pavement, he turned to the teen and said, "Wait here." He pointed to the front of the car he arrived in, but his attention was less on securing her in the back seat than on his colleagues, one of whom was charging up the stairway, no doubt on his way to assist the sheriff. Maria said nothing and moved to comply.

"That's it, sir," the pilot told Krebs. "The shot takes most of the battery; the drone has to get back to base or set down."

"Get it back, then," he replied, "we've seen enough." He turned to the mayor and, with his still unmasked contempt, said, "Happy now? Looks like two down." Then he walked toward the door.

"How much will it cost to fix them?" Haddad asked, referring to the expensive tools he worked hard to obtain.

Krebs stopped, turned, and stared back: "I meant two people dead."

CHAPTER 44:
THE BEST OK POSSIBLE

THOUGH HER HEAD THROBBED, AND BLOOD STILL SEEPED through the gash on her forehead, Maria' body was stock still while her eyes surveyed her surroundings at a frantic pace. They hurriedly darted around to access her options unfolding in the busy scene around her. She looked over at Bert's pick-up and could see that there was a figure in the passenger seat, but the sun's bright glare on the windshield prevented her from seeing who the person might be. She looked over where Max's body lay, only to witness the two men from the ambulance gently lifting him onto the wheeled stretcher they brought. Max's face was covered. One of the policemen came running down the stairs and over to his cruiser. He opened the trunk and hoisted what looked like a large black backpack onto his right shoulder and retraced his steps to the stack. Maria started to calculate how long it might take her to run to the woods, knowing that if she picked her moment correctly, the preoccupied people in the area might not see her.

But then there was the stranger's message tempting her to investigate. If it was true, the reunion would be the watershed moment she'd dreamed about for the last several years. If it was false, another painful heartbreak awaited, followed by another cruel confirmation that nothing good happens in life.

For his part, Miguel's heartbeat raced as he found it difficult to follow Bert's instruction to stay seated in the truck. He could see a teenager waiting near a police car, a young girl, but, from that vantage point and the years of separation father and daughter had been forced to endure, he wasn't sure it was Maria. The man judiciously watched the bustle of activity with the same scrutiny his daughter used, two people trying to avoid notice and any potentially consequential interactions with authorities in such an inhospitable environment they had to navigate. Of the three options human beings have in coping with threats of any sort, fighting was out of the question. That left freezing or fleeing; while Miguel could only do the former, Maria was inclined to the latter.

Back on the stairs midway up the stack, Bert looked over the still motionless Frank. The slim, steep pathway was awkward, making for a difficult assessment of the man's injuries. What was certain was that his friend still had a faint pulse.

Seeing the people around here still preoccupied, Maria sensed her moment was at hand. Either action was a massive risk, and the fearful nature of it was all she could think about. She took a deep breath and decided to run like hell to the possible safety of the woods, half a football field away. She sprinted away from the police car like a frightened gazelle.

Miguel watched her run. Sensing it was his moment also, he got out of the truck and the rusty old door on the Ford creaked loudly. Whether it was the brick walls of the surrounding buildings that made the sound echo, or the heightened stress hormones in Maria's body that made her hearing more acute, or some mysterious element of physics of soundwaves, or the guardian angel of Providence, no one could say but Maria stopped midway to her destination, exposed. She knew she would regret it for the rest of her life if she didn't turn around. So she did.

There he was, a figure standing still with his arms at his sides against an old brown truck, its open door behind him. He carried the build of her father, but not the youthful face she remembered, for this person looked more wrinkled and careworn. If one word described his countenance, it would be *please*. Miguel raised his arms apart, imploring, and open to welcome his daughter's embrace. Maria now started to run to her father.

Crashing into his chest, she released a floodgate of tears as she buried her head and arms around her father, who cradled his arms around his long-lost daughter, his treasure, and bent his head down over hers. His eye teared. They said nothing for a long while, savoring the moment they both imagined during years of wrenching sadness, miles and miles of strenuous effort and worry, and the roller coaster of emotions that come from unanswered questions and the absence of communication from each other. Wanting to look her in the face, Miguel loosened his arms to release her, but Maria still held on tight, not at all interested or ready to let her father go, even for an instant.

Eventually, Miguel softly said, "I missed you, kiddo."

It was a pet name Maria had not heard in years. *Kiddo*. The happy flashback it caused was like a chemical reaction that, once ignited, couldn't be stopped. With that one unassuming word, always issued in the bond of love between a devoted father and his daughter, came a wave of comfort, memory, and contentment the girl had not felt since she was a child. The term brought her memories of ordinary and happy days in Omaha when her family had just finished a meal and the casual conversation that invariably came with it. He'd always use it at bedtime after the nightly storybook with his "time for bed" instruction that preceded it.

Maria relaxed her arms and looked up to find her father's face. His eyes spoke volumes: joy, heartbreak, relief, and gratitude all wrapped in a blink-less gaze. She wanted to keep that image burned in her memory, every wrinkle, blemish, black hair follicle, and smudge of dirt, before it faded. "You've got a bad cut," he observed, noting her bruised head.

"I'm OK," she said, "more than OK; the best OK you could possibly be."

CHAPTER 45:
ANOTHER BONDAGE

IT WAS AS DIFFICULT FOR BERT TO ASSESS FRANK'S INJURIES as it would be for any trained paramedic to extract information from an unresponsive patient, precariously perched upside-down on a narrow iron stairway suspended some one hundred feet or so above the ground. He used his fingers to detect the veins in Frank's neck and felt a tinge of relief when he could feel blood still moving through them. He bent down closer to his friend's face to confirm that he was still breathing. Another bit of life confirmed. He opened Frank's eyelids and didn't like what he saw.

Bert knew he could not yet move the large man, even if he wanted to, without first trying to determine if any bones looked broken or if there were any apparent external injuries. Seeing none as he scanned, he reached into his bag for the C-collar he could use to stabilize Frank's neck. He could see the slender missile from the drone still protruding from the center of his chest.

By then, one of the emergency medical technicians from the ambulance had chugged up the stairs and arrived behind the sheriff. Bert said, "Male; approximately 50 years of age; stunned by electro-taser; unconscious and non-responsive to light. Possible spine injury. Call it in; we need a litter up here fast." The EMT used his radio to reach his partner on the ground.

It took some time for Bert and the others to carefully maneuver themselves and Frank's injured body onto the rescue stretcher they would use to gingerly bring him safely to the ground and to the second ambulance that arrived on the scene.

"Think he'll make it?" one EMT asked the sheriff.

"Maybe," he replied, the word dripping with both concern and fatigue. By then, other police officers had also appeared and a group of three started entering the Mills to evict and arrest anyone trespassing inside.

As the ambulance sped away, Bert walked back to his truck, where Maria and Miguel were still basking in the emotions of their reunion. When he approached, it was not clear to the man who was smiling more, father or daughter.

Shortly behind Bert walked another patrol officer. Turning around, the sheriff recognized him from his years on the job. He shot the man a firm stare. "They're with me," he affirmed with authority. The officer acknowledged the "back off" message and retreated. Heading back to his truck, he looked at his passengers and said, "Get in; let's get you two to the farm."

Maria looked at the stranger who rescued her. "What about the Boss?" she asked.

Bert looked at her puzzled. "You mean Frank?" he asked.

She nodded.

"He looks bad," he answered. "After I get you to my friend Estelle, I'll go the hospital and check."

Through a side door near the perimeter of the forest at the far opposite end of the Mills, the disheveled group of the marginalized and homeless people headed out of the Mills, carrying their few belongings or whatever useful item they scrounged from the creepy maze of old, mostly forgotten brick buildings that had given them a tiny crumb of shelter. Derek held a bundle of folded plastic sheets and a blue tarp, and

Margie chose a box of plastic cups and flatware. Others carried milk crates with pots or the few formed plastic chairs no one else would want.

They crossed the growing lawn, green with another advent of spring, and moved slowly to the woods beyond and through another slit in the chain-link fence that would soon be repaired to protect the new, historic showplace in this corner of the state from people like them. Soon enough, the townsfolk of Hallet Springs would hear the news that the Mills would be rehabilitated, and the region would have a strong new magnet—this time an historic one—to draw economic progress. All the more reason, they would say, to show visitors that there was no poverty, hardship, or need anyplace in town, so stepping up any displacement of "people of concern" or the clamping down on kindness was even more of a good idea.

The people leaving the Mills moved to another form of disenfranchisement, a bondage of sorts, in stark contrast to the vast openness of the White Mountain National Forest towards which they were headed. Unlike an imprisonment signified by barbed-wire fencing or the chains of slavery, this form of hell, born out of poverty and social neglect, was as expansive as a wilderness with every bit of the danger but nothing of the charm.

They walked slowly and at the edge of the woods, Tommy Hodges was the last one in their number. He stopped a moment to look back at the buildings, knowing he would never see Bristol again, nor be sheltered in the filthy old musty rooms of the Mills, nor have any meal or feeling of belonging at St. Theresa's, or any image of the Boss's smiling face or his comforting words. He turned away and entered the woodlands, calling out to Margie and the others, "Sorry I'm slow, you guys—wait up."

EPILOGUE:
TWO YEARS LATER

MARIA STOOD ON THE HILLSIDE AND CINCHED UP THE BUT-tons of her jacket as the cold light mist in the air gave her a chill. Beyond the resplendent color guard standing at crisp attention alongside the brown oak casket, the acres of precisely laid ivory gravestones of the fallen were a distracting and haunting image. Row after row, slope after gentle green slope, section after section, the pattern of white markers stirred powerful thoughts and feelings in the woman that added to the resurfaced grief she had been feeling for days. *So many dead*, she thought to herself, *and now one more.*

Never having met the soldier they were laying to rest, the chap-lain's eulogy recounted much from the military service record of Lt. Frank Stringfellow. As he quoted heavily from his Medal of Honor cita-tion, his recounting of the soldier's career taught most of the mourn-ers there things they had never known about their friend, all of which seemed both surprising but readily convincing. Maria knew that she would long remember the chaplain's closing sentence: "Heroes never want to be known or remembered as being called a 'hero.' Heroes just help people."

One of the soldiers moved off to the side of the group with digni-fied precision, making a straight line away and an abrupt right turn. The trumpet she carried shone brightly as if its silver metal had received an abundant share of polish and caring. Maria thought to herself that she'd never seen anyone play a musical instrument up close before.

But that was only one of the pearly string of "firsts" that flooded into her parade of thoughts as the soldier began her slow and wailing notes, the sound filling the air with a sad solemnity that no other melody could create. Maria thought of the first day Frank started to talk to her back home in Hallet Springs and the gentleness of his smile, which somehow conveyed that he was trustworthy and keen to help her. Not realizing it at the time, she now was convinced that the man's caring eyes reminded her of her father's eyes and that, just perhaps, the two men shared the same essence, strange as that may sound.

In stark contrast, she thought about the first man who violated her so many years ago as an innocent adolescent and the physical pain, emotional scarring, and crippling nightmares she still experienced from time to time. The memories of her frantic flight from state to state as she vainly tried to outrun the emotions that dogged her—each day the first day of another struggle to eat, find shelter, and survive—were duller now, but not so settled as to render them painless.

Flipping again, she thought about the first day of her reunion with her father, after all those miles of searching and years of separation they both endured. The feeling of his embrace in the back parking lot of the Mills on that fateful day when Max perished and her friend in the coffin saved her life on the stairs was visceral.

She thought that Frank wasn't the only one who fatefully entered her broken life in New Hampshire. Estelle, the woman who gave her father a job and both a home on her dairy farm, was like a second mother or grandmother to the girl, exuding both caring and routine in the physical and emotional sanctuary of the home she made for them. Though Estelle was too ill to make the trip to Washington, Judy Coble was not. Standing next to Maria at the grave, she had become like a supportive aunt over the last years. Noting the tears in her eyes as the music moved her, Maria slipped her arm around Judy's and the two women huddled close, magnetized there with a stronger bond that only grief seems to produce. Then Maria wondered about whatever became of her friend, Sister Isabel—another first messenger of kindness and hope— who set in loving motion the pathway she followed to struggle with and recover from the traumas she shouldered.

Both these strong and somewhat rebellious women encouraged, pleaded, and then almost demanded that Maria begin talking to a counselor. Anabella Carter, the next pivotal female in the young girl's life, helped her mental processing of her experience of trauma and became her expert companion, drawing upon both her professional training and personal experience with sexual violence. This quiet and unassuming social worker not only helped Maria heal, but also guided her to find the confidence and courage to face adulthood with a brave mix of hurtful memories and slices of happiness sufficient to make the future seem bright. Her maturation would continue.

All this reminded her of the last lecture she attended in her art class at George Washington University, an educational adventure and opportunity funded mostly through Estelle's generosity. It was about a form of Japanese art called *kintsugi*, whereby the artist purposely smashes a valuable porcelain object and mends the shattered pieces with a bonding agent mixed with a precious metal like gold, silver, or platinum. The beholder then sees a restored item whose flaws are accentuated and made beautiful; pieces fused together and made stronger than they were before yet retaining their original form. Rather than hide imperfections and fractures in the object, these are accepted and celebrated as an equally valid part of existence.

As the soldier finished playing Taps, Maria thought that maybe she was like someone who endured the shock and blows of a traumatic youth and was now gluing the pieces together to make herself better, perhaps stronger. Someone as unique as the woman she was meant to be, but also new and better through it all.

The soldier walked back to group with same stern and precise motions she used to depart from them. Before making it back, three Marine helicopters crossed low and loud over Arlington and filled the air with the unmistakable sounds of rotors on their way to the Pentagon or the White House. Bert looked up, as did the others there, momentarily distracted from the graveside service by the powerful noise.

Bringing his gaze back to the coffin, he too thought about his friend inside and wondered if, to him, the sound of helicopters wasn't an intrusion, but something associated with impending danger or welcome rescue. How accustomed Frank must have been to the sounds of the various machines of war that punctuated his life in service to his country, he thought. No doubt someone worthy of the Medal of Honor must have had a barrage of experiences—sights, sounds, and feelings— that sculpted his being as surely as a hammer and chisel shapes granite with the permanence of every strike, both good and bad.

Bert thought of his own last year or more of consistent efforts at navigating the Army bureaucracy to get his friend the final resting place in Arlington, the hallowed ground for centuries of national service men and women whose white stone markers stand as an army of silent sentries on one hillside after another in this sacred place. This was nothing compared to Frank's journeys and the arc of his life. While some may have thought that Frank's final moment in life was nothing more than a misplaced event not suited to a decorated, professional warrior with limitless potential in civilian life, Bert believed that his valiant protection of Maria on the stack that day was more than fitting. It was a demonstration of courage, defiance, and protest, emblematic of the man's values. He was, after all, a man who fought for others.

Next to the retired sheriff was another displaced lawman, Jason Krebs, a fellow Army Ranger, now working for a private security company in New York City. Dismissed from the Hallet Springs police department for losing two expensive drones in one operation, he, and Bert, both knew that his firing was necessary done so that Mayor Peter Haddad could resume his journey to higher political office in New Hampshire without the blemish of the fiasco that claimed the life of a real American hero. Now, right around festival time, Governor Haddad made yearly return visits to Hallet Springs.

Without any remaining family members there to grieve Lt. Frank William Stringfellow, Bert arranged a special gift for Maria. After the color guard painstakingly removed the flag draping the coffin and meticulously and precisely folded it into the triangle befitting this symbol of democracy, the soldiers handed it to the commander of the guard with stiff formality and decorum. He pivoted smartly on the grass and walked over the mourners. "On behalf of a grateful nation," he said, bending down in front of Maria.

ACKNOWLEDGEMENTS

I AM DEEPLY GRATEFUL TO MY SISTER, SUSAN MIELE, NOT only for her wise and careful review of my manuscript but also for her unfailing love and support for this endeavor and for every twist and turn of my life. I am beneficiary of invaluable feedback from dear friends like JoAnn Fenton, Marcia Lehman, Eileen Fernandes and Brian Donovan. Their comments, corrections and encouragement have been a true gift. I am also thankful to an author I have never met, Daniel Joshua Rubin, whose book on the essential elements of great storytelling arrived in my life just at the right time.

To my fellow professionals working in the field of community mental health, I wish for the world to acknowledge the powerful impact you make on people's lives every day, even if they aren't always visible or public. Never lose sight that the person you are with your dedication, talents, and training, as well as the hope you bring to people who need you are all potent factors you add to your tasks each day.

To anyone struggling with challenges to their mental health and wellness, I ask you to always remember that you are not alone. There are people in your community who want to help you. The efforts you make to find them, trust them, and work with them through the trial-and-error process of treatment is worth it, because you are worth it. Keep looking until you find the expert mentor that help you find your way to health.